The Best Asian Short Stories

2021

The Best Asian Short Stories

2021

Editor
Malachi Edwin Vethamani

Series Editor
Zafar Anjum

Kitaab
Singapore

KITAAB

First published by Kitaab,
an imprint of Kitaab International Pte Ltd
10 Anson Road, #27-15, International Plaza,
Singapore 079903

Kitaab International
Singapore

ISBN: 978-981-18-0038-2

www.kitaabinternational.com

Contents

Introduction

The Best Asian Short Stories 2021 is the fifth volume in this series. This collection brings together the work of twenty Asian writers and writers residing in Asia, namely from Canada, India, Malaysia, Japan, Philippines, Singapore, United Kingdom and United States of America. This publication is a part of Kitaab's efforts to provide a platform for Asian writers to publish their work.

Anthologising Asian short stories written in English is an important and significant effort in the international literary arena of Anglophone literature. This collection of regional writing in English brings together writing from most nations where it is national literature. As early as 1982 McCabe recognised the "(t)he multiplication of Englishes throughout the world and their attendant literatures" (1982:18). Singaporean poet Edwin Thumboo in 1991 called for the recognition of these writings as national literature and to dismantle the post-colonial literature label that is still associated with these writings. However, the notion of national literature can be problematic in certain countries where language policies and politics, in former British colonies, may not be welcoming to writing that is not in the national language. Malaysia is a case in point, where only writing in the national language, the Malay language, is recognised as national literature. In this light, anthologies like *The Best Asian Short Stories* series provide platforms for writing for all Asian writers and make their work visible and accessible to international readers.

Readers of *The Best Asian Short Stories* series will immediately recognise the diversity and multicultural Asian dimensions in these stories. The new Englishes phenomenon has provided the vehicle for Asian writers to use Asian English varieties of the English language. These writings confirm how Indian writer Raja Rao's clarion call over seventy years ago has come true:

> We cannot write like the English. We should not. We cannot write only as Indians. We have grown to look at the world around as part of us. Our method of expression therefore has to be a dialect which will someday prove to be as distinctive and colourful as the Irish and the American. Time alone will justify it.
>
> (1943: viii)

Each story in this collection testifies to the vibrancy and variety of writing in English in Asia. As you read the stories in this volume, you will recognise the many varieties of the English language these writers employ. Singaporean English is evident in the opening story, *Anniversary,* in Cyril Wong's description of his two characters' taste for local food:

> Adam used to be amused by my love for Malay food, for *nasi padang*. "You're the only Chinese person I know who eats *belacan* by the spoonful," he once commented. He rarely eats *nasi padang*, maybe because it reminds him of his repressive childhood. ... He would devour anything from rice with roasted pork to *wonton* noodles, while I would order exclusively from the Malay food-stall.

In *The Seal Carver*, Elaine Chiew draws from Chinese vocabulary to refer to food, family relations and making of the seal or the Chinese 'chop'. Its effectiveness is most apparent in her use of the Chinese expression "yi mo yi yang" which describes the image of the former lover's daughter and the effect it has on the seal carver:

> It isn't her prettiness that makes him suddenly awkward and tongue-tied when he presents the chop, but the fact that if he dares say it, she is yi mo yi yang – the exact replica – of her mother in her twenties, the same lily-pad face, the same dimple in one cheek, the sparkly eyes, the soft sable hair; it's like encountering Xiao Fen all over again ....

While most writers incorporate vocabulary and expressions from the local languages into their narratives, Terence Toh in *Bloom* does something unusual. He presents a whole dialogue in the Malay language. This verbatim reportage of the dialogue presents an authentic situation which is common in multicultural and multiracial Malaysia where interlocutors often unconsciously move from one language to another. The dialogue is crucial in the story, and though it contains many non-English words, Toh provides sufficient clues for the readers to know what is happening:

> One day at work, he received a phone call. It had been about two weeks after Gowri had first been admitted.
>
> It was an unknown phone number: Jian obviously did not know the number of the hospital. And yet, somehow, before even picking it up: he *knew.*
>
> He felt his head spin, and nausea built up at the bottom of his throat. Part of him wanted to ignore the call. And yet, he picked it up.
>
> "Hello? Ini Encik Chong Jian Beng?"
>
> "Ya."
>
> "Ini Dr Nurul dari Hospital Pantai." A brief pause. "Saya amat sedih untuk-"
>
> Jian did not register the rest of the message. He was too busy weeping.

The Indian English variety is apparent in the stories by all the Indian writers in this collection. I highlight two writers, Gankhu Sumnyan and Smita P Mukherjee, where elements of Indian culture are evident in their stories. In Gankhu Sumnyan's story, *Local*, a rude youth insults one of the older characters, comparing him to the red saliva that results from chewing *paan* (betel quid):

> "What the hell are you wearing? What is that red coat?" a third asked.
>
> "Village head-men wear this," Techa smiled.
>
> "Makes you look like *paan*-spit!!"

In *The Monstrous Hermit,* Smita P Mukherjee's description of the surreal re-marrying ceremony between the police officer Jaywant and his dead wife, Bhavna, is reminiscent of the Hindu wedding ceremony where the groom leads his bride round the sacred fire:

> The hermit inches towards Jaywant and with swift movements he takes Bhavna's sari *palloo* and ties it to Jaywant's belt that held his trousers.
>
> "Take the *pheras* around this pious *agni*".

The use of both Hindi and Sanskrit words which are related to the wedding ritual provides a reality in an illusionary ceremony that only Jaywant can see.

The main theme of this volume is the new normal. The use of the expression "new normal" came into currency with the emergence of the coronavirus pandemic in early 2020. Little did we know that this global pandemic will rage with such virulent devastation of human life both in terms of the livelihood and fatalities. In the new normal, as presented in these stories, the characters wear facial masks, work mostly online from home, are encumbered by various restrictions imposed through periods of lockdown and come to terms with the sudden loss of loved ones. Some glimmers of hope emerge as the world sees the numbers begin to decline. But with each decline, a new variant of the virus emerges to test the resilience of the human race.

As can be expected, many of the stories on the theme of new normal dwell on death. A young woman talks to the ghost of a man who had died of the virus. Their encounters have a significant effect on the young woman's love life. A policeman who had infected his wife grieves over her death and his yearning to fulfil a vow to her draws him to a hermit in a Hindu crematorium. A young man loses his partner to the virus and struggles to find meaning in his life after her passing.

There are many other stories to tell in this time of the new normal. A partner prepares a meal on the anniversary of their relationship. Their relationship is one that has been tested by differences in race and background, as well as the perennial conservatism and political correctness of the society they are forced to navigate in. A son makes a journey to return home as his business fails. The journey home brings back nostalgia of what he had left behind and he has to prepare himself for what lies ahead for him. A character returns to a place after 30 years and sees how the place has been gentrified. His encounter with a young visitor reveals inter-generational attitudes towards the same place. An apartment dweller's preoccupation with a possible rat infection during the lockdown presents an opportunity for her to discover the plight of a fellow apartment dweller. The pandemic affects families in unforeseen ways, and they need to take an evacuation flight to a new land that offers sanctuary. The preparation, flight and the arrival are fraught with anxiety of what lies ahead for all of them.

Roy Tristan B. Agustin's *Killing the Councillor* provides some dark comic relief in this collection as his characters bungle in their attempts to kill a politician during the pandemic. Their desperation leads them to consider using a blind masseur as the assassin. Christina Yin's *A 22nd Century Au Pair* employs myth and speculative fiction. Set at a post-pandemic time, the protagonist meets a stranger who might show her and her wards a new way of living freed from their current restrictive domes.

As one might expect, the new normal also results in the emergence of new jobs which become available to those who have lost their livelihood as the result of the pandemic. Vicky Cheong's *Safe Distancing Ambassador,* a euphemism for another form of policing public behaviour in Singapore, is an unexpected feel-good story about an encounter between a sympathetic safe distancing ambassador and a Nepali clothes merchant who is desperately trying to make his business survive in these hard times.

The stories which touch on additional themes fit well with the stories on the new normal theme. Ivy Ngeow's *Dog-sitter* provides a dark mystery element to the collection. *The Seal Carver* by Elaine Chiew is a story when the past comes back to haunt the protagonist in the form of his first love. A misunderstanding that goes on the infect the present.

Kiran Bhat's *April 15, 2021: The Day of the Sun, Pyongyang, North Korea* presents the constant fear of being under surveillance and the need to be super-patriotic in case one is found be disloyal. A child is taught to toe the party-line and be vigilant on what he says in public.

Han-jo thought long and hard and said, "My drawing comes first."

Mother went up to the boy and sealed her hand right over his lips. "Do not ever talk that way." He wanted to say something again, but she slapped him before he dared. "Come on, put on your bag. And don't talk while we are outside."

Namrata Singh's *Hiraeth* as the title suggests recounts and contemplates the protagonist's journeys to find her own space and place of belonging. The story is told through the use of thought presentation and the reader is drawn into the protagonist's private struggles. Andrew Innes's *The Short Story Collective* presents the price an imaginative writer has to pay for his betrayal of a drunken hanzaki (salamander) who had told him a story and "The Story could not pass beyond the boundary of the riverbank and be shared with others.".

Bhaswati Gosh's *Apu's Goals* is a rather deceptive title for the story. The story revolves more around Apu's father's obsessive interest in his son's life. It is a story of a father coming to understand that his son is growing up and has new interests besides his studies and sports. Danton Remoto's *Red Leaves* is a coming-of-age story of a young man confused about his sexuality. The cold city of Baguio in northern Philippines provides a foil to this tale of unrequited love.

Perhaps the most unconventional and experimental story in this collection is the second story in this volume, Sudeep Sen's 3-part short story titled, *Black Box: Etymology of Crisis*. The story dwells on the use of light and darkness suggesting what is revealed and what remains hidden, what is secret and who holds the power to keep it secret. There is a sense of isolation and alienation and of death and silences. The troubled state of mind of the unnamed protagonist is revealed to the reader:

> It is very late at night and I am knackered. Yet, I cannot sleep. All night I dream in fragmented images. Memory plays tricks with my mind. Her story, his story, my story, history — all collude and conflate.

Despite the sombre theme of the new normal, the twenty stories in this volume are far from depressing. They are entertaining and thought-provoking. They present genuine and authentic human experiences that readers all over the world can relate to.

Malachi Edwin Vethamani
October 2021

CYRIL WONG

Anniversary

Heat is key. "Nothing beats making your curry paste from scratch," says the website I stole the recipe from. There is something profound about knowing the exact constituents of your food, the sensorial tactility of every ingredient, every unit that makes up the eventual thing, so as not to take the completeness of that finality – the paste, the curry, then the dish as a whole – for granted. The part of me that aspires to be vegetarian, even vegan – since I'm now a Chinese lapsed-Catholic-turned-Buddhist – contemplated replacing the *hae bee* and *belacan* in *sayur lodeh* with vegemite, but this being the first time I'm attempting this dish, things may go wrong if I wildly experiment. The paste would make for a watery curry to be slathered over rice. Add turmeric for the yellow colour, but the resultant gravy in the wok would still be thin and depthless, even after dashes of coconut milk. Therefore, spiciness is important. Heat is everything.

After soaking in water and chopping up the lemongrass (discarding the rigid green tops, retaining only soft and fragrant stems), shallots, garlic, red chillies (keeping seeds in, since heat is crucial), ginger, galangal, *hae bee* and candlenuts (they shine like moonstones once washed and cut, I think, not that I have ever encountered a moonstone in real life) for rapid grinding later in the food processor (no arduous pestle-and-mortar action for me: I'm not *that* hardcore about doing things the traditional way; good enough that I've decided against using readymade paste purchased from the supermarket downstairs), I dump everything into the blender. Turning the machine on, the sound the grinding makes is like an unremitting moan.

It's the school holidays, in the thick of the coronavirus pandemic, the new normal inspiring – more like forcing – me to experiment with food at home. I'm also at home cooking dinner for my boyfriend because it's our eleventh anniversary as a couple today; eleven years since we first met in a bar in Chinatown, introduced to each other by mutual friends. However, my time in the kitchen is producing metaphors about my relationship with Adam, full of implications that I'm not sure I can properly digest. Surely Adam and I don't have a *depthless* relationship.

Superficially, friends point out that we are opposites. I'm short and slightly stocky while Adam, due mostly to genes and weekly classes of yoga and Pilates, is tall and slim. Adam left home in his twenties, both literally and figuratively; he abandoned not just his conservative Muslim parents, but also the religiosity and the cultural conditioning that accompanied his childhood to teenage years. With gorgeous eyelashes and fair skin, Adam sometimes looks Eurasian and raises no eyebrows when he orders from non-Muslim stalls at the hawker centre or imbibes alcohol in bars and clubs. To friends and colleagues at the credit card company where he works, he is simply "Adam" instead of "Muhammad Adam Hakeem" and in our home, we always call each other "baby".

Adam is the talker while I hardly talk at all – sure, as a teacher, I talk in the classroom, but that's different; teaching Mathematics in a secondary school is usually never a rewarding two-way conversation – which can suggest that we have little in common. "Maybe the sex between them is *just that good*," I've heard one of my bitchier friends explain, as justification for why Adam and I have stayed with each other for over ten years.

Adam might be the social one, but I believe he shares my penchant for silence; it is typically hidden behind the general ease of his affability. That outward friendliness allows him to survive in a work-environment that he can manoeuvre in without offending anyone. With friends, talking is his strategy for keeping them mostly entertained. The art of saying much and saying nothing at all, simultaneously, has been an art he has mastered and secretly enjoys. Unlike me, Adam has long discovered ironic ways of speaking that ensure that he reveals nothing about his more complicated or profounder views on love and life.

Alone together, we actually barely speak at all. We tease a lot, yes. We also touch each other all the time, which has perhaps led me to assume that there was no need for excess verbiage.

Is the heated fervour of physical intimacy all that defines us, then, since we refrain from volubility? Is our relationship as diluted as the soup now coming to a boil on the stove, made from blended paste and cups of water; barely thickening even after I hurl coconut milk into the mix straight from a can? Could the fault rest with me for not ever beginning a longer conversation in the first place, one in which we might open up about more than everything?

What if talking never becomes our thing? What if I lack trust in words or the limited ways in which language can frame complex truths? What if I don't think that conversation is essential for revelations about the self and an ever-unfolding understanding of our deepest feelings?

Now for other ingredients needed to complete the curry: firm tofu I fried beforehand, kaffir lime leaves, chicken stock; then vegetables I cut up which slide from the chopping board and into the wok; cabbage, carrot, snake beans. My workstation beside the stove has never looked so colourful, decorated with motley bits of ingredients. The kitchen has never smelled so fragrant, thanks to my curry languorously bubbling.

Adam used to be amused by my love for Malay food, for *nasi padang*. "You're the only Chinese person I know who eats *belacan* by the spoonful," he once commented. He rarely eats *nasi padang*, maybe because it reminds him of his repressive childhood. We hardly cook at home, even during the weekends. The routine is to buy food from the hawker centre downstairs and consume it unceremoniously in front of our television. He would devour anything from rice with roasted pork to *wonton* noodles, while I would order exclusively from the Malay food-stall.

"Don't your taste buds rebel against a lack of variety?" he once asked.

"My tongue isn't slutty, like yours." He rolled his eyes.

Absently, he might nonetheless pick bits of *sayur lodeh* and other ingredients from inside my open packet of rice. I know better than to say anything whenever he does this. I know a part of him still misses the food he grew up eating.

Soon, the cooking is done. I transfer curry into a pot and carry it carefully into the living room. I set the table with bowls of rice and chopsticks – a touch of Chineseness, just for fun – and cannot wait to catch the look on Adam's face when he comes home and sits down to eat.

*

The television is on. Adam has had a long day. He plonks down and digs into his food beside me at the dining table. I watch his flickering profile as he picks up his chopsticks and his rice bowl. He spoons curry into his mouth. After chewing on some cabbage, he pauses and turns to me. "You didn't buy this from downstairs?"

"No. You like?"

"You didn't blend the paste in properly. I can still chew on the ginger. And it's too spicy."

"Sorry, first time la."

"The chopsticks are a nice touch."

"Thanks."

Adam stops chewing and gazes at a vague point between the bowls on the table.

"Oh wait ... is it today?"

"It's okay. I didn't expect you to remember."

"Sorry, baby."

"No, really, it's okay."

I feel bad that my cooking did not make him feel nostalgic for the best parts of his childhood. I feel stupid for trying to achieve this through food. I still don't know why this is important, not losing out on better aspects of your history, even as the worst parts – in Adam's case, the conservatism and homophobia – tend to eclipse everything else.

Life has been kinder to me. After my parents died, I moved out, sold our family home, bought a flat, stopped going to church, dated whomever I wanted, and finally persuaded a man to move in with me. No drama; no trauma. I simply bided my time, as if coming to the end of a surprisingly bearable prison term, before entering a bright future as a queer atheist. I loved my parents even though they understood nothing about my existential challenges. I love my late parents – I just love my life without them more.

Adam had to uproot himself. He suffered inwardly, more than I ever have. For him, the past – he shot me down once for bringing up his childhood; it was something he refused to discuss at length – was like a proper jail; full of pressures to become the perfect Muslim son. There was much resentment that he had to exorcise before becoming capable of self-acceptance, even love.

Yet what are we without our past?

Am I enough to ground him, since his past has let him down? Could our life together serve as the foundation for a wholly-happy-Adam far into the future? Am I overthinking everything? What makes me believe Adam isn't already complete and whole, right here and now?

I realise Adam has been staring at me, such thoughts still flouncing through rooms of my mind. "I didn't mean to criticise your cooking," he assures me, smiling, but his eyes slightly narrowed.

Not wanting to worry him, I smile quickly. I notice a piece of cabbage has landed on his collarbone just inside his work shirt. "So long already and you still can't use chopsticks properly," I tease him, attempting to seem playful.

I reach in and pick off the cabbage with my fingers, tossing it casually into my own mouth. A trace of curry is left where the leaf had landed. I rub my thumb along his collarbone to wipe it off. Instinctively, my little movement slows.

He is looking into my eyes and smiling broadly. At nearly the same time, we both start to giggle. My thumb never leaves his body. I start to rub an invisible stain higher up along the side of his neck, swiftly warming to my touch. Silence conjoins us. His eyes are suddenly wistful.

I fail to notice when the news comes on; the television feels further and further away. My thumb presses against his pulse pushing against the skin beneath his jaw. I envision a whole network of veins and arteries spreading out like branches of an inverted tree from where my finger is firmly planted upon his quickening heartbeat; a tree that extends eternally downwards towards a spaciousness, so sacred and distant that neither of us – no matter what questions we ask or how deeply we might hope to thrust into each other – may hope to reach.

SUDEEP SEN

Black Box: Etymology of Crisis

for Neelam, Kabir, Angad & Rocky

1. BEFORE: *Talk, Trailer, Fore Play*

"Prisoners of drops of water,
we are nothing but perpetual animals."
— ANDRÉ BRETON & PHILIPPE SOUPAULT,
The Magnetic Fields

A high-voltage swivelling lighthouse beam blinds us in this controlled darkness — Virginia Woolf or Robert Eggers are not present here to write their scripts. Shrill echoey electromagnetic sounds shriek, deafening our wavering eardrums.

Behind a lit translucent cloth-screen, a man in a wood-chopping motion wields his axe. His long hair glimmering halo-like — a chiaroscuro. He shines his shoes, breaks bread. He rummages through a box to a find a length of gauze to bandage his eyes, his mouth. His nose, stuck-shut by black tape.

On his bare body, he places fresh flowers on his skin, every hair follicle marking its petaline scent on a digital oximeter — measuring his pulse-beat, heart-rate, his blood oxygen levels — every new-fangled indices of health, trendy obsessions of these pandemic times.

On an empty chair, sits a bodyless form — legs crossed, no spine, a jacket hung on the chair's frame, a spotlight glaring on it. This light moves, trailing a pair of footsteps, following electrical wires to a set of old switches blackened since war-torn blackout days.

A female form scribbles text on a notebook — *all work and no play* — in robotic repetition. Metronomic words leading to more words in silence — but speech cannot be silenced under any circumstance.

There is agreement and contradiction in this duality — a bipolar tension of ego/alter-ego, of fulfilment and vacuity in our unstable psyche. The graph is not constant or regular like sine or cosine curves — the mathematical grid inexact, unsure and asymptomatic like the contagion surrounding us — trying to resuscitate every molecule of breathable air under our masked pretences.

Parallelly, a film unfolds in the black box — the eye of Kabir writes *dohas* on an old tin trunk, the couplets composed in cinematic frames, its edgy noir feel obliquely reminiscent of *Mehsampur.*

In *the company* of *dark matter*, I try to trace my steps of sanity in this thick heavy air as we sit at more than an arms-length fearing human touch and disease.

What convoluted times we live in now — where being human is inhuman, where free-thinking is dissent, where being democratic is anti-national. Even the 'black box' of a crashed airplane storing facts cannot reveal the facts — everything in done in secrecy, everything is subterfuge to maintain the sub-altern, everything is about power or the lack thereof.

*

2. After: *Play, Black Box*

It was the best of times, it was the worst of times.

— Charles Dickens, *A Tale of Two Cities*

Under a conical thatched roof held up by bamboo armatures, the *misen-en-scene* —

four tin trunks painted black containing personal and household items, two off-white gold-bordered cloth curtains, a metal kettle, a large white shallow tray to hold water from spilling out, a metal black chair, a white bicycle, lots of white flowers, black electrical tape, two long bamboo poles, a pair of shoes, two empty transparent polythene bags — all framed by three more bamboo poles set up as a goalpost, or a proscenium marking out territory to contain spillage of any narrative beyond silence.

The theatre walls are painted matte black, the floors tiled in clay terracotta. There are three lights that hang from the ceiling, a whirring fan, two spotlights, and old-fashioned wooden switchboards with clunky round black switch fixtures.

The lead actor, a soloist dressed in black, lies askance on the carpet on the centre with a low wall of loosely stacked bricks forming a horseshoe enclosure.

In is silent here and our eyes are led by lights that train our sight to follow a story. It is a gaze that looks outward and inward. Words are minimal, metronomic, repetitive like a refrain mouthed by an invisible chorus. But there is no ensemble cast or musicians.

*

A white bicycle stands at an angle, alone — white flowers lie scattered, upturned on the floor. Piece by piece, petal by petal, I pick them up — stick them onto my bare body, on my eyes, nose, mouth.

I get onto the cycle — slowly start pedalling, circling the outer periphery of the brick enclosure, marking my tracks. I gather pace and more pace, circling round and round at breakneck speed. I disembark— start unpeeling the flowers off my body … and start running, circling round and round like a falcon.

Turning and turning in the widening gyre / The falcon cannot hear the falconer; / Things fall apart; the centre cannot hold; / Mere anarchy is loosed upon the world, ….

*

I sit on the loose bricks that form an enclosure, a geometric U-shape. I sanitise my hands, look at my hands closely surveying my destiny — wear latex gloves, put a pair of shoes in a transparent polythene bag — and say: *"Eya sab ko chahiye nahi!"*

Dateline: March 25, 2020. I start counting from 1 to 2 to 3 to … bang a steel plate with a stick — keeping up the beating until the cacophony is no longer discordant.

*

The futility of the country, endless. No earnings, no hope: *"I want to go back to my home"* … 485 kilometres … I start to count down the kilometres as I drearily trudge along the highways and on rail tracks with a trunk on my back like a homeless migrant. All transportation is shut down, everything immobilised — our mobility too is immobile — *"I can't go, can't reach home!"*

I am craving for a home-cooked meal, a simple meal — but instead all I have is a stale sandwich that might have been donated by someone who took pity on me.

*

Sanity, insanity, sanitised — I give my half-eaten sandwich a stray animal and insects. Both animal and human reduced to one, on our knees, by the powers to be. Everything is shut — door, window, sky, auditorium, stage, audience — no one is spared.

What does an artist do? Storytelling, *dastangoi* — stage, kings, *ghungroos* — story of a sparrow, wise folk tales — anything, any tales to keep our sanity and imagination intact, alive.

*

The overhead lights dangle precariously on wires that might short-circuit any moment — like a pendulum clock, it wavers counting down time. *Ghungroos* become an instrument to auto-tune dissonance in place. A moth sits on the white screen, its wings wingless, awaiting flight.

Sparrow speaks to an ant, the ant to an elephant — everything is a deal, deal without a deal, deal within a deal —

*

Dateline: April 24, 2020. Body, corpse, futility. My cadaver tries to sit up, ascending with the help of crutches.

I spot a squirrel. I walk, walk, walk. *"Let's go for walk, ... baby, let's talk ... "*.

Two transparent polythene bags. I fill water in them using a kettle, and then tie them on the bamboo crosspiece. I pierce the bag carefully with multiple holes. The piercings induce rain. Rain is the only hope.

*

Chair with a wet cloth, bodyless, waterless, hopeless — nullity — everything, all life-source is pushed away —

But still, one is hopeful — writing on soil — scripts of hope, future.

"Hello! Is there anyone out there?" — just for a moment I am reminded of the Pink Floyd, but that may be misleading. *"Hello, hello ...!"*

*

Four tin trunks. Two of them the same size. Ideal furniture.

He opens a trunk that contains stories, cloth, a blue floral-printed woman's top — vesture of memory, hope, ... now asleep.

Only in dreams, is there hope — hope of embrace, humanity, scent of my beloved's garment all life-source I can't hear or smell her —

*

"Where are you?" I can't hear you, touch or feel you. All senses have evaporated. I have nothing. I have everything. All my mere belongings in a trunk. I stack the trunks up in ascending order, and open the smallest one on the top.

On the obverse of its lid is pasted a 10-digit number. Can I call for help? Or is it just a missed call?

Om, om, om, … breathing – *pranayam.* Back to the beginning. Black box.

*

3. There After: *Memory, Will*

We look at the world once, in childhood.
The rest is memory.
— Louise Glück

It is very late at night and I am knackered. Yet, I cannot sleep. All night I dream in fragmented images. Memory plays tricks with my mind. Her story, his story, my story, history — all collude and conflate.

The trailer I saw before was only a glimpse. The film is still being cut. We might yet change the narrative. But do we have control over our own destiny or karma's fate? Jump-cut, dissolve, fade. The parallel sprockets of analogue film-reel struggle to run smoothly on its spool.

It is all digital now — memory is not an issue, megabytes abound in tiny microchips. Yet it is all about memory — real, virtual — inscriptions on epitaphs, coded hieroglyphs, ink, text.

Will. Our will. A will on a parchment that was never written. Will to live. What will it be? *"Is there anybody out there?"*

ELAINE CHIEW

The Seal Carver

Through the louvered window of Clifford's second-floor studio on Koon Seng Road, he, bent over a stretch of rice-paper writing the characters 永远 (forever) with a brush, hears, 'Hello', and then again, 'Hello'. The second call is louder and when he looks up, there atop the brown limb of the tembusu he spots a glossy black bird, a mynah. Its bill reminds Clifford of those American sweets his wife is so fond of – orange fading to a yellow tip – candycorn. On her last trip to visit their sons in San Francisco, she had brought back five bags' worth. She eats them like sunflower seeds, sir, their Indonesian helper had said. Indeed she does, and diabetic to boot, but any attempt to chasten her only infuriates her.

His studio is located in the back of his father-in-law's shophouse, also their home, and overlooks a small green field, and the sole distinctive feature is this aged tembusu that provides welcome shade from the afternoon sun slanting into his study. Clifford knows well all the different breeds of birdlife that frequent this patch of geography, given his love and artistic practice of painting huaniao and Chinese calligraphy, and yet, how strange that he has never seen a mynah before this.

The mynah looks at him. Its throat convulses, as if about to speak again.

"Hello, birdie." Clifford pauses; the interruption has caused him to make an unbecoming smudge in the dot character stroke of 'yong' and the 'strange-shaped stone' stroke now resembles a smirking mouth more than a stone. Where has the mynah come from, and will it stay if he tries to coax it to come to him? The bird continues to observe him out of the corner of its eye, as if discerning the tidal flows of qi in its own good time.

Abruptly, it flies off. There and then, he decides to call the mynah Clifford, as a gesture of vanity, but also of self-deprecation. He hopes it will return.

*

Yesterday, out of the blue, a blast from the past. Xiao Fen, his xuemei from university from thirty years ago, found him on Facebook and contacted him, ostensibly to commission a seal chop for a new business she has started with her daughter Ching Hui, come back for good from London – a bakery in Joo Chiat – and her message had read, "Hello Cliffie, I can't believe our paths have not crossed before this..." and his eyes had glazed over, the rest of her message refusing to take purchase in his mind, because he was instantly transported to an image he hadn't thought about these many years – him and Xiao Fen, buck naked on the twin-sized bed in a friend's flat they had borrowed, their smooth thin bodies revealed in a lightning flash gaze in the mirror, wrapped around each other like two cicadas, all arms and legs entwined. The image brings with it a nostalgically sweet but blue feeling. Xiao Fen hadn't wanted to lose her virginity, so she had suggested alternate means of pleasuring each other. Just what were these alternate means? In answer, her eyes sparkling with mischief and laughter, she had pushed his head down towards her belly. Three months in between monsoons spent in this sultry way while their friend was in Kota Bahru on art tutelage with a master, three months pleasuring each other without threatening her virginity, because he and Xiao Fen would never wed (she was betrothed to another, someone better-suited, an upper-crust Chinese with credentials and ambitions to match, handpicked for her by her wealthy parents). He suddenly remembered a Polaroid he took of them together – he with his arm slung around her shoulders, the two of them staring unsmiling into the camera held at arms-length, a cigarette slouching from the corner of his mouth alá James Dean, both without a stitch of clothes on. He remembered it was taken close to their parting as the date of her wedding loomed. She was so full-of-life, so mischievous and cupid (lining up cut guava on his stomach and sprinkling plum-salt on them and saying 'oops' every time the salt missed the guava; weighing his testicles and trying to guess how many grams they were) and yet, so thoughtless about a life to be lived without love, but was that not youth, you spared little thought for the future? No woman had made him laugh quite like that ever since. Definitely not Seok Kheng, his wife.

Where has that photograph gone? He begins an urgent search through his personal effects, desperately sure that he had never thrown it away, the sole memento mori of their time together. Seok Kheng comes in as he's rummaging away, dust floating up from the papers and miscellany like pollen; she throws him a curious glance and sets his tea on the table. "Can you make sure you tidy up before the afternoon viewing?" The shophouse which has been their home for twenty-odd years belongs to Clifford's father-in-law, the 'business magnate' as Clifford likes to refer to him tongue-in-cheek. It may not be their home much longer as Charles wants to cash in, buy himself and them condos out by the coast in Pasir Ris. Clifford does not want to live in Pasir Ris, with its social image of being sandwiched between the ghost-infested hospital of Changi and the charging wild boars of Sengkang, but he will have no say in the matter, as has been the case for his entire marriage with Seok Kheng.

He flaps his hands at her, no point going into words, their conversational exchanges are often, to his mind, like environmental discharge, a by-product of a married life focussed on purpose and utility, a form of waste that lays daily siege to peace of mind and heart, highly toxic. When she goes on her annual sojourn to visit their children, now emigrated to San Francisco, it's the most restorative and peaceful three weeks of his year, and he often finds himself counting down the days to when she leaves. Thinking of his wife while searching for the photograph of past love, this is scandalous, his mind cleaved and divided while his heart feels snagged in turbulence, and it completely destroys his mood to finish the painting of a lotus pond on a rainy day with the couplet he wants to write on the side.

In her message, Xiao Fen had asked to meet to discuss the commission. She had exclaimed that she was happy to see that he had indeed fulfilled his ambition of being an artist – dedicated to his Chinese paintings and calligraphy while maintaining a seal-carving business; she had even come to one of his exhibitions in the past at the Chinese Cultural Centre, though she hadn't thought to contact him then. And why not? He wonders. Why now, and not then? She had dashed off a few quick lines about her current life: widowed, her message said, and her daughter Ching coming back had been a boon. The bakery idea felt like a lease on new life. Widowed was another word he chews over, along with the tough beef in oyster sauce Seok Kheng made for dinner (she refuses to upgrade to FairPrice Finest, saying the downmarket FairPrice saves money). He marvels at Xiao Fen's casual revelation of intimacies; they haven't been in touch for decades, and with one correspondence, it feels as if they are once again, sitting on a bench by the side of a park connector, whispering dirty salacious things in each other's ears and popping peanuts into each other's mouths. The memory brings him a tinge of sharp pain, but it's pain he welcomes, almost as if he's watching an old beloved movie. The way they had kissed, all tongues and teeth, no lips, as if that's how kissing was meant to be done – and lo, after months of limpness, his little cricket jumps to life. At the dinner table!

*

Charles has never called him 'useless' to his face, but he needn't do, it's insinuated in numerous words and gestures (when Charles comes over for the weekly ordeal of family dinner, he would examine Clifford's latest painting and execute one of his stock coded responses: the tap of his chin with one finger – not bad; the suck of teeth at the corner of his mouth – definitely could be improved; the soft 'tch' preceding exhaled breath – no good very bad one.) Many years ago, not long after Clifford married Seok Kheng, there had been a man-to-man discussion. "Look here, what do you want to do with your life?" Charles had levelled him with a piercing stare, and Clifford hadn't been able to answer. He had an art diploma, he was good with his hands and had been working in a Chinatown business that made traditional shop signage and billboards, but the pay was a pittance, and no way could he support himself, let alone a wife. But Seok Kheng had fancied herself in love with an artist, and in the devastation he felt after Xiao Fen's wedding, which he didn't admit even to himself, a numbness had set in that was glacial, and every day, he painted in a subconscious attempt to thaw, and sometimes succeeded, because the way ink bled into rice paper – tiny florets of washed ink tissuing into fibrous ecru – was so beautiful and tender his eyes would tear up. Eventually, Charles had set them up with the shophouse, the seal-carving business which he had had to learn on the double, and arranged for a gallery to take on his paintings to sell. In Western art circles, as Clifford has come to learn, Charles would have been a sort of patron, and yet, what patron seeks to undermine his client whenever he has a chance? His attacks are never vicious, and yet, one less-than-artfully phrased question could decimate Clifford – "why always the lotus?", Charles had asked once with a sneer. It was on the tip of Clifford's tongue to quip, one could paint lotus blossoms ad infinitum to the day one died and never reach spiritual enlightenment, but 'the business magnate' would see that as a slight on his artistic perspicacity, as indeed it was intended to be, and it didn't do to bite the hand that fed you.

It's getting towards one p.m., the time of his meeting with Xiao Fen. He has suggested that they meet at a kopitiam on Old Airport Road; he has no wish for Seok Kheng to encounter Xiao Fen, who has no knowledge of this past love. He arrives at the café, all sweaty and bothered for fear of running late, and just as he is scanning the QR Code for TraceTogether, a voice behind him says, "Cliffie!" followed by a finger-prod on both sides of his waist. He jumps, whirls around and unmistakably, even with the face mask, it's Xiao Fen – older, yes, her hair now cropped to a fashionable bob instead of the waist-length coil he used to love running his hands through, but her eyes are surprisingly free of corner wrinkles and just as twinkly as before. It hadn't occurred to him to feel self-conscious prior to meeting, but now he is beset with embarrassment as he thinks of his pot-belly, his balding head, his deteriorating eyesight. The young man he was – whom she had nicknamed "My Asian Tom Hanks" – where has that boy gone? They both stand there with eyes scouring for the ravages of age and time, long enough that people bump into them before they recover their senses.

Sitting down at a corner table after ordering, he looks at Xiao Fen, jabbering nineteen to the dozen; apparently she is going by 'Synthia' now, spelled with an 'S' not 'C', and she proceeds to detail how three decades of housewifery has led to a reawakening after her husband died of colon cancer last year – carpe diem, she says, with gusto, her hands waving about. Next she's on about her only child Ching, who has a pâtissier degree from Le Cordon Bleu, and her gorgon of a mother-in-law, who owns the bakery chain Tung Wah, that battle-axe's closely-guarded baking secrets, and how she herself never believed that she has any affinity for baking, despite being in a family with a food-conglomerate business, and how she has just started a baking club right here in Joo Chiat, imagine that, and the entire time he sits there listening, nodding his head, this single errant thought sears its way through his mind: does she not remember how hot they used to be for each other, how incendiary, and also how ferociously ignorant they were? How could she sit there slurping up bak chor mee and issuing forth speech bubbles of inane chatter? And he echoes her in chowing down like an imbecile. Has he nothing to say to this past love, or to be deathly honest, this sole love? She pauses, sips from her longan juice, and then leans closer, "How are you, how is life treating you? Happily married and all that?" As their eyes lock, he imagines what he thinks are trapped embers of a dying love, dying but not dead quite, and the blood coursing through his atria and ventricles pulsates wilder, raking through an emotional acre he couldn't have imagined still exists at the sundown of a man's life, and yet, here it is, a truth one would scoff at if told, that love, specifically his love for this woman, has remained frozen for thirty years, and because frozen, it has become snow-white and pristine, a perfectly unblemished preserved thing. Like the marbling of soapstone.

*

He spends all morning looking for his chisel-knife with the flat blade, finally locating it where it has been all along, in his knife kit, and then spends the whole afternoon choosing a suitable soapstone, picking one up, putting it down – Qingtian or Changhua or chicken blood, not that it much matters, it's just the colour of the seal, but normally not so indecisive, he simply can't make up his mind. By the time he feels less mentally manic, it's four o'clock, and the chop is due for delivery tomorrow. He glances out the window, and is surprised to see the mynah there again, a shred of lettuce leaf drooping from its mouth which it must have picked up from a garbage bin somewhere. In one gobble, the leaf is gone, and the mynah steps daintily along the branch, cocking its head, eyeing him. He goes downstairs and brings up a dish of blueberries which he sets on the windowsill, gently calling out to it, calling the bird by his own name, and it feels hilarious. In another life, he might've been a bird just like this one, free to roam open skies and undulating landscapes, alighting on bough or bower or gazebo, tethered to neither role, expectations nor status; in another life, he might've married the girl of his dreams, they would have three daughters together, and each would be named consecutively, 'Lian-One, Lian-Two, Lian-Three', a tribute to the lotus blossom.

He whistles and whistles, but the mynah won't come. It simply gazes at him, flaps a glossy wing, and then, audibly, says, Hello.

Hello, hello, he shouts back, inexplicably joyous.

He finishes the carving by dinner time, places it in its silk brocade box in readiness for tomorrow. Xiao Fen has left all the decisions to him; he chooses the Qingtian stone for its lovely jade colour, he carves in intaglio, the 'yin' style, so that the characters would show up in white on a bed of cinnabar red, and he uses an ancient flowing script to write 'Yip Ching Hui', the daughter's name. Xiao Fen had said at lunch yesterday that she would like to introduce him to her daughter; already, in carving the seal, he feels a karmic link he is hard-pressed to articulate. Over the course of lunch, he and Xiao Fen had slipped into a mantle of 'old friends', though it felt artificial to him, and he sensed, more than saw the evidence, of a surge of feeling underneath Xiao Fen's cool, chic demeanour. What if he were to propose that they continue keeping in touch, now that they have resumed contact, and what if, one day, he were to give her that photograph he has in his possession? What will happen then? What does he want to happen?

At dinner, like an eerie eavesdropping electronic device, Seok Kheng starts banging on about her pal from the baking club, Lisande, whose ex-husband has recently found himself a new squeeze, younger by a good ten years. She harrumphs, The girl must be barely out of diapers, and Clifford wants to argue: that would mean she's still a toddler while Lisande's husband is in the throes of puberty and equally not culpable, but he decides to keep his mouth shut; they have been here before, and the last time, she almost poked his eye out with her chopsticks while she ranted about aging men and their perverted need to hold onto youthful vim and vigour.

*

He isn't sure what preconceptions he might've had, maybe none, but he isn't quite prepared for how pretty Ching is. It isn't her prettiness that makes him suddenly awkward and tongue-tied when he presents the chop, but the fact that if he dares say it, she is yi mo yi yang – the exact replica – of her mother in her twenties, the same lily-pad face, the same dimple in one cheek, the sparkly eyes, the soft sable hair; it's like encountering Xiao Fen all over again, and it puts the brain in a kind of spin, because the real Xiao Fen is standing next to him, proffering a gula melaka chiffon cake even as he continues to stare almost balefully at Ching, which seems to make her uncomfortable, as she tugs at her crop-top and shifts her hair to one side of her neck. They are at Seok Kheng's mansion of a house on Duku Lane, and he is awed by the splendiferous trappings of wealth on display – the Ming Dynasty vases, the contemporary sculptures, the swimming pool, the porcelain vat full of finning koi, the chandeliers (there are at least three in the living room alone), and also, his sudden face-to-face encounter with a 1.5 metre scroll of sanshui by a fellow artist and rival by the name of Tatt Boon, whom he regards as an empty-headed imitator.

During the serving of cake and tea, he makes a faux pas. The first forkful takes him by utter surprise – he's not much for cake, but the graininess mixed in with a certain softness on his tongue in that first bite swamps him with a memory from the past, and the words roll out of him unbidden: "Remember, Xiao Fen, that day we were strolling in Chinatown? You were so hungry you bought a single angku from this kueh shop, and then you spotted this crying boy, no more than five probably, and you offered him the angku and immediately got scolded by the shop-owner for it. She reprimanded the customer instead of her son! But when she disappeared to the back, you gave the angku anyway but he wouldn't stop crying, remember that? You told him that you would tell him a story but he must finish eating by the time you finished telling your story. Did you know that the entire time I was filled with so much anxiety, not because the mother would come back and see you, but that I wouldn't hear the end of the story before she came back?"

An awkward silence descends after Clifford's voluble speech. He reddens, catches mother and daughter exchanging glances. Ching's mannerisms become stiff and formal, and when she inspects and tries the chop, her thank-you afterwards is frosty. Suddenly, he suspects that she probably had known nothing about her mother's past romance with him. He's not sure why she's offended, but there is nothing he can do about it now. When Ching excuses herself to get her cheque book, he manages to catch Xiao Fen's eye. "Good cake," he offers timidly.

"Cliffie, why did you bring all that up?" Her casual tone is belied by her taut smile. He scratches just above his ear, casting around for something more to say. His glance falls back on the cake and in that moment, notices that Xiao Fen has mashed bits of it with her fork into a flattened mass.

"You have never learned to apologise," she says quietly, "have you?" The statement, so at odds with what came before, floors him, hinting at something out of his ken, something inapposite to the history of their involvement with each other, imbued with a mystery of perspective he hadn't discerned. "Apologise?" he cues.

She shrugs. "Never mind, I guess you don't remember."

*

Clifford goes for a long walk afterwards, his mind awhirl with questions: from Duku Lane, he turns down Duku Road, crossing Joo Chiat, his head down, just ambling, not noticing the scenery, the surrounding activities or the late afternoon heat. Whatever did Xiao Fen mean by 'apologise'? Had he ever done anything in their relationship that he needed to apologise for? Wasn't she as enamoured with him as he was with her? Or has she changed her mind in hindsight, and the memory of their love is beautiful no longer? This unwanted revision of past memory pains and angers him. Was that why she contacted him now, and not before? Did she wish him to 'apologise'? But for what? His thoughts run around in circles, and before he realises, he has ended up in Paya Lebar Square. He buys a large meat bao, removes his mask, eats it sitting on a stone ledge, and the taste of it disappoints him: so salty and pedestrian, not a bit of uplift on the tongue. In the past, there was pride in making a good pork bao, skill and art were involved, now everything is just motion and pushing food out for mass consumption. Seal carving too will die out one day, and seal carvers with it. He watches people flow around him, going about their quotidian activities in the new normal, seemingly oblivious. We are swimming in a sea of death, he thinks, and this subcutaneous knowledge, obstructed from view behind these masked faces, nevertheless is lodged just underneath the skins of each and everyone. Like flashes out of the blue, do they remember how things used to be? The tragedy is this: what could never be etched or engraved is the microscopic gap between perception and reality. It exists in all that we can't see.

*

The photograph of him and Xiao Fen that he had been searching for lies on top of the black lacquered box containing his knife-kit, the first thing he sees when he gets to his desk after his walk. It not only jolts him, but for the first time, a hard bolt of shame tunnels through him. Seok Kheng comes in with his cup of tea just then, rattling the lid on top of the cup, and the photograph slips from his fingers. She says, "I found it on the floor, it must have fallen from your papers. Past amour, is it?"

He flushes, picks it up, turning it over to its white back. "It happened before we met."

Her demeanour is deliberately calm and chill, and it scares him. "Oh, I don't care," she says, "Everyone has a skeleton or two. Why did you never mention her?"

"Like I said, it was before we met."

His wife, true to her nature, simply says, "She must not have loved you all that much, considering that you didn't succeed in marrying her. Look at that sour expression on her face. Taking a naked picture together, that's brave of her. Very European leh, how did you persuade her?"

Then, he remembers, the memory seeping through him like inkwash. They had quarrelled moments before the photograph, she had had to leave for a wedding photography shoot and it had reminded them that their moments together were dribbling down to the end. He had wanted to say, don't go, or even don't leave me, but instead, said that they should have a photograph together, for memory's sake. To commemorate their lust. Naked as they were on the bed, and him moments before, mouth buried between her thighs, and that feeling of sinking into her, he could process neither the ending sure to come nor the irony of being together like this, and he took up his camera and said, Let's seal our time together, entomb it in a photograph. She lashed out at him, calling him inconsiderate, out of his depths, and they started slinging words like hot stones, until finally, droplets of tears leaked out of his eyelids. Yes, he was the one who had cried. She remained dry-eyed, and this angered him too. He lit a cigarette, puffed on it, slung an arm around her, pulled her close and took the Polaroid photo without her permission. It would seem that indeed, he had something to apologise for.

He's still looking at Seok Kheng, aghast, when the mynah interrupts through the window, but this time, chirping distinctly, Goodbye, Goodbye.

*

He dashes out of the house, the photograph clutched in his hand, at first just to escape having to answer his wife, then he finds himself running in the direction of Duku Lane. Breath heaving, legs pumping like pistons, sides aching, the distance seems insurmountable, as if he would never get there before his breath runs out, and he has this thought: just what exactly is he trying to salvage? His pristine memory of a frozen past? The delicate potentiality of a renewed liaison? Or is it because the power of the unsaid has the ability to break you? When he gets to the front of Xiao Fen's house, the automatic gate is just swinging open, and a car is being reversed out. It brakes. His peek at the car's rearview mirror reveals Ching, Xiao Fen's daughter. Their gazes clash in the mirror. She gapes. He doubles over, hands resting on his knees, gasping for breath, drool and sweat dripping from him. Ching gets out of the car and walks over. "Uncle, is everything okay? My mother is at her Pilates session, and I'm about to run some errands and then pick her up." He doesn't answer, and she asks again, "Is something the matter?"

He waves one hand in denial. It hits him then: if only Xiao Fen could have been there, would he have shown her the photograph? What would begin with that simple gesture? In his head, he imagines handing the photograph over to Xiao Fen, seeing her take it, looking at it, her eyes widening, her mouth falling open, an expression overtaking her face, a film of emotion not dissimilar to the face she used to make whenever she orgasmed.

"Uncle?"

He looks up. Sweat is pouring from him, so much sweat that his vision dims. Through it, he sees that it is her. Xiao Fen, come back to him, from all those years ago, her limpid agate eyes, the smooth sheen of her face. He holds out the photograph to her. "I'm sorry," he sputters out. "I am so sorry." Her glance automatically falls on the photograph, then her face pales. He thrusts the photo at her again. She takes a step back, a look of hesitancy mixed with alarm overcoming her features, and the instantaneous judgment forming in her eyes – he could identify it: *off-his-rocker, pervert.* He stops short, suddenly realising what he has done. He retracts his hand like a turtle retracting its head, and the other hand covers his face in mortification. "I'm so sorry," he says again, but this time for something else entirely. He whirls about, walking rapidly away. She calls out once, "Wait..." but she doesn't repeat the call, and he doesn't have the guts nor means to explain, just as he hadn't had the guts nor means those many years ago to retain Xiao Fen in his life, or even to call her just to apologise.

What-ifs and what-could-have-beens abound in any one life, and just one of these might have altered the course of his life permanently, as well as the lives it touched. Sweat continues to stream from his pores, drenching his shirt. In fact, sweat continues to pour from him for days and days afterwards, mysterious, odourless. In the middle of that same night, he awoke to the sounds of Seok Kheng's quiet sobbing, and it pained him. No, one did not suffer a loveless marriage alone.

In the year that follows until they move to Pasir Ris, the mynah never returns. One memory, though, solidifies, and it troubles the one before, the way a wrinkle does pristine, unblemished rice paper. As he was retreating from Xiao Fen's house, he had looked down at the crumpled limp photograph in his hand. His thumb had punctured the paper in his pell-mell haste, leaving a tear exactly where his left breast was, the fissured line resembling the first cut a blade makes into soft stone, that moment pregnant with all the possibilities that the carved character has yet to become.

DANTON REMOTO

Red Leaves

Under the pine trees, three girls were walking to the Session Hall in Teacher's Camp, their light-brown uniforms blending with the softly falling dusk in the mountain city of Baguio.

I slung my blue jacket on my shoulders and stood up from the stone steps of Benitez Hall. My classmates had gone to the hall ahead of me. The sun was beginning to dip behind the trees, leaving awash of colours—pink and salmon and red, with tints of grey that deepened with the night.

The emcee was a short young man with hair slicked to one side. He introduced the Director of the 20th Quezon City High School Seniors' Conference, a big, muscled man with a voice that matched his build. The emcee also called onstage the coordinators for accommodations, meals, security, secretariat, and socials. Polite applause. From where I sat at the back, the newsletter coordinator was a plain-looking girl, tall and skinny. The coordinators were last year's students; this year, they volunteered to help run the conference.

The French windows in the newsletter room were wide open. A chill wind roamed inside. I buttoned my jacket and turned up its collar.

"Hi!" called out a voice that was warm and even. I turned around. The newsletter coordinator. She was nearly as tall as I, her head tilted regally to one side. She had a big mouth and bee-stung lips. She looked like a model.

"Hello," I said. "I'm Danilo Cruz, and you're the newsletter editor, right?"

"Yes, I'm Roxanne, Roxanne Gonzalez." She had high cheekbones and a wide forehead. Her jaws were angular, the kind of face you'd see on a magazine cover. Her eyes were large, and they had a way of turning brown in the light. But when she smiled, I thought I saw sadness in those eyes.

"Please fill in the personal data sheet. We'll wait for the others to arrive." She turned around and walked to the door, pasting a piece of paper scrawled with "NEWSLETTER" in blue pentel pen on the door. Her shiny hair flowed down her shoulders. Black Levi's hugged her long long legs.

Roxanne presided over the meeting. "Jhun-Jhun, Let-let, and Mai-Mai, please you can interview the delegates for the *Gazette* issue. Ask them about the trip from Manila. First impressions, fresh impressions."

"What about me, Roxanne?" said the guy from across me. He looked like an airhead, one of those guys who had nothing between his ears, except earwax. His name was Jonathan Livingston Sy Go.

"Okay, Jon. Can you write an editorial based on the theme of the conference? The theme is —"

"Oh, yes, I know: 'Youth: Moral Values in the New Decade.'"

"Oh, how nice to know that *you* know the theme of the conference. Now write an editorial, please, around 250 words, okay, Jon?" Beneath the cool voice, I noticed a quick temper. And then she looked at me.

"Danilo could you please do the literary page?"

"Okay. Will do." Then I smiled to catch her attention.

She ignored me, then she added. "Please turn in all assignments by five p.m. If there are no more questions, you may go to your rooms and rest. There's an acquaintance party tonight. Enjoy."

Everybody stood up and left the room, except me.

"Aren't you going to the party?"

"No, I've two left feet, you know. How about you?"

A sigh. Then: "I've to finish this for a paper in my class." She showed me a small book bound in black cloth. *A Farewell to Arms* by Ernest Hemingway. "Don't let me keep you here," she said.

Oh, you only want to continue reading the love story of Catherine and Lieutenant Henry, I wanted to tease her, but all I said was goodbye.

Inside my room, I took off my jeans and changed into the blue jogging pants that my father gave me last Christmas. I lit a cigarette, a habit I began only last month. Like many of my classmates, the first time I smoked I did it in the bathroom of our house. It must be those adverts (*Come to Marlboro country*), with the sexy cowboy in tough brown leather jacket and boots, because I had a hard-on the first time I smoked in the bathroom of our house.

The cigarette butt glowed. Smoke quivered in the air. I wanted to be alone, to think, because I was confused again. I heard the wind, a sound lost instantly amongst the pine trees. I thought I heard a familiar voice, floating from another country. I stood up and closed the windows. What shall I give the Gazette? A poem, perhaps?

I picked up my blue ballpoint pen and yellow pad paper. Writing. Writing was like a sudden urge, an itch, a lust even. The words ran inside me, like blood.

*

In the province of Bulacan, I saw farmers in threadbare pants and faded shirts. Behind them lay the fields heavy with ripe grains. When we reached the province of Pampanga, a mountain broke the smoothness of the horizon. Mount Arayat. The familiar mountain of memory. They said that many rebels still lived there. The original inhabitants of the Philippines, the dark-skinned and curly-haired Aetas, also lived in the higher reaches of the mountain. Above Mount Arayat, the sky was an immense blueness.

We stopped for lunch at the Vineyard, a restaurant in Rosales, Pangasinan. After lunch and pissing in one of those toilets where you held your breath so you would not have a migraine later, we went back to our buses. We passed a bridge with steel girders and high arches. But below it lay burning sand and stones, not the mighty, roaring river I had expected.

When the air became raw and sharp, I knew we were going up Kennon Road. Suddenly, smoke came from the hood of the La Mallorca. "The bus is burning!" cried the girl behind me.

The driver stood up, a stocky man with a beer belly and skin the colour of dry earth. "We only need water. Don't worry, we'll be all right," he said. My teacher, Mrs. Genova, noisily volunteered her Tupperware filled with water. We snickered.

Then we continued with the trip. Mountain and sky, river and ravine. I was a small waterfall. They said it was called the Bridal Veil Falls, the water falling down the side of the hill like a thin and white veil. But the sight of a landslide made us shift in our seats again. It was a four-month-old landslide, caused by Typhoon Miling. One side of the mountain was gone. But the landslide had created a wide and calm lake. From the lake, a young tree was beginning to grow.

And when we reached the city of Baguio, the first things I saw were the poinsettias, like blood on the face of a hill. My Biology textbook said the red petals of the poinsettias were not really flowers, but leaves.

Thus, you can say that the poinsettias are masters of disguise.

*

I would have awakened later but for the noise in the room. "That Ruby from Holy Family Academy has a very soft body," said Bing Bong.

I plumped my pillow into a fat missile and aimed it at him.

"You're just jealous. Where did you go last night?" asked Bing Bong.

Mario was my new classmate. He was wearing only his undershirt and his shorts, showing his young, hard biceps and hairy thighs. I always looked at him surreptitiously in our Physical Education class, when he would be wearing his abbreviated shorts and sleeveless shirts.

And now Mario said, "I saw him in the newsletter room. Seems like he's making a pass at the newsletter coordinator. Remember the *Vogue* model?"

I wanted to say, "You're just jealous, Gerry," but I held my horses. I found Mario cute, and he always teased me. He must have sensed that I liked him, even if I did not show it directly, which was my wont. I said, "Hey, I wasn't making a pass at her." Then: "But of course, I'd love to —"

Mario just smiled at me, a wicked glint in his eyes.

*

After breakfast, we went to the Session Hall. The list of delegates and the groups they belonged to were tacked on the bulletin board. I belonged to Group 5, with my classmates Edgar Allan Pe and Daffodil Tulip Pastilan. During the first session, Daffodil was elected secretary and I, chairman. In the afternoon, Attorney Honey Boy Velez in a dark-blue suit bored us to death when he gave a two-hour speech on the theme of the conference that began with national hero Doctor Jose Rizal's quote, "The youth is the hope of the Fatherland." Rizal must be break-dancing in his grave by now. I sat at the back and did some doodles.

After the sessions ended, I left my essay in the newsletter room, with a short note for Roxanne. After dinner of fresh Baguio vegetables and sweet-and-sour fish *escabeche*, I walked back to the room and saw her, but she was busy reading Hemingway. On the table lay my essay, unread.

I rushed back to my room, hands deep in the pockets of my jacket, gnats of annoyance following me. Nobody, nobody ignores a frigging Aries. My classmates were all there. Mario said that we should drink. We pooled our money together, then sent Nick, Gerry and Mandy to smuggle a case of beer. We tried to be quiet since drinking was against the house rules, but as the empty beer bottles multiplied, the noise level also rose. My classmates told stories and jokes about women with boobs like the bumper of a car, or what they would do if they met Bo Derek on the beach. We smoked and drank and burped. A haze began to form before me, followed by a hiss of words: *"I like you, Danny, but I'm sorry..."* Sheena had said that evening in their yard, the garden perfumed with *ylang-ylang* and jasmine. *"My family is moving to Canada in summer. Let us write to each other. Good luck and best wishes...."* The beer bubbled and foamed, and I drank my San Miguel cold and bitter. So many departures and so few arrivals. Afterward, I was so drunk I just staggered to my bed and fell asleep. *Good luck and best wishes.* As if she were congratulating a mere acquaintance on graduation day. Sheena and I had been dating for a year, watching films at Virra Mall and fumbling with each other's clothes in the dark. But being bred in Catholic convents, she had her rules. The navel was the border zone. Everything below was a no-no. So while watching *Blue Lagoon* I would give her a French kiss and run my tongue around her nipples and try to pull down her Bang Bang Jeans, but she always slapped my hand. The noise of a hand being slapped would bring snickers from the other lovers around us. We would stop, look at each other, and then begin kissing again. I whispered to my Catholic girlfriend that the pillar of salt wants to see the burning bush but she would not hear of it. She would just kiss me back and embrace me tightly, running her fingers down my spine. I always went home with a bad case of blue balls. Those were, ah, truly painful moments.

The sunlight streaming from the window woke me up. I got up from bed with a morning hard-on. My classmates were still asleep. All bombed out. Mario was on the bed next to mine. Such luck. His grey, woollen blanket had already fallen on the floor. He was wearing his white jockeys. He also had a hard-on, which tent-poled his jockeys. I had to tear myself away from the Tower of Babel so my morning could begin.

It went to the bathroom and took a shower. I washed and lathered my face, and then I shaved. I remembered my dream last night (Mario and I taking a bath together, at dawn, our fingers exploring each other's bodies), and I slapped cold water on my face. I had to pull myself together, because later in the day would be the panel interview for the Ten Most Outstanding Delegates of the conference.

The Director, the Conference Secretary, and a man introduced as the dean of an Opus Dei university interviewed us. The results would be added to the scores each candidate got for their performance during the conference. We were interviewed individually, behind closed doors. It was all beginning to sound like the Miss Universe beauty contest, and so while they interviewed me, I sat straight, with my right foot pointed forward.

The first two questions were a breeze. The Opus Dei dean, who looked like any of your kind uncles, asked the third question: "What do you think of such adolescent preoccupations as masturbation, drinking, and drugs?" He spat the word *adolescent* from his lips as if it were some illness.

I was uneasy because I had expected a question about the conference itself. He was sooooo damned smug. I said, "Well, sir, I think drinking is not so bad, especially if done in a social setting. Smoking you can do if you want to have yellow, nicotine-stained fingernails. Drugs, I would like to believe, would be too expensive for high-school students like us."

"So do you smoke or drink or take drugs?" he asked, taking off his thick glasses that looked like goggles, and then fixed his sharp eyes on me.

What the hell do you care? I wanted to tell him, but I kept my cool. He who blows his top first, loses. "Of course, as I said, I would drink socially, especially if my peer pressure me. I smoked for a while, but the nicotine stained my fingernails and teeth and so I stopped. Drugs? I jack off, like everybody else. I drink beer, yes. Drugs? I don't even know where to find them, maybe you have an idea where?" I would have rambled on, but the dean had told me to stop.

During the awarding ceremonies, after the emcee had called the names of the tenth down to the second Most Outstanding Delegate, I knew that I had lost. I was sitting beside Mario, inhaling the fragrance of his *Brüt*. The night was cold and our warm thighs were grazing each other. I was thinking of the many things I could do to his hairy thighs when my name was called as the Most Outstanding Delegate. Mario gripped my hand tightly, and then he hugged me. I wished he would never let go. But he did, eventually, and so I walked to the stage and received my heavy gold medallion and a certificate done in sheepskin. My classmates' Instamatic cameras kept on popping.

The Opus Dei vote could only pull me down a few points, I heard later from the grapevine that always clung and grew after the results of any contest had been announced. After the awarding ceremonies, there were some more boring speeches. I asked Mario, "Would you like to take a walk? It's cooler outside."

Down the footpath we walked. Dusk had already settled amongst the leaves, and the air was heavy with the clean fragrance of pine. A moon hung in the sky, ripe and full and yellow, like a harvest moon. Is there still a man on the moon? I wondered suddenly, remembering our housemaid Ludy's tale one childhood night so many years ago. But I let the memory go.

Mario and I sat on a concrete bench encircling a dry fountain. A mermaid in stone sat in the centre of the fountain.

"Congratulations again," Mario said as he sat beside me. Vapour rose from his lips as he spoke.

"Thank you," I answered. He looked good in his black long-sleeved denim shirt, with one button down, and faded blue jeans. His eyes were big and penetrating. I wanted so much to touch his face and tell him I like him. I knew he knew what I wanted to tell him, but the words remained frozen on my tongue.

It was he who broke the awkward silence. "Perhaps we should be heading back?" Then he snickered. "I think any moment now a snowflake would settle on the tip of my nose."

Which I would melt with a kiss, I wanted to say, dangerously witty to the very end. But all I could say was "Yes, you're right." Then I swallowed all of them, down my gut, all the words I wanted him to hear. Suddenly, the brightest young person in this gathering was struck dumb. *Like gold medallions to the thumb.*

We walked back to the hall, the heavy darkness and mist smothering us. We sat down and tried to do small talk amidst all that noise. I knew then that he had already let me go. I was crushed, but being an Aries I never showed my defeat. Early on in life I had learnt that you could always sheathe everything with irony and wit.

The farewell party went on. The DJ played that stupid song about Wolfgang Amadeus Mozart. But when he played "Morning Girl," Mario suddenly stood up. He walked clear across the darkened hall, to a girl in a pink and frothy dress. Barbie smiled and stood up and walked with him to the centre of the dance floor. His arms tightened about her waist and they danced so close to each other. For once, I wished the dean from the Opus Dei were here, to tell Mario that there should be distance between him and his doll "so your respective guardian angels could pass by."

I wanted to laugh, but I was afraid my face would crack from all the sadness inside me. Quietly I slipped out of the room, ignoring everybody who was congratulating me. All along, my gold medallion as the Most Outstanding Delegate hung in my chest. I only forced a smile when I saw Roxanne, who was asking me if I had seen my essay in the last issue of the *Gazette.* I just nodded, and walked away. I was walking into a door, another door, an infinity of doors.

Down the stairs I ran until I reached the dark yard. My arm brushed against the poinsettias hanging like bouquets in the empty air. But when I turned to look at them, small beads of water were glittering on the red leaves.

IVY NGEOW

The Dog-sitter

He took a long, hard look and then he said OK. David Soh had never had a dog before but then he'd never lost his job before. There was a first for everything. His 22-year-old niece Stephanie, who'd never worked a day in her life, now fancied "a change". She was going to America to "check out" a course. It was all right for some people.

She'd offered to pay him RM200 a day. Expenses on top. David was not in a position to say no. All he had to do was to keep the dog company, take him for walks, feed him. Seemed like the easiest job. He thought back when he was in PR a year ago, managing a tech firm's marketing and web strategy. He hadn't found anything else since. Soon he would be handling a dog, now *that* was a different animal.

Having to bite down on his pride, whenever he dropped by at his brother's place, did not make it easier. His brother and sister-in-law ran different businesses morning to night. He never saw them. You wouldn't know they lived here. He looked around him, at the dark granite patio with a hammered finish where the dog had been padding around since living here. The dog's house alone was a palace, a mini sandstone temple with built-in Italian spray taps for washing the stainless steel water and food bowls.

There was no denying that his brother had done well for himself. 5,000 square foot designer house with swimming pool and electronic gates in Mont Kiara, with far-reaching views of Klang Valley. A new black Range Rover, his brother's spare family vehicle. And a couple of "less rugged" vehicles such as a tiny sports Mercedes, which was Stephanie's, and a Prius (the wife's shopping trolley).

"His name is Keane," said Stephanie. She wanted a personal maid just for herself and she got two; a big dog and she got one and now she'd decided she'd die for a film studies course in San Francisco and that too was in the bag.

"Pardon?" Said David, distracted when he looked straight into the dog's soul, if there was such a thing, and the dog stared back.

"Keane."

Keane was like a long-lost friend, found again. The dog's eyes had the sad downturned look of an ancient lion, yet he was not old. He was only four. In human terms he would be a young, fit, hot-blooded man, chuckled David. The opposite of him. He was a slight, bespectacled middle-aged anyman, an ex-manager type with no interests except lunch or golf and even that was now a fantasy, like going to the moon. His only thrill had been dragging himself to a sports bar in Bangsar Village to watch Liverpool's Champion League matches at 3am. Perfect for the unemployed. Golf, private health insurance, gym membership and lunch at the club had been the perks of his job. His world.

He stroked the dog's head tentatively.

"He OK one, Uncle. You can sayang him. If he don't like you, you will know straight away one."

"OK," David laughed. Keane's tail, wagging continuously, slapped Stephanie's thigh. His jaw hung open in a drooly smile. The dog shut his large sad eyes like it was rare to be shown affection from anyone, apart from Stephanie who was now "too busy". David's hand moved to tickling the dog's neck which David enjoyed almost as much.

Keane was an enormous black and copper-coloured Rottweiler, Shar Pei and something else mix, which gave him his huge melted candle look. His neck alone was the size of a small motorcycle wheel. Stephanie was already his third owner as he was abandoned, abused by various other dubious owners and then finally brought to the animal shelter. No one knew where he came from originally. Stephanie felt sorry for him, adopted him from the shelter six months ago, sent him for training, and now had decided she needed to party for about two months in California.

David took on his new "job" with the gusto and enthusiasm of discovering a new bike hobby. After Stephanie left, he went from his modest apartment in Sunway every day to his brother's Mont Kiara resort-style mansion. He picked up Keane and drove around in the Range Rover. They went everywhere together, mostly exploring nature reserves, caves, big parks, long walks. David started enjoying avoiding people while improving his fitness. Why on earth did he ever need a gym? Dumbbells were dumb. Dogs were smart. He already started to feel odd stabs of grief that when Stephanie got back, he'd have to say goodbye to Keane.

Sometimes he waved to neighbours, acquaintances and other dog owners or walkers. Maybe he'd dog-sit as a career. Working his first 3-hour shifts before 9am, getting fit, taking care of animals. Never having to schmooze or talk to colleagues or arrange meetings again. Lunch on the go. Keane didn't like to sit around panting in kopitiams. David imagined himself doing job applications and LinkedIn all afternoon with the TV on low and the aircon on high. Then back for another 3-hour shift of more dogs, from 5 to 8pm.

He shopped for food at the vet (none of that rubbish from Carrefour), weighed the right amount for Keane's breed, age and weight, showered him every two weeks, dried him with a fluffy extra-large beach towel that he bought from Jusco in a pack of three. His brother and niece would surely give him a reference. Alia, one of Stephanie's personal maids, was relieved. Indonesian and Muslim, she did not want to care for canines for cultural reasons.

One of the places he liked to explore with the dog was the hills at around 5 am when Bukit Kiara Park was cool and calm, with the hum of insects and birdsong. David would turn left after the Pizza Hut and start the steep ascent before finding a parking spot for the Range Rover. Keane was keen. He'd always jump out of the boot, casting a glance of approval towards David before he dashed into the bushes to sniff around and find treasures such as the scent of a jungle rat or a flying squirrel in the dense, ancient rainforest.

After almost two hours of hilly jungle exploration, occasionally David would buy takeaway breakfast on the way home, prata or chee cheong fun at the TTDI market before peak hour traffic started to build. Also, it was probably his only chance in this lifetime to show off the

Range Rover. He was almost 60 and had been hanging on for his retirement package from the tech PR industry before shit happened, so why shouldn't he show off the Range Rover? He always got ta-pau because he knew most people wouldn't welcome an enormous and not very handsome-looking dog into their cafe or kiosk. Though of course, to David, who was not in the least biased, Keane was cugly. Cute ugly.

One morning, when it was still dark, it started to drizzle after they arrived in the park. Mist covered the paths a few meters in front of them. David proceeded with caution but Keane relied on his sense of smell and confidently strode off looking for marks and scents of anything he could chase or actually catch. A long-tailed civet cat, a fox.

David looked up at the trees. They were at least 50m high. He had his waterproof hooded walking jacket on. He pulled the zip all the way to the top and tightened the knotted toggles around his neck, so that the hood stayed on, not slipping back. He checked his phone was on full charge, as he'd need a torch at some point. In some parts of the forest, it was eternally dark from the dense tree canopy. He glimpsed a faint figure in the misty distance. Surprised, he stared. It was unusual for this time, when day looked like night. Keane let out a low growl, and his hair stood, that motorbike-wheel neck stiff as steel.

David felt a chill. Keane had changed. Icy sweat poured from David's brow, steaming up his spectacles. A tourist guide in Sarawak had once told him an Iban proverb: "when you know the jungle and a friend very well, you know well this is not the jungle and the friend you know."

Keane suddenly charged off towards the ghostly figure without even a glance back. The copper-colored, short-haired body bolted into the darkness of the jungle. "Keane! Keane?" David shouted. "Come back! Oh God. Keane!" The dog did not return.

A few shrieks. Then it stopped. David waited. Was it a monkey or a human? He shouted the dog's name again, as he ran through the dense forest, between the fallen trunks, over roots, dead leaves, probably even snakes. There was no path, this was the real jungle, no one had come with a parang and cut out a nice tarmac walkway. It was covered in thorny undergrowth and branches. It was hard to tell what was plant or what was space in the darkness.

David tripped and fell. He hit his head on a log branch protruding at an odd angle. He felt the hot trickle of blood turning cold against his forehead skin when he touched it. "Keane," he moaned. "Where are you?" He got up and tried to run to where he thought Keane went. His phone. Where was his phone? He had to find that too. It must have dropped out. "Keane!" he screamed.

The dog returned, calm, wagging his tail. "Oh my God," he said. The dog's jaws were wet, dark, glistening. "What did you do? What the hell have you..." In his jaws was David's phone.

David held his breath. He stared at the dog, unable to read his expression. He took the phone from the dog. When David shone the torch of his phone, Keane's grinning teeth were covered in blood.

"Oh my God," he gasped sharply and his hand flew to his forehead.

The dog led him by looking at him and walking, walking and looking back at him. Shaking, he followed the dog.

As there were no paths, the dog jumped over the uneven ground, roots and bushes while David had to climb his way over, covered in cuts and bruises.

The dog stopped.

Something like a lying human form twitched on the ground. He switched on the torch on his phone. "Oh shit," cried David, his voice trembling. "Oh shit, shit, shit," he roared. He clamped his hand over his mouth, the other still shining the phone torch. He leaned towards the bulky figure. A man. A fly already landed on him and buzzed like a little doorbell. "Oh God, Keane, what have you done? No, no, no. Oh God," David's knees had gone soft as tofu, and he lost his balance.

He reeled backwards, light-headed. He vomited white froth which ran over his waterproof jacket. It tasted of acid and diesel. His stomach was empty. He had been looking forward to having breakfast later before returning the dog to his brother's house. After David was sick, he sat down on a log and calmed himself. Rain fell on and around them. He stared blankly, telling himself in a trance-like voice don't black out, Uncle. Don't pass out. Wake up.

Minutes passed or maybe half an hour. He had no idea how long. He steadied himself while looking at Keane. "What did you do, Keane?" He wept. "I can't believe it. Why, Keane, why?"

He checked the man's pulse. Nothing. They sat with the man for a while. His face was a mess, like pasta sauce or a pizza. No one would be able to tell who this was. Keane had completely taken off the man's face, his nose and lips were missing. The man's teeth were exposed in a horrible monkey grimace. His neck was severed. Was that a windpipe? David leaned towards the rest of the body and peered.

In the man's hand was an umbrella. It was half open. The man had huge walking boots, and a tracksuit, a baseball cap with some team logo. A walker. He obviously had started to open the umbrella and it was extended to the second extension point. It started to rain. Gradually bigger proper drops fell, which penetrated the dense foliage.

He held and glared at the man's hand, slim, wet, cold. It was a white man.

*

He looked at his phone which calmed him for a second. "Keane," he said. "Let's cover him up. We'll come back later." He got branches, twigs, huge palm leaves the size of his 60" TV. Keane wagged his tail and assisted him in gathering material and covering the body.

He drove like a tyrant on acid. Adrenaline coursed through his veins and every breath he exhaled was an attempt to retch. Oh no. He knew the disastrous consequences. They would take Keane away, put him down. David would be in court in some stupid suit he last wore at a team meeting. No more dog sitting or any work at all for David. Stephanie would not talk to him. No one would. He was hideous as the dog. Both monsters. Pariahs. They went back to the Mont Kiara mansion. Breakfast was definitely cancelled now. He had lost his appetite.

No maids appeared. He pressed the remote control and the electronic gates of hell slid open. They were both wet and stank of mud. The rain had washed off the blood on David's cut when he fell over, the vomit, everything.

Thunder roared as David traipsed across the manicured lawn, kicked a dropped frangipani flower and raided the gardener's storeroom behind the palace that was Keane's kennel. The dog followed and watched him. David found the biggest shovel he had ever seen. Naturally his brother had to have the biggest and best of anything, including gardening tools when he didn't even do any gardening. He then put a kerosene lamp, a waterproof oilcloth sheet and the shovel in the Range Rover boot. "We're going back, Keane."

David dug for two hours in the downpour, which, by softening the ground, had made it looser. And there were no walkers or trekkers in weather like this. Great. When he thought it was deep enough, around 3 feet, he simply rolled the body into the grave. The next stage was easier than the first. Grave-digging was now a new update for his LinkedIn profile, he grimly thought, under Volunteering. After the body was buried and the grave well-concealed with the original assortment of tree branches, foliage and giant leaves that Keane had brought, David thought he'd move an entire small tree, roots and all, for good measure. He planted it in place and made it all natural, no bare earth showing. When he looked back at the dog, he swore. He couldn't believe it. The dog was holding in his jaws the bloody corpse's baseball cap. What. The. Hell. He would have to dispose of it ASAP. He snatched it from the dog who surrendered the cap dutifully.

*

He did not go back to Bukit Kiara Park. He dreamt of the man every night. In some dreams, the faceless man talked to David and Keane, like friends. David woke up each time, gasping and trembling. Every day, palms sweating, he checked the news online in the Mail and Straits Times. He also had kept the baseball cap that Keane had clung onto. Manchester United. He had not noticed the logo at the scene of crime though it was familiar enough from those days of watching a stupid match and being handed a beer and a bowl of nuts at 3 am in a sports bar on Jalan Telawi 1. It seemed like another lifetime. He snipped the blood-splattered baseball cap into a thousand pieces with scissors and put them into 3 different municipal bins in TTDI.

A week after the incident, *The Star* ran a missing person appeal. A 65-year-old tourist from New Zealand was on a two-week holiday with his children and grandchildren and staying at the Bukit Kiara Equestrian and Country Resort. It appeared that he did not come back to the hotel seven nights ago.

According to BBC, a family friend said Tim Vale, despite his mental health issues and the medication he was on, enjoyed being out alone in nature. The friend also said the family had called him for breakfast that morning, but he was not in his room. Sri Hartamas OCPD Supt Mohamad Nor Ali Hishamuddin confirmed the family, "comprising a couple, an elderly man and a 10 year old child", had checked into the resort a week ago. "However, the family lodged a report after they found that he was missing at 8.30am the following morning," he said. A police team assisted by personnel from the Fire and Rescue Services Department had conducted a search in the area. “We are continuing with the search and we have also informed all district police chiefs to assist,” he added. “Anyone with any information needs to contact the Sri Hartamas police desk.”

Days went by, perhaps another week. He lost track. No news from his brother, sister-in-law or niece. They were busy living their important and hectic lives. David’s eyes were bloodshot. He was unable to concentrate on anything. Meals, TV, football. He had lost weight and looked old. He was too ill to go on anymore long walks. He only needed to stare at the dog and tears came. Keane was possibly the only thing he’d ever loved. How awful it was to find out this way. He’d never loved his wife and there were no children. They separated five years ago when he was 54. She’d had enough, he didn’t blame her for that. He had too.

Guilt consumed him. He observed Keane swallow meals as before, with a normal appetite, a sense of resignation, duty and dignity. Never blame the dog. Always blame the owner. But Stephanie was not in the country. How could anyone be blamed but him?

Seven weeks with Keane. Now it was all over. He wasn’t able to put that poor family out of his mind. A holiday of a lifetime in KL? Not so much. He knew he had to say goodbye to Keane and confess his crime at the Sri Hartamas desk on Jalan 26A. He was looking the directions up on Google Maps when he noticed that a WhatsApp message came in. Stephanie was arriving the next day. She said she was just leaving Los Angeles International. Would he be available to pick her up at KLIA at 8:20pm the following night? He replied OK. She sent her flight number.

Right, he thought. Stephanie would never forgive him whether or not he owned up so he might as well. Just as he shut his WhatsApp, his Facebook newsfeed came up with a photo of the missing man, Tim Vale. He had not seen the photo in any of the other tabloid news he had been scouring.

David's heart banged like a drum.

It was not the man.

He brought the screen in his hand nearer to him as though he was back in the forest that day. This was a bald man with glasses and far older than the man Keane killed, who, when the baseball cap fell off, had a lot of dark hair and was relatively young. 30s or 40s.

A more chilling realization came to him: who the hell did Keane kill? He found no more missing persons reports. "Keane. Shower time. Chang ek leow," he said in Hokkien. Stephanie said the crap previous owners didn't talk to him. At the training school she had sent him to, Keane managed to learn some basic words, like lai (come), cheh (sit), khoon (sleep), chiak (eat) and of course, chang ek (shower). He wanted to protect his secret language with Keane. It might be their last day together.

*

"I want to talk to you about the dog," he said driving Stephanie home from the airport in the Range Rover.

"Yes, uncle? But I am very tired now." She yawned. "Not going to ask me how was San Fran?"

"No, I need to ask you something else."

"What lah?"

David stammered. "W-what... why... what happened to Keane in his previous life?"

"Uncle, why did you not ask before?"

"I didn't know what to ask. I have never had a dog."

Stephanie hesitated. "Wait... what's happened?"

David was choked up. He had to pull over at the next toll booth. He was prepared to tell Stephanie. Everything. But first he said quietly, "Is the dog from a shelter?"

She didn't answer.

"IS HE?" He shouted.

"NO," she yelled back. "I didn't want you to know. He is... you won't tell my daddy, right? Promise me you will not tell him anything?"

"I won't. Why should I? I have not talked to him in years."

Stephanie smiled sadly. "Keane's previous owner is... called... Mike Thurton. English. A bastard in Bangsar. He was my..."

"Oh... you-- were--?"

"Just a fling," she said sullenly.

David did not reply. He did not care. He just cared about Keane. After a slight pause, he asked, "why is he awful?"

"Mike lived alone, loved long walks. Nature. Had the boots, the kit. But he is violent. Abusive. I don't know why he started beating Keane. Mike inherited the dog from his ex-wife. That is why I am the number 3 owner. The wife went back to the UK. He used to punish Keane, with an umbrella. And to this day Keane freaks out and growls when he sees an umbrella, any umbrella, especially if it's the extendable, foldable kind. I tried to report Mike but he threatened me too."

She shuddered and shook her head, burying her face in her hands. David thought this was unusually sensitive for Stephanie, perhaps she was tired from the flight. She took her hands off her face and looked alarmed.

"He OK?" she bleated. "Everything-- OK?"

"Of course, he's OK. Having the time of his life."

"Oh, Uncle! I'm so happy to hear that." She clapped like a child, with grateful wet eyes as if being told she would be going to Disneyland.

"What was Mike like?" said David. "Was he into football?"

"Yaya. He's English, lolz," she said without a trace of irony or a laugh.

"What team did he support?"

"Uncle. I hate football. Please take me home now. I am tired," she whined. He started the engine and they set off.

"I just have one more question," he said as they pulled out onto the highway.

"What lah?"

"Can I keep Keane after tomorrow?"

"Oh sure, I can't have him back. I have signed up at the University of California San Diego. Yep! I am going to be making films! Is that cool or is that cool? Watch out, Sundance! But now tell me why you were upset?"

"I wasn't. Your dog missed you, that's all."

"No, he so does not, lolz."

She shut her eyes on the rest of the journey home. They arrived at Mont Kiara. David pressed the remote and the electronic gates slid open. As he parked and got out, the dog came racing from his sandstone mini palace.

*

David went to wake the passenger. Keane barked and wagged his tail on seeing Stephanie. She opened her eyes. "I just remembered, Uncle," she said, "it might have been Manchester United."

BELA NEGI

The Way Home

Shekhar hurriedly handed his I-card and road permit to the cop who was leaning in impatiently through the car window, his facemask hanging carelessly around his neck. He suspiciously observed Shekhar's delicate features, his fair skin that was somewhat puffy and sagging with ill health rather than age. "The hills are yet free of the disease and you want to carry it here", he stated accusingly.

"My mother is critically ill … I have travelled all the way from Mumbai to see her," Shekhar replied feeling more fraudulent than necessary.

"But your permit is only till Kathgodam." He thumped the car top and barked, "Turn it around". As the car started, he got onto his scooter and in a great rush to get somewhere, disappeared around the bend. Shekhar ordered the driver to continue, reminding him of the exorbitant amount he was charging for this journey, hoping there would be no checks after this.

As they left the foothills the fairly broad road wrapped itself around the hills, gently working its way up. Shekhar looked at the pine forests with unfamiliar eyes. Large sections of hillsides had been ravaged by landslides and the building of this tarred road had altered the perspective with which one viewed the valley. The bare pine trunks that scrolled by in an almost perfect rhythm lulled his anxiety and he fell into a distracted slumber. His head slumped back over the seat top and bright sunlight through the rear window lit his face, so when the car swung around a sharp curve and woke him, his eyes still carried red blurry remnants of sunlight.

The road had become narrower and steeper as they climbed higher. The cold crisp air revived his tired nerves and put some colour to his pallid skin. He looked at the network of steep tracks on the slope across the valley. The sight of a lone woman trudging up slowly with a large sack on her back, stirred in him a long-forgotten feeling. Over the noise of the car, he could hear the faint jingling of the river far below and the quiet swishing of a thousand trees that thickly layered the uneven mountains.

Earlier they had passed the occasional vehicle, but for the last hour the road had been completely deserted. The driver was beginning to crib audibly and the sky, a morose grey, rumbled ominously. Google Maps was of no use in this area, but Shekhar sensed that they were approaching his village.

The three small shops along the road were completely dilapidated. Shekhar peered in and called out even though there was no one in sight. The weary driver began to blow the car horn petulantly. Shekhar turned hurriedly to get into the car feeling sure that the lively marketplace of his village was just a little further when he stopped short in his tracks. Right in front of him was a towering boulder, its broad rockface tilting slightly onto the road. It was unmistakable. He turned around in surprise to look at the crumbled shops again, then at the wild chestnut tree a little ahead. His heart began to race. Unexpectedly and without ceremony, he had arrived.

The driver was reluctant to leave him here in the middle of nowhere but Shekhar assured him that his village was a short walk down the hillside. Receiving the generous fare, which was a large chunk of Shekhar's savings, the driver became cheerful and shouted several greetings. But Shekhar was already moving down the dirt path, a small bag in hand, wondering to himself where they had shifted the marketplace.

Recent rain had made the muddy slope slippery and he walked with cautious steps, while taking in everything around him. The oak and rhododendron trees that shaded the path, rustled softly in response to his gaze. It seemed to him that each stone, each shrub had preserved itself for him, unchanged so that he would be able to recognize his way home. Further down, the terraced fields were overgrown with tall weeds and the path became a thin parting between the vegetation and sometimes, disappeared altogether. They must have made a broader motorable track right up to the village, he thought, which explained the disuse of this path. He was surprised to see how every turn returned to his consciousness like muscle memory, as if he had never been away. Instinctively turning left when the path forked, he remembered himself as a boy running up this slope through fields of mustard. His younger sisters would tag along shouting at him to slow down when he moved too far ahead. Babu, his father, would be loping up the hillside, his thin tall figure clad in a dhoti and coat, late for the morning puja at the temple, of which he was the priest.

Shekhar learnt that going downhill could be as tedious, if not more, as climbing up when the knees had gone city soft. He sat down on a boulder to rein in both the breathlessness and apprehension he was feeling, one aggravating the other, making his thoughts wander in zig zags just like the trail he was on. Babu … would he still be alive? He could expect him to be completely unreasonable and unbending in accepting him back.

Getting up and moving down again, he was reminded that mountain paths could be deceptive, destinations that appeared close shifted further as one moved towards them, the gaze not accounting for the numerous upheavals that remained hidden in the folds. Soon he caught sight of the tops of numerous rows of houses and his nervousness returned. Part of him wanted to turn back and not return to what he had left so long ago. But there was nothing left in the city. He had run huge losses since the pandemic broke out and was forced to sell off his small transport business to pay the bank loans.

The village consisted of several rows of houses, each separated by fields and now the topmost row was in sight. How would he greet Ija, his mother? She would embrace him dearly, but he would remain unmoved and aloof, he told himself. His sisters would no doubt have married and gone away. But would his baby brother fight with him when he claimed a portion of land where he hoped to rest for some time?

He had expected the village kids to have spotted him from a distance and come running to him, clamouring for city treats, wanting to know his intended destination, running ahead to announce his arrival to the household. He had stuffed his pockets with sweets remembering the disappointment he had felt as a child when an outsider arrived empty-handed.

He quickened his steps towards the first house in the row, puzzled by the complete silence and apparent disrepair. He moved past it quickly and stood a moment in front of the second house. Holding his breath, he climbed the narrow stone staircase that led into the courtyard. Scattered recollections of a forgotten home reconstructed themselves in the image of what he saw before him. However, the simple stone structure appeared so small and the sprawling courtyard of his memory was only a few feet wide. But there were no signs of life and all the doors were locked. Where had they gone? Seized with a sudden desperation he began to knock on all the doors, calling out loudly for Ija, hoping that one of the windows would fly open and her unaged face would peer out of it. Perhaps there were attending a function, he thought hopefully, but seeing the state of neglect he knew that the house had been unoccupied for a period of time. The neighbours would surely know of their whereabouts, he assured himself. He peered to look down at the other rows of houses, but the overgrown fields impeded his vision. Drained by the long journey he slumped down onto the parapet to gather his thoughts. His eyes moved over each part of the house, acquainting himself with it again - the worn-out wooden railings, the carved doors and windows stripped of all paint except in a few dark green patches, the tall grass that had sprouted in between the stone slates of the roof. His eyes finally rested on a courtyard stone which he expected to see broken and with a small part missing. But he noted that it had been repaired. As Shekhar sat there, forty-four years old, slim but soft around the middle, the chequered beret on his head shading his green-brown eyes, his face lined with numerous regrets, his mouth drawn thin to disguise the feeling of desolation that followed him like a shadow, he remembered himself as the nine-year-old who had left this home.

Being the eldest sibling, he would take care of several chores to make life easier for a fragile Ija. He remembered her as being continuously pregnant. He had learnt to cook at a young age for when on those rare occasions Ija was menstruating, she was confined to the cowshed. Apart from his three younger siblings, she had delivered two still-born babies and with each birth she became more pinched and frailer. Being an upper caste brahmin and additionally the temple priest, Babu took pride in in creating elaborate rituals at home and would fly into a rage if things were not exactly as he was accustomed to. Shekhar would have to wake up early in the morning to recite mantras with him before helping Ija out and rushing to school. Babu had ambitions for Shekhar to become a government officer and Shekhar had to be very conscientious about schoolwork. Part of his being was devoted towards impressing Babu and part of it was employed in softening Ija's life. His diligence didn't go unnoticed by Babu but was accepted without a compliment. And with every display of sincerity from his son his expectations rose and his temper became aggravated when he found Shekhar faltering on the smallest count.

He had gone over that particular day in his head several times, tempering the details in his retelling of it to a few trusted friends. But sitting here in that same courtyard by himself, thirty-five years later, he let it come back to him with as much faith as he could repose on his memory. Babu was away to preside over a puja in the neighbouring village. Drinking water needed to be carried to the house from a well about half a kilometre away, and because Ija was not well, Shekhar had excused himself early from school. He was on his second round of ferrying water home when he found Babu sitting in the courtyard, tired from his excursion and scowling fiercely. Realizing that his day had not gone well, Shekhar put down the water vessel as quietly as possible and announced to him that Ija was ill. Babu rose and leapt towards him, "So is that an excuse to miss school?" He grabbed a surprised Shekhar by his collar. "You want to be tied to your mother's skirts or do you want to be a man of some worth?" The humiliation that he had suffered at the puja fuelled his anger and he began beating Shekhar mercilessly. He flung the copper vessel full of water down the slope. Shekhar heard the receding clanging as it rolled down the hillside. Babu grabbed him again and flung him to the ground with all his might. A sharp broken edge of a courtyard stone pierced his right temple. Seeing blood Babu withdrew. Ija rushed out but became paralysed seeing her husband's fury. The baby in her arms had started bawling loudly. "Get that baby to shut up!" Babu barked at her and turning to his wounded son he said condescendingly, "Go get the *ghada* back, I'll prepare a *patti,*" and went in.

Shekhar rose from the ground pressing his throbbing, bleeding temple, gulping down his sobs and shame, and under the shocked watching eyes of Ija and the neighbours left the house, ostensibly to retrieve the water vessel. But that display of arbitrary and unreasonable savagery had in a moment snapped that cord of reverence that tied Shekhar devotedly to Babu. As he walked down the village path listening to whispered commiserations from neighbours, he wanted, with the same earnestness that he had earlier sought his father's approval, to hurt him grievously.

The years that followed were a blur. His first few stops were in towns not far from his village, cleaning tables at roadside dhabas. At that time the distance had seemed immense and not wanting to risk being found he changed his surname. When his anger subsided, it was shame and fear that kept him from coming back. For he had lived with people of all castes and religions and the Brahmanical scruples of his father would not have allowed his re-entry into the house. As he had struggled in the world for the last thirty-five years, moving up slowly in life, being in a big city and in a failed marriage, his village became the vision of all that he had missed in life. Had they looked for him at all? Did his father regret his actions? Had his mother been able to protect the younger children? These unresolved questions had haunted him all these years and kept him tied to a childhood that he had lost too early. Years later he had reverted to his original surname, partly as an attempt to establish a connection with his past and partly, to claim his elevated status of a brahmin. The thought of returning had come to him several times, but with the passing of years his courage had faded.

As the monsoon evening fell on the valley, a dense fog arose from its depths, creeping silently like a demon into the courtyard, wrapping the house in a layer of mist, preparing to confound this man who thought he had found his home. Shekhar pulled himself together to seek the neighbours when his eye fell above the doorway. He was reminded that an image of Lord Shiva used to be embossed there but which was missing now. Perhaps he had walked into the wrong courtyard! it struck him, beginning now to notice other inconsistencies. Feeling hopeful he quickly ran down the dirt path but was dismayed to find the next house also deserted and in a greater state of disrepair. His used to be the second ... no third house, wasn't it? Maybe more houses had come up after he left, he thought.

As Shekhar moved from one row of houses to another, past the fields that separated them, the mist rushed towards him riding on a strong gust of wind from the valley below, silently erasing the village from his view and adding to his confusion. Every house in the village was built in more or less the same fashion and each presented some anomalies from his memory of the home he had occupied so long ago.

He could barely see the path in front of him and with every step forward, this homecoming that he had been thinking about for years was moving away from him. He beat down the thorny weeds that blocked the path to the last row of houses. As he groped his way down to the edge of the village, he realized that it was entirely deserted.

The thick mist hung absolutely still now and with night descending, its pure whiteness sullied into a dull grey. The rising sound of the cicadas pierced through its seemingly impenetrable shroud, pronouncing the silence of the entire valley. His legs quivered with exhaustion and his heart was limp with profound disappointment.

He began to move back tentatively to retrieve his bag, taking one step at a time, not wanting to risk a fall down the slope, when a sudden gust of wind cleared the fog around him and a dark doorway revealed itself to him. He peered at it in the fading light. A lump formed in his throat as he looked at the carving of Lord Shiva above the doorway. He had found it! How had he missed it before? The wooden door gently beckoned him into the warmth of its fold.

He decided it would be safer to retrieve his luggage in the morning. The rusted padlock on the main door gave way after a few hard pulls. The door creaked softly as he pulled it open. He got onto the other side quickly, shutting out the devilish fog with relief. He stood in total darkness. Switching on the light on his mobile phone he climbed the narrow mud-coated staircase that led to the rooms above the cowshed. The room on the right of the staircase used to be his father's puja room but was now bare. He peered at a frayed calendar on the wall with a large familiar image of goddess Laxmi smiling benignly. The date read July 2013. That was the year floods had devastated the hills and probably the year his family had moved away. Where had they gone? What had they done with the goats and cows? he wondered as he moved through the rest of the house.

The house had a dusty and stale smell, however the indescribable feeling of finally being home was sufficient comfort for his exhausted body. He inspected every bare nook and corner, a calming warmth spreading inside him. Finally, he came to the room he used to sleep in, keeping that for the last to savour at length. He collapsed onto a bare coir cot which sagged under his weight, its rough cords biting into his skin. He was terribly cold and looking for some kind of cover he found an old sheet and a pillow in a corner of the room. He had to curl his body as tightly as possible to keep himself from shivering.

It began to rain hard. The water bombarded the stone-tiled roof like metal pellets but was unable to drown a doleful wailing sound that was unsettling him. He listened to it intently. It sounded like a woman in mourning. He thought of Ija wistfully. His lasting memory of her was her face transfixed with fear and her body completely subdued into inaction on the day he left home. Over the years the extreme guilt that he felt towards her, the deep suffering he knew he had no doubt caused her, and his inability to do anything about it, had transformed into a resentment which became more overpowering than the anger that he felt towards his father. However deep down he had been sure that she would still be waiting for him.

He dug his face into the pillow which, though musty, brought back to him her smell – a mixture of scented soap, mud, grass, and through it the cleanness of her soft skin – a smell that he often woke up to all through these long years. Unlike Babu, Ija had always been passionate in her display of love for him. When Shekhar grazed the goats in the pastures near the forest she would slip away from home with humble treats from the kitchen hidden in the folds of her ghaghra. Amidst the muted shuffling of the short green grass she would hug him dearly to her breast. On rainy nights like these she would sit patting him to sleep, her face weary of that unending burden that life had apportioned to her, her fair skin worn-out to a permanent jaundiced pallor. And now the thought of her made him want to go out and soothe that dramatic wailing that the mischievous wind had conjured.

The cheerful and raucous twittering of birds outside belied the cold dark gloom of the room that Shekhar woke up in. It took him a long moment to remember where he was. The pillow that he had hugged to himself all night was caked with stale brown layers of perfumed hair oil. He threw it away as its sharp putrid smell stung his nose, surprised that it had smelt different in the dark of the night. Sunlight had crept into the room through the cracks in the wooden windowpanes and filtered by dense cobwebs, it cast a dim pattern on a framed photograph on the wall. Stiff with cold, Shekhar got up with difficulty from the sagging bed and took the frame off the hook that it hung precariously from. It was covered with a sticky layer of dirt.

He dragged himself out into the golden warmth that had filled the pale-coloured stone courtyard. As he sat on the low broad parapet his limbs began to thaw immediately, and eager to get a glimpse of his family, he pulled out the photograph from its cracked frame. He looked at it for a long time. An unknown family stared back at him. As he looked up he experienced an illusion of the mountains across receding from him. He steadied himself, holding onto the parapet to keep from falling off. He threw away the photograph. He turned to look bitterly at the house which became a stranger to him in an instant.

Everything was still except for thin sheets of clouds that swept swiftly across the sky. He had heard of entire villages getting deserted in the Uttarakhand hills by villagers desperate for job opportunities and easier lives but had never in his wildest imagination thought that his would be one of those ghost villages.

His stomach protested with a loud grumble and he was reminded that he hadn't eaten since the previous afternoon. Was it only yesterday that he had arrived? It seemed like a long time ago.

His bag lay in the open in a courtyard, completely soaked. He opened a packet of biscuits and hungrily went through it. Feeling a little sick after that, he threw up. He had no drinking water, so he glugged down half a bottle of juice. He decided to go to the school that was high up on the ridge to his left, hoping to find someone there or on the main road that went past it. As he moved through the eerie silence of deserted rows of houses he was disconcerted by small details – a bamboo basket outside a door, a rusted sickle hung outside a window, a faded shard of a sari clipped onto a clothesline – it seemed as if any moment people might emerge from inside and have a late start to this day.

Several thoughts swirled in his head as he trudged up. How should he go back when he had no money left? How should he locate his family? The land was there for his taking but was that all he wanted? How would he prove to the next person who came along that this was his land? What had he hoped to find here? What had he ...? Feeling jumpy and agitated he fumbled and slipped several times and took many wrong turns.

Stopping for a breather he spotted some houses on the mountain across the valley. He looked keenly for some signs of life, but they too seemed deserted. He remembered that the village was Tallagoan, where craftsmen lived. Considered to be of a lower caste, they were separated clearly from the higher castes, who lived in Mallagaon, Shekhar's village, by a considerable physical distance, to avoid any unnecessary contact. Babu would not let even their shadow fall on him and purified himself whenever their paths crossed.

Resuming the hard climb he finally arriving at a clearing, completely exhausted.

The school building was in ruins. Broken down mercilessly. The forest had taken over, throwing curly vines across dilapidated walls, sprouting seedlings of trees where once children had sat on cold cement floors poring over books. He waded through the wet vegetation thinking of the endless hours he had spent, even in the short span of his life here, diligently parroting teachers.

He found a small classroom which was somewhat intact. The floor was littered with soiled books and broken desks as if a sudden storm had swept everyone away. He walked around the room, hoping to find maybe a phone number scrawled on a notebook, or some clue to help him to proceed from here. He spotted a chart which hung askew on a wall, no doubt the handiwork of a young enthusiastic teacher. It mapped the migration of people into the Uttarakhand Himalayas over the centuries. While Babu would claim that they had lived in this land forever, Shekhar remembered Ija telling him of how they had come from so many parts of the Indian subcontinent, seeking a safe haven from persecution, humiliation, defeat and sometimes in search of opportunities, land and even God. In the generous embrace of the mountains, they forged their identities but only to differentiate again, humbling and oppressing some and elevating the others to power. Ruing at the pointlessness of an education that had made them forget how to use their land, of how to treat each other with dignity, of how to keep their children safe, Shekhar gulped down the sour taste he still had in his mouth from retching in the morning. He looked with despair at the torn charts that lay scattered on the floor, formulas and alphabets, failing to assemble into any meaning.

Outside he sat looking at the blurry pale blue infinity between two mountain ridges, the plains from where he himself had returned and where all the people of this area had gone, to merge with the unknown multitudes. He continued to sit holding a blank gaze, there was no course of action to deliberate on, all roads had come to a dead-end.

As the day wore on, the mist began to rise again from deep down in the valley. Looking for something to anchor his thoughts on Shekhar watched it rising in a hypnotic upward swirl, gently erasing everything in its path, when his eyes fell on a tendril of smoke rising from one of the houses in Tallagoan. Goggling his eyes with his hands he discerned a dot of movement in one of the courtyards, like a sweep of dark skirts.

Feverish with excitement he was racing down the path. There was still time to make the long walk to the other side before dark. The woman would definitely have an address or phone number of someone from his village, he thought as he doubled his speed. The path plunged straight down to the riverbed, not rising and falling as most mountain paths do, as if making up for the numerous disappointments that had been heaped upon him in quick succession.

He stumbled across the shallow stream which was lined with long moist ferns and, undisturbed by humans, thick moss had spread itself out lavishly on the boulders along it, making the walk very slippery.

As he started working his way up the other side he came into the fold of the mist and had to concentrate on every step he took. When he reached the edge of the village, he discerned that the houses were much smaller here. A stack of handwoven bamboo baskets lay neglected in the corner of a courtyard, and a similar air of desolation hung in the air. Shekhar tried unsuccessfully to recall the name of the boy from this village who was in his class and who he had been instructed to discreetly avoid in school.

He moved desperately through the mist, that was thickening around him rapidly, from one locked door to another. Had he imagined that vision? He had to stop soon as everything around him disappeared from sight. He looked down to see the foggy remnants of his own body, and in a blink he was completely swallowed by the encasing greyness. He stood still listening to his breathing. It was as if only his thoughts existed, and all that he had ever been was erased in that moment.

It was hard for him to guess how long he stood there before he heard the soft tinkling of a bell. The image of a shrine came to his mind, a small one inside a house, illuminated by a robust wick, orange light falling on little pictures of deities, his mother's tall back bowing down to them. He was not bound by faith to this vision, but by the memory of warmth and security it had evoked so long ago. If it is possible to feel deep sadness and a sense of complete fulfilment at the same time, that is what Shekhar experienced at that moment.

A strong gust of wind dissipated the fog and the world around him reappeared. Right in front of him was a large patch of marigolds. He caught a whiff of *prasad* being roasted in pure ghee. He turned around to see an old short lady moving towards him, wrapped in a black ghagra and stole. "Lalit you are back?" she cried "I knew you would come home." She reached to take his face in her rough hands, her cataract ridden eyes peering out of her dark wrinkled face, "I have waited for you." He bent down towards her, deciding to be what she wanted him to be. As she crushed him to her breast, he smelt scented soap, mud, grass and yes marigolds.

The next morning, she gave him a handful of seeds to sow. The monsoon was upon them and they had not yet sown the crop for autumn. He walked past the fruit grove to get to the fields. A snake that was sunning itself under the *kaku* tree gently slithered away. Shekhar plucked a *kaku* that was half eaten by birds and bit into it. As he tilled the land Ija cooked the afternoon meal.

TERENCE TOH

Bloom

November 2020

The caladium was dead. There was no doubt about it.

Its large heart-shaped leaves had curled up at the edges. Once a vibrant shade of red and green, they were now a sickly shade of brown, with the brittle texture of old paper. The plant used to stand tall and proud, like a general on guard. Now, its stems drooped forward, its decayed leaves brushing against the ground as if kow-towing.

Jian shook his head. *Bloody ungrateful thing!* And he had lavished it with so much love, too. Watered it regularly. Pampered it with dollop after dollop of high-quality fertilizer. Protected it from the ravages of aphids. Even re-potted it recently. Everything the damn gardening manual had told him to do!

Yet its corpse lay there, mocking him.

Jian was tall and lanky, with an almost pallid complexion due to regular time indoors. His dark hair was spiked and styled to resemble a sleek shark's fin. He also had one of those faces that seemed perpetually marked with a scowl, even if he was really bursting with joy underneath.

Today, however, the displeasure on his face was real.

The potted plants stood on a four-storey rack at one corner of Jian's tiny little apartment. Close to the balcony, the largest natural light source in his place.

For months, he had been looking after these ungrateful things. He maintained their nutrients better than he maintained his own diet. By every right, they should have been thriving.

And yet, they weren't. This was the eighth plant dead this month. If this continued, there would be nothing left of Gowri's garden by the end of the year.

Goddamnit. He was a serial plant murderer. Nothing thrived under his touch. Even the hardiest cactuses died under his care. If plant lives were held in as an high esteem as human ones, he would have been arrested and executed long ago.

It wasn't fucking fair. He had done his best! And he had never even signed up for this, for God's sake.

If only Gowri was still here, Jian thought sadly. Some people had green fingers: she had green palms and hands and arms and a whole body. Everything blossomed in her presence: she was a veritable goddess of greenery.

That was Gowri for you. So full of life.

It had been over two months, and yet Jian still felt her absence: it suffocated his soul. He never knew that nothingness could feel so heavy.

His head started to ache: a rage was coursing through his bloodstream. Jian clenched his fists: suddenly, more than anything, he just wanted to strike back at the unfairness of life.

Jian tilted his head back and screamed his lungs out. “FUCCCCCCCKKKKKKK!!!!’

His voice echoed loud into the night. All his neighbours were probably at home to hear him: where else could they go, during these peculiar times? But Jian did not give a damn. A fury frothed within him. His head felt like a kettle at boiling point.

Jian picked up a nearby chair and hurled it against the wall: its pieces collapsed beside his sofa. His next target was an old vase. He flung it on the floor, and it smashed into a thousand pieces: the sound was peculiar music to his ears.

Jian then picked up a flowerpot and threw it out his balcony. It hit the rail with a smash, its pieces dropping behind the air-conditioner condenser.

He was struck by regret at the precise moment the pot left his hands.

Fuck. Jian fell to his knees, the boiling rage in him suddenly replaced by stinging sorrow. That had been one of Gowri’s favourite snake plants. A memory flashed in his head: Gowri smiling as they walked through a nursery hand-in-hand, beneath the morning sun…

Leave the plants out of this. They were innocent.

Jian bit his lip. He had never hated himself more in his entire life. *You gave your word, Jian. What kind of a man are you if you can’t keep it?*

*

January 2020

In a way, this whole thing had started due to a careless chef.

Under normal circumstances, Jian and Gowri would probably never have met. Let alone spoke to each other. He was a marketing specialist at a multinational corporation in the heart of Kuala Lumpur. She was a freelance artist working out of her mother's flat in Subang Jaya. Two souls as different as cats and cauliflowers.

But what were the odds? Apparently, they shared a common friend. And this friend had invited them to a birthday party at a swanky restaurant in Bangsar.

Jian and Gowri had both attended. This had been early 2020, months before the pandemic unleashed its full wrath around the world. A simpler, more innocent time, when most people only thought of 'Corona' as a beer from Mexico. A time before phrases like 'social distancing' or 'flattening the curve' had strong-armed themselves into daily vocabulary.

The guests walked mask-less into the party. They hugged and shook hands freely. No one's temperature had to be recorded.

Jian and Gowri sat opposite each other. Yet they did not speak, both their attentions stolen by other guests. They might have just gone on separately, their lives never intersecting, had Jian not been served with the worst meal he had ever had in his life.

He had ordered a garlic steak, 'well done'. What he received, however, failed at every sense of that phrase. The meat was rubbery, and oozed crimson the moment he plunged his knife into it. The sauce was watery and the garlic bits were burnt. And dear God, was that a hair he saw among the fries?

Jian had complained, and the head chef-a distinguished looking French man in his seventies- was summoned. He apologised profusely and agreed to exchange his meal.

"I am sorry, I don't understand," the head chef kept repeating. In all his decades of experience, he had never messed up a meal so badly.

And the girl opposite him had laughed.

"That is super cool," she exclaimed. "Like, I'm sorry about your meal and all, but think about it. You are a miracle of probability!"

Gowri was a small and slender woman, with scarlet highlights in her hair. Her ear-rings were shaped like tiny dreamcatchers, and a large purple flower peeked out from behind her right ear. She looked like she would break out into a hula performance at any second.

"What are you talking about?" Jian fumed.

"That chef must have cooked thousands of meals in his life. And you are his FIRST mess-up, apparently. What are the chances? The food gods either really love you or hate you." Gowri laughed again, and Jian was suddenly aware of how beautiful she was. "Maybe you should go and buy 4D numbers."

"What? Why?"

"Clearly you are a man against the odds! Maybe you'll get super lucky again. Win the big jackpot!"

"I don't think probability works that way," Jian had scoffed.

"Hey, no harm trying," Gowri said. "Also, I think you deserved what you get. Why lah, you come to a place like this and order a steak WELL DONE?"

Normally, Jian would have ignored this rebuke, or even perhaps even been offended. But somehow, there was something about the way this woman spoke that made him smile.

Jian responded with a joke. Through the strange sorcery of good conversation, this led into a discussion of culinary dos and don'ts, and then transformed into a comparison of worst dinner parties ever. It ended up a bitchfest about the state of cuisine nowadays.

Jian usually treated small talk the same way he treated other small things such as children or viruses. As nuisance that should be avoided as much as possible. And yet, he had enjoyed the conversation. He had never met anyone so witty before.

Numbers were exchanged. A first date was held, which led to a second, then a third, and the two stopped counting after that.

They went to the cinema and to the aquarium and to the park. She introduced him to Shah Rukh Khan films, and he opened her eyes to the magic of K-pop. They walked hand-in-hand through the mall, gossiping loudly about any interesting strangers who crossed their path. They cycled through the neighbourhood, stopping at intervals to pluck flowers or pandan leaves. They made love in four-star hotel rooms and in the dusty backseats of their vehicles. They experimented with art in ways that always ended in them shedding their clothes and rubbing their paint-streaked bodies against each other. Gowri was a freak, always ready to start something. And Jian was always along for the ride.

Four months after their first date, Gowri moved in with Jian. But she did not come alone. She had a little jungle with her: an assortment of potted plants of all colours and sizes.

"They're my babies," she said, barely embarrassed. "You don't mind if I put them here, do you?"

Jian didn't. He would have put up with a sewage plant in his apartment if it meant Gowri would be close to him.

They bought a four-shelf plant rack from IKEA and put it up. Jian's balcony, which he hardly used, now stored Gowri's watering cans, fertilizer bags, and other gardening necessaries.

For a while, things were predictable, but good. Every day, Jian would rise early and go to work, where he would bury himself deep in the ways of marketing. Gowri would rise at noon. She would tend to her plants and work on her art. Then Jian would return from work, and good, sweet love, would be made.

Jian had to admit: it was nice returning to a house filled with green. Especially after eight hours in a the most sterile office known to man. To spend nights with a warm body pressed against his, and wake to fresh kisses in the morning…that was pure bliss.

But alas, all good things never last

*

August 2020

Gowri had to lie down: she was coughing violently.

Jian wanted to drive her to the doctor, but Gowri turned him down. She should minimize all contact with him for a while. Just in case she had..you know what. She dared not even say its name: somehow, even saying it might make it real, invite it to come.

She took a Grab to the nearest clinic. Jian had trailed behind her in his own car.

The doctor confirmed their worst fears. Gowri was in serious condition and had to be quarantined immediately.

"But how?" Gowri had wailed. "I haven't gone out in months!"

"It's hard to know how this happens," the doctor shook his head sympathetically. "You can pick it up from anywhere. Sometimes, you get the germs off a lift button, a door handle, a food container. I'm so sorry."

Normally, patients with slight symptoms would be moved to a quarantine centre in Serdang. A 50-minute drive away. But Gowri's case had developed far beyond that now. She needed intensive medical care, immediately.

An ambulance was called, and Gowri was rushed to a nearby hospital. Jian wasn't even allowed to accompany her.

The next weeks were a bit of a blur. Jian visited her every day he could, even taking leave from work to do so. Mostly, he wasn't allowed to see her. But somehow, it just felt good to be under the same roof as she was. He would always be there for her. As close as he could get.

Jian was in no way a religious man. But he had never prayed more in his life than when Gowri had been admitted. Surely, surely, the universe would not be so cruel to take away the person he loved most, would it?

One day at work, he received a phone call. It had been about two weeks after Gowri had first been admitted.

It was an unknown phone number: Jian obviously did not know the number of the hospital. And yet, somehow, before even picking it up: he *knew.*

He felt his head spin, and nausea built up at the bottom of his throat. Part of him wanted to ignore the call. And yet, he picked it up.

"Hello? Ini Encik Chong Jian Beng?"

"Ya."

"Ini Dr Nurul dari Hospital Pantai." A brief pause. "Saya amat sedih untuk-"

Jian did not register the rest of the message. He was too busy weeping.

He drove to the hospital, and helped her family claim her remains. He helped with all the insurance claims. He went to her funeral, which very few people were allowed to attend. And there he delivered an eulogy of the short, but wonderful time they had together.

Jian was no writer, but the words of the eulogy flowed freely within him. Perhaps it was because he was being haunted. Not by her ghost: that would have been preferable, if only because it meant getting to see her again.

Instead, he was haunted by memories. The first time they had kissed. The little fights they had had. Her in a bikini, lounging by the beach at Pulau Perhentian. Her in tears, after a beloved plant had died. Her radiant smile after he told her he had just got a promotion. Her waking him up at 3am once, just so they could gaze at how big the moon was tonight. All these little moments, like delicate dandelion seeds in the wind, tossed about, never to return.

One memory stood out the strongest.

After the diagnosis. The two had been sitting at the clinic's reception, waiting for the ambulance that would take her to the hospital.

"Hey, cheer up," Gowri had said. She forced a smile. "I'll be back before you know it! No need to get so emo, okay?"

Jian couldn't think of anything to say. He wanted to just take Gowri's hand, squeeze it, assure her things would be alright. But Covid-19 meant he couldn't even do that.

"It'll be fine," Gowri said. She had always been an insufferable optimist."I'll get through this."

"I hope so," Jian said.

Just then, the Grab car arrived outside: a silver Proton Saga.

Gowri stood up. "Don't forget to look after my plants, okay?"

"I will!" Jian replied.

"That's not enough," Gowri said. She coughed a little, before smiling. "I need a formal declaration. Can we call a commissioner of oaths?"

Despite the sombre mood, Jian found himself grinning behind his face mask. This was a popular joke between them.

Jian raised his hand, and recited in mock formality: "I, Jian, do solemnly swear that I will watch over these plants with my life, under penalty of my balls dropping off."

Gowri laughed. "You better make sure! I tell you, if I come back and find all my plants dead, you're gonna get it!"

She blew him a kiss. "Take care, baby! I'll see you soon."

Gowri stepped out of the clinic, and into the car. She waved from the window, and then she was off.

Jian could not hug or kiss her goodbye. He would carry this regret for the rest of his life.

*

October 2020

A few weeks after she passed, Jian packed up all Gowri's personal possessions, and everything that reminded him of her. A difficult task, as that was almost everything in his apartment. He put everything into a spare room and locked it.

It would have been easy to get rid of her plants as well. Gowri had many friends who were also avid gardeners. They would have eagerly claimed the plants she had left behind. But doing that would have been...wrong.

Gowri had entrusted him with her plants. They were her babies. Her legacy. He couldn't just give them all away.

A promise was a promise. Granted, Gowri had probably not intended to bequeath them to him permanently. But he had told her he would take care of her plants, and so help him, he would do it or have his balls drop off.

How hard could it be anyway? Jian thought. There are so many gardeners out there...

After a week of amateur, mostly improvised gardening, however, Jian suddenly looked upon gardeners with more respect. Apparently, just watering the plants daily was not enough. Some plants even seemed to suffer after he did that. There was a lot more that was needed to be done.

Jian bought as many books on gardening as he could. He went online and looked up videos and *How To* articles.

Different plants, it seemed, had different needs. Some needed lots of water, while others needed moisture only about once a month. Some needed one type of supplement, while some needed another. And they all needed to be weeded and pruned and re-potted and so on.

At this point, Jian was starting to worry about what he had gotten himself into.

The first step was identifying the plants. This involved a lot of Googling, but Jian was soon inducted into the world of philodendrons and fittonia and monstera and peace lilies. Good God, who named these things?

From there, it was a matter of identifying plant needs and satisfying them. Jian bought fertilizer and gardening tools. He started going to nurseries: Gowri once told him that the best ones were in Sungai Buloh and Klang, both places at least half an hour's drive away.

From there, Jian started making charts, recording each plant's water and sunlight needs. He bought a humidifier and an indoor hygrometer and sprays of insecticidal soap. Jian even started wrapping plastic sheets around the plant rack at night. According to the gardening handbook, this was a handy way of maintaining the moisture in the air.

Gardening had benefits. Previously, when not with Gowri, Jian would spend all his time at the cinema or the bar. The pandemic, however, had stopped all that, along with every other leisure activity in the country. Gardening gave him a purpose: kept his head, heart and hands occupied. It was a nice break from his job, and Jian started looking forward to doing it in the evening after a long day's work.

If only you were here, Gowri, Jian reflected sadly. He would have appreciated her advice, her company, her laughter. Why hadn't he shown interest in this before? It would have been so much fun, tending a garden together.

His efforts paid off. Many of the plants thrived. Some, however, did not. Much of Jian's gardening was through trial and error. Sometimes, a plant would burn up after being left too long in the sun, or a flowerpot would be dropped out of carelessness, or a shrub would have its roots rot from over-watering. Jian would curse himself every time. Every dead plant felt like a betrayal of Gowri. She had loved each one of them in her own special way.

Still. Despite a disastrous start, 28 out of Gowri's 53 original plants were still alive under his care. More than half. That was good, right?

Jian worried though, about the future. He was now working from home, and so could tend the garden at all hours. One day, however, the pandemic would end, and he would be back in the office. Would he still have the time and energy to keep these plants alive? Perhaps he would need to hire a gardener.

*

October 2020

As it turned out, he would not have to worry about that.

For on one gloomy October day, Jian lost his job.

He was sitting at his desk at home, when he suddenly received a message from his boss.

"I need to see you immediately," it said. "I'm afraid I have bad news."

He drove to his office: Jian had not been there in so long; he had always forgotten the way. There, he met his boss, stone-faced and sullen. He handed him a letter of retrenchment.

"I'm sorry," his boss said." But as you know, times are bad. We had to cut about a quarter of our staff."

The company had not been doing well for the past few months. And then Covid-19 had come around, and the death sentence had been sealed…

"Why me?" Jian had pleaded. "Is there some way I can appeal this?"

His boss said nothing. In some ways, he was even sadder than Jian.

It was odd, saying goodbye to an office he had not been to in months. There was a virtual farewell on Zoom from all his colleagues. Jian suffered through it, all the while haunted by a singular thought. How to find a new job now, in the middle of a pandemic?

He was optimistic at first. For the first three weeks, Jian sent his resume to any company that would read it. Applied for positions way too high or too low for him, tried his luck with exotic careers he would never have considered in other circumstances.

The fruits of his labour were rejection letters. He was unqualified for some jobs. Other jobs couldn't afford the pay he needed. Some places found his resume interesting but were not hiring. And a lot of places didn't even bother writing his back.

Days turned to weeks, and then months. And no acceptances came.

Jian stopped eating. At first, in a misguided attempt to save money. Then he just lost his appetite in general. He stopped watching TV, or reading. Nothing gave him pleasure any more. He would just sit on his couch and mope in the darkness, the lights off to save electricity.

It was also around this time his plants were hit by a disease.

Jian didn't know how it happened. To be honest, he had not been doing much gardening for a while. Ever since he had lost his job, he had little energy for anything. And looking at the plants hurt his heart. When he saw them, he remembered Gowri. What she would say if she could see him now? A washed-up man, unable to get a job?

Large grey patches developed on many of his plant leaves. This grey soon spread to their stems, and pale brown spots began to develop on their flower bulbs. Soon, the plants started to wither.

When Jian discovered this, he panicked. He did everything he could think of: add fertilizer, repot them, all the usual remedies. If anything, these only made things worse. A Google search revealed it was probably a bad case of botrytis, or grey mold: the only way to cure this was to cut away the infected plant parts. And Jian had acted so late that many plants were now beyond saving.

There was a spray helpful for situations like this: unfortunately, the pandemic meant many shops were closed to ward off Covid-19 infections. Keeping plants alive, unfortunately was not seen as an 'essential business'. Jian had no choice but to buy the spray online, and it could only be delivered in a week.

By the time it arrived, there were only 11 of Gowri's plants alive. This was the straw that broke Jian's back.

He spent his days walking aimlessly through his apartment, his curtains and windows always closed to maintain a perpetual darkness. Either that, or he would sleep. Jian would climb into bed, wrap the blankets into a cocoon around him, and sleep the pain away.

Sometimes he would dream. His dreams were full of Gowri, and all the wonderful times they had spent together.

He hated these damn dreams. They were dead delights, joys from a glorious past he could never return to. A stark contrast to how horrible the world was now. All they did was make him bitter and hollow.

*

December 2020

One night, he could not take it anymore.

Jian staggered out of bed. His hair hung over his face in tangled knots. He scratched his chest with an extra-long fingernail: he had not showered in almost a week. A straggly beard had sprouted on his chin. There was a foul mustiness in the air, possibly emanating from the equally unwashed bedsheets. His stomach growled, but he paid little heed to it.

5.15am. Jian walked to the bathroom. How long had he been asleep, he wondered. Did it matter? All the days felt the same anyway….

He was overcome by nausea, and he threw up in the sink. His temples throbbed with a harsh, stabbing pain: Jian desperately clutched the sink to avoid collapsing. His heart was heavy as sin.

What was the point of anything? This stupid pandemic had taken everything he loved. Why the hell did he still go on?

His first thought was to watch TV. Perhaps there was something interesting on, to distract him from his suffering. Jian staggered to the hall, but lost interest in his plan immediately.

Something else had grabbed his attention. A gleam of silvery light. The moon reflected in the glass door of the balcony.

As if guided by an invisible puppeteer, Jian found himself walking there. He had barely enough strength to open the sliding door open.

The night was warm, and almost silent. Fewer cars on the road, thanks to the Malaysian Movement Control Order. Jian walked over to the tall steel bars that formed his balcony ledge and rested his hands on the horizontal support railing.

He looked down.

Nineteen floors, a long way to fall. Jian felt a tinge of vertigo. He never had a head for heights.

A dark thought entered his mind.

Did he dare?

What else was left? Why stay? Did he want to see what else the world would take from him?

Jian extended his arms, like a diver. He gritted his teeth and grabbed the support railing. The ledge was too high to just jump off: he would have to climb over to the outer edge, and then let go. For some reason, he found this scarier than jumping.

For a moment, he was seized with doubt. But he braced himself. Better do it now before he chickened out.

Jian was not strong enough to lift himself over the ledge. He noticed the air conditioner condenser nearby and made his way to it.

Climb on top, and jump. Easy peasy.

As he was making his way there, he suddenly caught sight of something unusual.

A small green island, in an ocean of brown.

What the hell was that? Jian stepped off the condenser and moved to take a closer look. He hadn't come to this spot in …. God, he couldn't even remember how long.

A small green shoot, almost ten centimetres long, protruded from a small mound of earth behind the condenser. Tiny leaves were budding at its sides. Beside it, on the ground, lay several broken pieces of ceramic.

Jian gasped. It was Gowri's old snake plant. The tenant of the flowerpot he had tossed aside in a moment of anger, months ago.

Like the animal that gave it its name, this plant had been sly. Growing here in silence, despite being cast down into this God-forsaken spot. Somehow, it had managed to gather enough sun and air and earth and water and was thriving.

A memory flashed in his head: the first time he had met Gowri, months ago at that birthday party…

"Clearly you are a man against the odds," Gowri had laughed. God, she was so beautiful.

"A man against the odds," Jian repeated softly. Tears were streaming down his face.

He stepped away from the ledge. Instead, he walked back into his apartment, to the kitchen, where he poured himself a glass of milk.

When he had finished, he walked over to his rack of plants. Most were dead or withered from days of neglect. But there were survivors: they stood tall and strong, brandishing their fading greenness like medals of courage.

Jian picked up his shears, and carefully snipped a few blossoms. *These will go into a bouquet,* he thought. *Gowri will love them.*

He had not been to visit her since the funeral. Well, today he would go to her grave, and clean it up. Lay these blossoms from her garden at the spot she rested. It was only appropriate.

But not the snake plant. It had made a home for itself, behind the air conditioner. And there it would stay. Possibly until the end of time: God, that plant was hardy! It would probably outlive him.

Jian stood at the balcony. A cool breeze lapped against his face, and he smiled as he took in the scenery. The first rays of the morning sun were spreading across the land. Soon, the dawn would be here.

ROY TRISTAN B. AGUSTIN

Killing the Councillor

San Juliano was a small town placed neatly in a forgettable section of Luzon, where the provinces of Laguna, Cavite, and Batangas overlap their borders; resulting in a town belonging to no clear province. It's a quiet place, where the houses are small but neatly built. There are no flimsy shanties here. The houses, though they can be tiny, are all built from concrete and masonry. The rooftops are proper galvanized iron, not rusty, and the windows are all glass, all the doors all have metal grates. Very sturdy ones. The strange adjacencies the town had with these three provinces was a constant point of irritation for politicians as jurisdiction over it was never clear, and, thus, the town had the unique distinction of never having a mayor, instead, the town was operated by a mixed committee of representatives coming from the three provinces.

The town itself was happy without a clear mayor. The council was constantly arguing over tax and budget allocations, which meant that tax collection was a confusing and frustrating effort, and, thus, was often abandoned. The town itself, strangely enough, seemed to appreciate the lack of fiscal pressure, with the citizens taking it upon themselves to ensure that the surroundings were clean, and that order was maintained. As a result, San Juliano was spotless and crime free.

Of course, there was also the small matter of San Juliano being a town of assassins.

The confused jurisdiction was perfect for fugitives. After all, in a town where the police of any given province were not sure if they could even operate without violating the other two provinces' laws and statutes guaranteed that, for the most part, they stayed away from the town, save for a weekly visit to Aling Letty's mini-grocery and bar, which served as the official watering hole of the town. They never stayed long; the long, unflinching gazes of the townsfolk unsettled them and there was a distinct smell of gunpowder always lingering around the store, which worried the policemen. The shooting range in the basement, where the townsfolk got their practice in, was the culprit, though Aling Letty was always appropriately baffled by the questions visiting policemen inevitably ask her. "Why no, sir. I don't smell anything," was her standard reply, which was always corroborated by two or three locals. It was deep enough underground that the sounds of the guns were never heard unless someone left a door open, which they never did. But the smell of gunpowder still wafted out of the store.

In truth, the occurrence of fugitives was quite rare; they weren't welcomed by the residents as they often brought unwanted attention to the town, which did brisk business as assassins, particularly these days. Fugitives often simply disappeared after a few days, with no one remembering where they went, though their corpses often ended up in one of the nearby towns. Assassination was the town industry, and thus, no one talked about it. It was easy to arrange: a few thousand pesos would get the client a quick drive by, an additional few hundred will throw in the planted firearm, the head wrapped in cling wrap, and as was the fashion, the piece of cardboard placed on top of the corpse, declaring that the victim was either a drug dealer or a criminal. (Some enterprising fellow tried to charge per character, which did not go well.) The assassins of San Juliano were known for providing value for money when it came to killing people.

Of course, they never spoke about their real professions openly; they would refer to various other occupations as a way of talking about their work in the open without arousing suspicion. Danny Cruz, for example, was a tailor (he wasn't) and he was pretty good at it. His friend, Murph Santos, was just starting his own (not) tailoring business and Danny was excited to get his friend going in what was a very lucrative living.

Murph and Danny could not be more different. Danny was lean and sleek, as if he were designed to be a, um, tailor. He had wiry muscles, particularly on his arms, which, at times, looked like coiled ropes, especially when he was holding a gun. Murph, on the other hand, was round and large, but also smooth, as if he didn't have muscles but was instead a large, single piece of meat. Murph was, however, phenomenally strong, and could easily snap lumber in two. Both had been friends since they could remember, and while Danny was the quicker in wit, Murph was always the one who could be counted on to finish a job. And now, Murph has finally decided, because it takes him very long to decide, to join the tailoring business. Danny even set him up with a sweet contract: Kill the Councillor.

The Councillor was part of the town council that had control over the town but, unlike the other councillors who could be counted on to ignore their duties to the town, this one has shown a lot of interest in the goings on in San Juliano. Particularly, on the odd mediocrity by which the town's businesses plied their wares. The baker's bread was often old, the grocer didn't seem to care much about restocking her stores, not to mention the perpetual smell of gunpowder wafting from her store. The tailor never seemed to be making anything but was always taking down measurements on the phone. The Councillor wanted to be Mayor of San Juliano, not because he wanted to improve these industries, rather, he wanted a cut from their earnings. He knew their real business, of course. He'd hired the baker a couple of times for other tasks, which made the Councillor's political career a little easier. Now, it seemed that he wasn't happy just hiring from San Juliano; he wanted San Juliano itself. After all, how much money can one make just taking a cut from every member of the town's earnings? That would fill the campaign chest faster than the "commissions" he was taking from his infrastructure projects! And imagine, an entire town of people capable of getting rid of anyone he thought was a threat. That would be handy indeed for an up-and-coming Councillor with ambitions of, well, who knows how far he could go?

The town wasn't going to be used as anyone's exclusive bakery. Or tailoring service, for that matter. It was perfectly happy being independent. After all, it ensured that they never owed anyone anything. So, what could be easier than to get rid of the Councillor? For that, they needed someone who the Councillor was not aware of, someone who was not yet a baker or tailor. So, Danny volunteered Murph. It would be a great first job, and Murph would have the love of the town, who could then help him get even more contracts! It was perfect. Murph, of course, was excited. So was the town.

*

The contract was pretty simple. Danny took down the details, as always, with a pencil stuck behind his ear, another one scratching a long pad. Kill the councillor, get Php 10000. Not a bad deal, he thought. And it was perfect to get Murph in the business. After all, the man's been practising for years with Danny and truth be told, he had some skills. But Murph was also really lacking in confidence, partially because he was starting out so late, partially because he'd never done anything as ambitious before. Danny sighed and picked up his cell phone to message Murph.

-OY. You have a job.-

-Rlly?! - (Murph had a bad habit of abbreviating texts)

-Yah. Come over and I'll give you the details –

-K-

Murph was over in about ten minutes. He was sweaty with excitement, already carrying his leather clutch bag, presumably carrying his pistol. "Well? Well?"

Danny looked meaningfully at the bag, "Calm down, let me give you the details first."

"Ok." Murph slumped onto a stool, the bag placed in front of him. Danny looked at the bag again, this time making sure to stare at it deliberately, and stared back at Murph. "Oh, oh! Sorry." Murph put the bag down, away from view.

"The job is our new Councillor. Apparently, the town's gotten pretty sick of the guy, especially since he's insisting on deploying a police force in town. People think he's going to run for mayor, and he wants this town as part of his territory." Murph nodded solemnly.

"It needs to be clean, though, Murph. None of the usual walk up to the guy and shoot him deals. The councillor already suspects that we have some stuff going on, which is why he's so interested. So, if he's going to be killed, it can't be linked back to anyone in town. Including you."

"Oh. Well then the bag's..."

"Not going to be very useful this time. But there are other ways. We'll just have to figure it out." Murph looked disappointed, after all the shooting range practice, he'll have to come up with something different. Danny then said, "But. If you pull this off, you'll be in serious business!" That perked Murph up.

"Okay!! First thing then is to scout the guy out." Murph smiled and walked out, leaving his bag on the counter. "Oh, whoops! Going! I'll tell you all about it, Danny!"

That was the first of what became a nearly daily briefing session by Murph. He would run into Danny's shop and give a detailed rundown of the daily routines of the Councillor, who, frustratingly, wasn't very regimented. The times where he would have a routine schedule were often also the times when he was surrounded by the police or his own security. He had advance parties to scout any areas and was very careful when visiting any area, allowing his security people to do thorough sweeps. He even wore a facemask, given that there was this new COVID thing lurking, and he would avoid any areas with any active cases.

After a while, Murph was getting frustrated. There were no clear points where he could either cause an "accident" or get close enough to the councillor to deliver something like poison. A lot of times, Murph had to watch from a fair amount of distance. Even Danny, the experienced "tailor," was stumped. The councillor knew his stuff.

Murph, however, was undeterred and, eventually, he did come up with a plan, though Danny was truly shocked when he heard it.

*

"Let me just get this absolutely clear. You, the assassin, who was hired to kill Councilman Sanchez, subcontracted??" Danny's eyes were unusually large as he said this, which Murph took to be excitement. It wasn't.

"Um, yeah."

"Why on Earth would you do that?"

"Covid. You know, I just didn't feel secure enough to go out."

At this point, Danny slapped his palm so hard on his face, the sound echoed loudly through the old warehouse where Danny and Murph would occasionally wrestle. It sounded like a whip cracking. Danny's cheek was now red. "And you didn't think that the other guy would tell on you?"

Murph, at this point, smiled. "No, see, I got that covered."

Danny looked incredulous. Murph has so far not given him any reason to be confident. "Really."

"Yah! He doesn't know what I look like." Murph smiled and nodded, emphatically as if to pat himself on the back with phantom arms, since his were still crossed.

"I'm afraid to ask."

"The dude's blind! He can't see! He can't finger me because he never saw what I looked like!" Murph's grin was becoming annoying.

"Wait. The guy's blind?"

"Yup!"

Danny froze for a moment, pondering the possibilities. Was it possible that Murph, who had so far been dismally inept, actually stumbled on a brilliant idea? A blind henchman. It could work … could it? "Wait. How was he supposed to get to the councillor?"

"I thought that through, man." Murph walked over to the pile of steel beams on the side of the warehouse and plopped himself on them, still brimming with pride at his brilliance. He took out a cigarette and lit it with a match, no doubt stolen from his uncle's kitchen. The ember flared and then dimmed as Murph took a nice long drag. "The councillor loves to get massages. I found that out from one of the drivers, who was bitching about finding another masseuse since his boss insisted on rotating a bunch. Y'know, just to make sure nobody gets too familiar."

Hmm, Danny thought. That's not bad. "Okay. I'm with you."

"So, I know this guy, Jose, nice guy. Little short, balding, you probably seen him around ..."

"No, I haven't, Murph."

"Really? He's always by Mang Lito's store, you know. Trying to score some change from the customers. Never mind if they're just as poor as he is. He he he..."

"Murph."

"No? No bells? Really? He wears a sando most of the time." Danny's face darkened, which immediately jolted Murph's memory. "Oh, oh. Right. He also was training to be a masseuse, since all those *sosyal* types like to get massages from blind folks. Better sense of touch, or something. Anyway."

"Yes. Anyway." Danny looked impatient now, his feet tapping on the concrete, making little puffs of dust rise with each tap.

"Well, here's the genius thing. He'd go in, then do his massage thing. The councilman falls asleep during these massage sessions so all he had to do was massage the guy until he fell asleep. Then, when the guy's finally sleeping soundly, he whacks the guy with a hammer!"

"What?!"

"He whacks the guy with a hammer!"

"Wha, wha. A hammer? Really?" Danny was stunned. Murph looked tickled pink.

"It was in the list of things that the security people allow in. There were renovations ongoing in his house."

"So you get the blind masseuse," Danny repeated the words "blind masseuse" slowly, "to go into a man's bedroom carrying a hammer?"

"Yah."

"And then what? He just starts banging on the guy's head?"

"Yah."

"You're a moron."

"No, no, it worked! Well, it should have worked. Except."

"Except what?"

"The guy forgot where he put the hammer down. So, when he reached for it, he lost his bearings. You know. Because he's blind and he wasn't in familiar settings."

"Wait. So, you tried this already."

"Yah."

"Aaaand???"

"Well, Jose started banging around looking for his hammer, so the councilman woke up."

"And?"

"The councilman gave him the hammer."

"And?"

"Jose said thank you. He's polite that way."

"Oh God. And then?"

"Well, Jose thought about swinging at the guy, but it would look pretty weird, right? I mean, a blind man saying, 'thank you' and then suddenly swinging at the guy.

Not to mention the fact that Jose couldn't see anything, so a swing at the guy could miss, I mean, right? So, Jose got paid a nice 2000 pesos and was told to come back. The Councilman liked his massage. I got 1000 since I gave him the job. So, yeah, not bad."

Danny stood motionless for a good two minutes, trying to figure out what to say. His fists clenched and unclenched. On one hand, that was one of the most stupendously ridiculous assassination attempts he'd ever heard of. However, the guy got close. Closer than anyone had before that. Murph had some flashes of brilliance there. But then again, he just told a blind guy to beat someone to death with a hammer. It was, to Danny, an absolute mystery, his mind struggled to comprehend and decide on whether he should smile, laugh, or beat Murph to an inch of his life with anything he could get his hands on. Murph, God bless him, was still sitting on the steel beam, dragging on his cigarette like the story he told was nothing special. The boy could be a genius or an idiot. Danny, at that point, could not decide which. The contract, however, was still on. And they needed the Councilman killed or 10000 pesos was gone. That would be an utter waste. "Murph."

"Yah?" Murph blew a thick plume of smoke into the air.

"I. I," Danny couldn't figure out a reply, "Ah fuck it. Let's go."

"D'you hear about COVID, though, man? I hear it's getting pretty bad out there," Murph said, with a serious look on his face, "It would be scary if it got here."

"Yeah. That's scary," Danny agreed.

On the radio, they just started counting cases.

*

Murph looked bad. Pale, runny nose, swollen eyes. Danny was clearly worried as he saw his friend walk slowly to the table, beer in hand. There wasn't anyone else in the restaurant; Mang Ramon wasn't even really open; he was happy to have people in the place, though. Mang Ramon was behind the small bar, stocked with some Ginebra Blue, Tanduay gold and, of course, some Johnny Red. Fancy stuff. Murph was tired.

He raised his beer to Danny, "Hey Danny."

Danny raised his back, "Hey Murph. You okay?"

Murph smiled wanly, "Yah. Been a long few days. I got close to the councillor."

Danny stopped mid-drink and put down his beer. "Wait, you got close to the guy? I thought you didn't want to be close to anyone?"

Murph took a swig. "Yah. But it was an accident. I didn't even get a chance to do anything." He looked dejected.

"Well, how'd it happen anyway?"

Murph sighed, which seemed to be a lot of work for him. "I was getting my new plan ready. I was able to get a temp job at his house, y'know, the renovations..." Danny nodded. "Well, the renovations were going well. I got a job working the batch mixer for the cement. It was easy, I used to work that thing when we helped make Tita Rica's place, remember?" Danny nodded again. "Well, the idea I got was I was going to stack some cement bags and then just drop them on the guy. Simple, right?"

Danny replied, "Yeah, but you're gonna get caught. You're the cement guy."

Murph smiled triumphantly, "Ah hah! But no! I thought that through. I was going to rig it so that I was downstairs, with the Councillor, when it fell. That way, they won't think it was me. See?" Before Danny could react, Murph continued," I had the bags balanced on a plank of wood, placed juuuust a little too far, but not so far that anyone looking would notice. The plank was being held up by a bracket that I put there. Wood too. Nailed it to the frame of the house."

Danny interrupted, "Then you had a way of releasing the bracket, right?" Murph beamed at his friend, pointing the top of the beer bottle to his head.

"You were always sharp, Danny buddy. That's right. I had a rope tied to the nails. They weren't nailed in fully, you see, and a good tug would yank the bracket out of the frame and tip the plank over, dropping the bags. But, since the bracket would fall onto the ground I can reel it in with the rope before anyone notices and then get rid of it. Evidence gone! Plus, the Councillor dies, I get paid!"

Danny already saw a bunch of holes in the grand plan, mainly dealing with how iffy the method was. The rope could snap, or the plank could stay put and not fall. The direction of the bags fall was also another possible thing that could go wrong. Danny didn't expect this to work, but Murph certainly thought it would. He decided not to tell Murph his misgivings; the guy was clearly miserable as it was. Instead, he simply asked, "So, I guess it didn't work?"

Murph slumped on the table, sniffling. "Noo! I pulled the bracket when the councillor was walking right underneath the plank and the bags fell the other way! Kicked up a ton of dust. Everyone was coughing and covered in cement! I was able to reel the bracket in and keep it in my pocket, so at least I wouldn't get caught. But it did fall close to the councillor, close enough that he fell over and dove to the ground! I ran over, coughing from the dust, and helped the guy up. I wish I could have strangled him there, but his security people were running our way. I just asked if he was okay and he nodded, but he was also shocked at what happened. We were all grey from the cement dust and I saw the foreman run up to the second floor where the bags were. The next thing I know, I'm being yelled at for being careless. I could have killed someone for doing that. I was thinking, 'yeah, that was the point' but I didn't say anything. I just bowed my head as I got screamed at by the foreman, then by the councillor's head bodyguard. They fired me, then the bodyguard said "I know your face now. Don't you ever come near the Councillor again." Murph shook his head. "That's it, Danny. I don't think I can do the job anymore. They're onto me."

Danny looked sympathetically at his friend. "Well, you definitely can't just walk up to the Councillor anymore. But, um, I don't know. Maybe you'll figure out a way of pulling it off anyway. Cheer up, man." He tapped Murph on the shoulder. Murph didn't move. "Hey, that's not even one beer, man. Don't tell me you're passed out already." He slapped Murph's back harder, "Yo, Murph." Murph didn't move. His breathing was really laboured now, and he was pale. "Yo! Tito Mon! I think Murph needs to see a doctor!" Tito Ramon rushed out from the bar and saw Murph slumped over at the table, his back rising and falling with each laboured breath.

"Let's get him to the hospital, Danny." They both carry Murph to Ramon's jeep, parked outside, and drove to Ramon's cousin's clinic, not quite a hospital, but it was well equipped.

The hospital kept Murph for observation and, the next thing Danny knew, Murph was in the ICU, with tubes up his nose. Danny couldn't visit anymore; the hospital forbade visitors. Instead, the nurse texted him the results.

COVID. WILL ADVISE. Was all the text said.

*

The radio announced, a day later, that the councilman had tested positive for COVID and was in the hospital being treated. Murph was in the same hospital. Both of them contracted pneumonia. The councilman was immediately surrounded by the best doctors in the province. Murph, well, wasn't. Danny sat in his store; he still couldn't visit but he found a cousin who was a nurse at the hospital who kept tabs on Murph. The days in town slowed to a near halt. People weren't allowed out, barangay officials were announcing new cases and fatalities on bullhorns, urging people to stay home. Masked people walked quickly, looking around to make sure no one was near them.

The smell of gunpowder disappeared from the grocery store as Aling Letty, her face now hidden behind a surgical mask, conducted business from a small table at the entrance of the store. A line stretching out from the store's entrance was a common sight. The bakery delivered now, though it did nothing for the quality of the bread. Danny's business was silent. Even the tailoring business. Who needs new clothes when you never leave your house? The days became ones of simply watching it go by and hearing the news. The disease spread and more provinces locked down.

The councilman survived, but he didn't want to take the town anymore. If anything, he seemed subdued, as if the brush with illness and death sobered him. He now talked about feeding programs and helping promote testing efforts. He looked shaken, as if the experience changed something fundamental in him.

Murph passed away after a week in the hospital. He simply couldn't cope, and there wasn't enough medicine or ventilators to go around, so Murph struggled mightily for a week. Danny got to see him a few days before he finally passed. Murph smiled and weakly apologized for failing to kill the councillor. He promised to make it up to Danny, and said that he would try again, between heaving gasps for breath. Danny's last image of Murph, was him smiling, waving at Danny from the hospital bed, clearly tired, but still smiling. Danny's eyes were swollen for the rest of the day. Murph was cremated, the urn sent to Danny, who was his only relation.

There were rumours that went around that the Councillor was visited by someone during his stay in the hospital. The figure knocked out his security and was curiously not seen by any doctor or nurse. The figure, a large person, by some descriptions, loomed over the Councillor, who's eyes were bulging in terror. No one knows what was said; the figure was masked, but it was clear that the Councillor was shaken. His frantic attempts to call the nurse on the call button had broken it and, according to some people, he looked dangerously close to a heart attack which, had it happened, would have definitely killed him. But it didn't. The figure only stayed for a minute or so before it left silently, no proof of it on any CCTV cameras or from anyone who worked in the hospital. The mayor would fall asleep for the next two days before finally waking up and calling his staff, suddenly changing his plans.

He was asked once why he suddenly changed after COVID. Was the experience of the disease that profound to him? To which, the Councillor replied, "Yes, and no. During my stay, I saw what my life could have been, and I was made to see what really mattered. I'd like to say that I've led a fortunate life, and I forgot that. My experience in the hospital was harrowing, but it also was eye-opening. I was getting better while others weren't. I had a chat with... well, let's just say that he was a ghost -- he scared me. But he also showed me death, and how it happens so easily for some, but not for others. I didn't agree with that. Neither did he."

Needless to say, no one got paid. But the town stayed independent. People nodded to Danny's shop when they passed. Danny would nod back. Murph, who was somewhere in the back, on a shelf, would have been happy.

BHASWATI GOSH

Apu's Goals

It was not a big match, but I was nervous. In my more-than-forty years of football craziness, I had experienced countless nail-biting, fist-clinching moments whenever Mohun Bagan clashed with East Bengal. But this was going to be far more nerve-wracking for me. It was my son's first state-level match. He was the only high school student to make it to the state team; every other player was either college level or higher. Like all the milestones in his life, this was as much my test as his. As I joined the uproarious crowd milling into the stadium, I wondered if Apu would be more anxious than me. Knowing my boy, that was unlikely.

I took my seat and opened the packet of roasted peanuts I bought from a vendor outside. Until the match began, the nuts would be my welcome distraction. As I plopped the first few into my mouth, a familiar voice greeted me. It was Mr. Saha, my neighbour.

"So, Mr. Banerjee, how does it feel to see your son in action?" He asked.

"Well, I should be asking you the same. Rana's also in the team, isn't he?"

"He is. But just as a reserve player. Not like your Apu who carries the load of the entire team on his young shoulders."

His sarcasm wasn't lost on me. Yet, I couldn't agree more with him. As the goalkeeper, Apu did have a big responsibility. I passed some nuts to Mr. Saha and said, "Let's hope our boys do well."

"Of course, of course, I hope so. With Apu in the team, how could they not?"

God bless Mr. Saha; his words proved correct.

Bengal, the team Apu played for, scored two goals against opponents Punjab in the first half. But as soon as the second half started, the Punjab boys came back with a terrific goal. They looked focused to equalize. My eyes kept shuffling between the field and the dial of my watch. Every opportunity Punjab missed became a golden moment for me. Barely four minutes of match time were left when Kulwant, Punjab's star player, looked ominous. As he scampered towards the goalpost with the ball, the stadium went mute. Amid the silence, I could clearly hear Mr. Saha's latest remark, "*Ahh*, poor Apu, God save him the disgrace of Kulwant's goal."

When Kulwant went for the kick, a cloud of haze blurred my vision even as my mind raced faster than the ball. I could only see an image of Apu flinging his body across...his small, eight-year old frame diving in a desperate bid to save the ball, his coach cheering him on, Apu securing the ball to his chest ....

"Hurray, Mr. Banerjee. Our Apu has done it!"

Mr. Saha's frenzied call brought me back to the scene on the ground. I couldn't ignore his "our Apu". Evidently, Apu had managed to save the goal with a "heroic effort" as Mr. Saha put it. My days of taking eight-year-old Apu to the sprawling Calcutta Maidan for football practice seemed so prudent now.

At dinner, Apu relived the final moments of the match with me. I didn't tell him I had missed witnessing his goal-saving magic. Even as he spoke, gulping down his favourite fish curry and rice, I could see the spark in his eyes. I was glad that for once, we were in the same team—Bengal. I had always been a Mohun Bagan supporter, and that was reason enough for Apu to become a fanatic follower of archrivals, East Bengal. Every time the two teams fought, a mini cold war ensued at our home. If East Bengal won the game, I would be at the receiving end of a torrent of scathing comments on my favourite team.

"Let's face it, Baba; Mohun Bagan can never match East Bengal."

"Don't forget, son, East Bengal was born out of Mohun Bengal only."

"Please, Baba! Your lame historical references actually prove that you can't accept how pathetic a team they are now."

"I have seen more football than you, Apu. East Bengal is having a good phase no doubt, but Mohun Bagan is still the best. Just wait until the next match."

"You make me laugh, Baba."

So, Apu did have the proverbial last laugh after all. With his momentous save, he established that he knew better football than me. Did that hurt? Well, I could actually feel my chest swelling with pride. Funny, how losing the final argument can be so satisfying at times.

After dinner, I asked him about another test he was to face in three weeks' time.

"So, Apu, are we all set for the engineering entrance?"

"Hmm, more or less, Baba. Just have to buy a couple of books from College Street. Dilip has picked up some good ones from there."

Apu was barely five or six when I first took him to *boi paara*, the book bazaar at College Street. I would force my most unwilling boy to wake up early on Sundays, give him a bath, make him finish his breakfast – toasted bread, a boiled egg, and a glass of milk (back then, he swore not to touch milk the day he finished his schooling; he has since lived up to his promise). Then, we'd go book hunting. It didn't take Apu too long to look forward to these Sunday sojourns. He would rummage for hours through the piles of yellowed, ancient-smelling books, and hoard his own collection for the library that was building up at home. Russian folk tales and the poetry of Pushkin he collected in middle school, "Animal Farm", which he picked up at fourteen, some autographed books he was lucky to find on occasions, and the MAD comics he remained loyal to all through the years – our library housed a feast of books, from the rare to the odd, the bizarre (Apu insists he's mature enough to "handle those"), and the hilarious.

Thinking of the impending exam, I asked Apu, "Aren't you a bit late for buying those books?"

"Ah, 'guess I am, Baba, but what to do? This football business had to get in the way. But why worry; we'll see how it goes?" His blithe smile reassured me he was up for the challenge yet again.

In the days that followed, Apu hardly came out of his room. On a mission to grab a seat at the prestigious Jadavpur Engineering College, he momentarily gave up every bit of pleasure – TV, *adda* with friends at the Coffee House, and even his football practice – to prepare for the exams.

As I entered his room one evening, I saw on his table scraps of paper with a million unintelligible things written on them (I was an accounts officer; what would I know of physics derivations?), and five or six tomes lying open. Apu immersed himself into one of these; his glasses tipped on the bridge of his nose.

"Don't overdo it Apu," I said.

He looked up and smiled, only to get back to his reading material. Walking up to his table, I took the book away and closed it.

"Enough of that. Get up now." I said.

"But Baba..."

"Just take a half-hour break, Apu. Your brain needs charging up."

A shrug and a sigh later, he relented.

"OK, you go to the terrace, Baba. I'll be there in a minute."

"Done, son."

Apu made it an evening to remember. As he strummed the notes of "Purono shei diner kotha", a song by Tagore on friendship and nostalgia on his guitar, the motion picture of Apu's life unspooled in my mind. My wife's death, leaving me with three-year-old Apu; my struggle to be a father and mother rolled into one, often failing in both roles; images of Apu, the prankster; Apu, the friend; Apu, the rebel; Apu, the mock detractor.

"Good recharging session, Baba?"

"Um, most definitely. My idea, after all."

"You have to win, no?" Apu said and added, "So what were you thinking so deeply about?"

"Trying to decide if you're a better guitarist or football player."

"Guess I should just work towards being a decent engineer. And if I don't get back to studying now, I would be strumming mournful notes for the rest of my life."

"Or give football lessons to eight-year-olds at the Maidan," I yelled as he sprinted down the stairs.

Barely a week before the exams, Apu did start going out of the house. For "group studies", he told me. I'd never seen my son engaging in collective exam preparations, so this was new to me. However, he came back on time for dinner and seemed upbeat with his progress. That was more than I could ask for.

A couple of days before the entrance test, Apu had me worried with his lateness. He was usually back by eight or eight thirty, but that day there was no sign of him even at quarter past nine.

After pacing the balcony for more than an hour, I came down to the street with my flashlight. I am a paranoid father; I can't help it. Apu knew that – he always made sure I wasn't kept waiting for him. Except once. But back then he had no way of letting me know.

*

He was in class nine and his final exams were on, so he would return home early. I would take half-day breaks from work to be at home to cook fresh lunch for Apu. He loved steamed rice with butter and boiled eggs.

On the last day of the exam, he was late. Since he travelled by public bus with his friends, I wasn't worried at first. But after an hour's wait, I grew restless. On calling up at Samir's, the only boy in Apu's group who had a landline phone back then, I gathered he hadn't returned either. Cold sweat ran down my face. I left the house keys with Mrs. Saha and left for Apu's school. When the school guard told me the boys had left at the usual time, I nearly sank.

I checked at each of Apu's classmates' houses. The entire gang was missing. Frantic calls from the parents to the school authorities helped little. Finally, at five in the evening, the group returned, exhausted and triumphant at once. The glee in the boys' faces put a stop to the rush of premonitions I was having. A tired Apu, his shirt rumpled and soaked with perspiration explained the situation. His eyes beamed with the spark of an adventurer who had just returned from his Amazon conquest.

"The police stopped our bus and all the traffic at Tollygunj. And guess what the reason was?" He said, as the other boys started grinning.

"A rally?" I asked.

Diversion and blocking of traffic – even at rush hour, for rallies and processions – wasn't anything unusual in Calcutta.

"You got it. Baba. But it wasn't your regular political rally. The demonstrators were all carrying swords and daggers."

"What?"

Impishly delighted to spot a streak of fear in my eyes, Apu continued, "It was a procession of Sikhs – tomorrow is the birthday of their main guru. You should have seen them Baba – bright saffron robes and shiny swords. Wish I were a *Sardar*," He said, brandishing an imaginary sword.

"So what took you so long?"

"We decided to walk back."

"Don't tell me you walked the entire distance from Tollygunj to Lake Gardens, Apu."

"Oh yes, we did. And we had such fun. In fact, you all should do it too. The buses are no good; they only sandwich you with other people."

I didn't have to ask whose idea it was to trek all the way. The ringleader was not only smug about his own team's achievement; he also had some health advice for the parents.

*

That was the one isolated incident. Seeing my level of anxiety on that occasion, Apu took care not to get too adventurous at the cost of getting late.

But it was different now. All Apu's friends had phones, and there was no reason why he couldn't inform me about the delay. I called up Dilip to find out what was taking their study group so long.

"Study group? You must be mistaken, Kakababu. I haven't heard of any such thing."

"Are you sure...could Apu be studying with some other boys?" I asked.

"I doubt it. Apu and I discuss ideas over the phone every day. Besides, do you think he's a group-study type fellow, Kakababu?"

"Hmm, all right. Thanks for letting me know, Dilip," I said and hung up.

My heart ached – more with hurt than tension. Where did I go wrong? All through the years, I had been Apu's friend and confidant more than his parent. We disagreed and fought worse than siblings but made up in classic father and son style. For all our differences, he seldom hid anything from me. After all these years of raising him singlehanded, he lies to me! As I walked a few more paces, the flicker of the flashlight scraping my inner darkness, I saw Apu at a distance. He was waving at someone.

"See you tomorrow," he said.

"Not tomorrow. After your exams," came the reply.

"Oh yes," Apu laughed, "You made me forget."

"Bye, silly boy," she said.

I smiled and turned around fast to get back to the apartment before Apu spotted me.

Who knows if there were a few love notes amid the scraps I saw on his table the day we had our terrace session? I didn't bother to find out. For once, I felt happy to be cheated.

KIRAN BHAT

April 15, 2021: The Day of the Sun

Pyongyang, North Korea

It was more than a special morning. It was the day on which the sun, one hundred and ten years ago, bequeathed upon the earth the human form known as General Kim Il-Sung. He was to be the greatest military leader known to man. He was to be the man who took the most blessed tract of earth and made it into the country of respect and power known today as North Korea. He was the man who, along with his son, and grandson, parcelled the land away from those wretched southerners, giving his people all the security they deserved. So, it was important that on year Juche 110, after so many seasons of hardship and conflict, Mother's precious little nephew Han-jo paid attention to the proceedings on the television, which was broadcasting the ceremony at the Kumsusan Palace of the Sun. He, like any eleven-year-old with a talent, had spent his entire night celebrating the Kim family by drawing the most elaborate sketches of them that he could. They were clearly modelled of the official portraits of the Kims, which decorated the apartment.

"How are they?" he had asked a little earlier, while Mother had been feeding him his porridge.

They were in fact lustrous, the figures surprisingly well-defined for a boy of his age, but Mother did not want to stroke his ego. She said, "The colour you have drawn

The General's face is a disgrace. He is lighter skinned than that. Take another piece of paper and do it again."

By the time he had finished with the second rendition it was getting late, and he had to spend his last few minutes in the house completing the math homework he was supposed to have done the day before. The boy was shivering. Mother's sister had been so eager to get to work that she had forgotten how cold the mornings can get. Mother went and put in another yontan into the ondol. The charcoal creaked and crackled, and the air grew warm.

When Mother returned to the living room the soldiers on the television were marching across the screen, flaunting their military prowess. First were the rows of men in their green uniforms, marching in unison, kicking at a right degree angle with their hand in salute. Behind them followed the women. The army general would soon give a speech to the nation, outlining his plan for the year ahead.

"Look how handsome the army general is," Mother cooed. "Someday, that will be you."

Precious little Han-jo broke into the widest smile and giggled exuberantly to himself. He was clumsy while he was working. He reached over to grab another pencil, and in doing so knocked over the family portrait.

"Be careful," Mother said, and she picked it up and dusted it with her palm. This was one of the few portraits that the family could afford. In the centre stood her stubborn stalwart of a sister In-hee along with her husband. Han-jo was a baby at the time, and he lay in her arms. Mother was right next to Father, and Son was in the picture beside them. This was the only time Son had ever seen his cousin, as a baby. "It will be fun," Mother said. "You and your cousin, playing around."

"Yes," Han-jo said, not giving it much thought.

Mother felt a bolt of joy travel her spine, and she grinned widely. She wanted to tell him then and there that her son was just a night away from coming home, but she couldn't. Anyone who returned too publicly would be detained by the police, sent to a labour camp, beaten to near-death, and forced to go on camera to talk about the horrors of life in the West. Father was paying a lot of money to sneak him back through the border from China. Mother respected this decision by keeping her mouth shut.

Mother put the portrait back on the table. "You know, you and your cousin, your age difference, it is like the age difference between me and your mother."

This was not something Han-jo cared to think about. He was more interested in finishing the last sections of his math, as well as eating his last spoonful of juk. Nevertheless, Mother was staring at this portrait, particularly at herself standing beside In-hee, smiling politely, a little glimmer in her eye. It was often said by strangers whenever Mother and In-hee walked together that they were the spitting image of each other. Mother would smile and thank the passer-by, but in all honesty she saw little of herself in her sister. Maybe it was because she knew about In-hee's bad temper. She spoke her mind at any opportunity, and she was quick to criticise others. When she smiled it was a genuine grin, with the brunt of the happiness coming from the eyes; but when she was angry, even if she did not speak, everyone nearby would know about it. She was also shorter than

Mother and had a mousier face. And, of course, she had a better-fed frame. She also had enough money to buy certain make-ups, which plastered her face white. This was because their mother had remarried after Mother's father died of pneumonia, and her stepfather, who was In-hee's father, was much wealthier. In-hee's husband had also climbed the ranks of the WPK Central Committee, so their side of the family was much better off.

It was time to get going. In-hee's apartment was south of the city centre. School wasn't particularly close. "Come, get ready," Mother said. She picked up Han-jo's backpack and strapped it onto him.

"No, no, no," he shouted, and pointed to his sketch. "It needs to be done again."

Mother smiled. "I am sure it is more than good enough. We have to leave now. Otherwise, you will miss the programme they are planning at school."

Han-jo thought long and hard and said, "My drawing comes first."

Mother went up to the boy and sealed her hand right over his lips. "Do not ever talk that way." He wanted to say something again, but she slapped him before he dared. "Come on, put on your bag. And don't talk while we are outside."

Mother locked up the house and they passed through the grungy hallway. There was a fumigated smell to it, but the overall impression was of mould. It was growing all over. They entered the elevator, but they didn't descend alone. Another woman was already inside, on her way to the festivities. A light blue choson-ot covered her entire body. She was as short as Mother, but with much more plucked features, like a real-life Korean doll. If only the poor girl's skin was not so freckled, her hair not so thin and unkempt.

"Happy Day of the Sun," Mother said. The woman smiled and repeated the same. "Happy Day of the Sun." Mother continued, "We are the luckiest people to have him."

"We are the luckiest people, indeed."

The woman was smiling and nodding to herself, but making sure to avoid eye contact. Mother just wanted to take a brush and straighten the poor girl's hair. People in this land weren't the richest, but that was no reason to neglect one's appearance on a day like this. Mother rummaged through Han-jo's backpack for the comb. But no sooner had they reached the ground floor than the woman darted out of the lift and disappeared into the street.

They stood at the intersection and waited for the bus. Even with a sweater and jacket, the wind was strong enough to sting Mother's arms. She hated this aspect of age; feeling the cold, even when it was mild. Beyond the intersection a row of poplar trees were blooming, and beside them a huddle of pines. Each tree was manicured to such perfection—the delicate angles of its branches, the gentle fullness of its leaves—that Mother could not be sure whether they were the work of human hands or just a beautiful accident of nature. What reminded her that she was in the city was the noise. On every corner loudspeakers blared songs of glory to the Kim family, and on every streetlamp hung ribbons, their reds and blues and yellows as bright as choson-ots. Few people were outside except for Mother and a police officer wearing a wide blue cap and flamboyant blue coat. When she caught Mother's eye, Mother instinctively looked away; then she remembered that she should look, and so she smiled and said, "Happy Day of the Sun."

"Happy Day of the Sun," replied the officer, turning to watch a man leave his apartment and head towards the bus stop. The bus arrived soon after. It was a white bus with a single red streak, the same that Mother had taken when she took Son to school. And today, as then, it was overcrowded. Though Mother's hair was not yet grey, she had the comportment of an older lady, and for that reason she was usually able to get a seat. But today there were too many woman and men who looked much older, so the two of them were forced to stand amid the mass of youth and sweat. When one of the youths got off further down the road, Mother carried Han-jo in her arms and elbowed her way through the men and women on their phones to grab a seat. They were all looking at her. "Happy Day of the Sun," Mother said to the woman next to her. She was an old lady with very frilly grey hair. "Happy Day of the Sun," she responded. The woman noticed the boy in Mother's arms, clad in his blue school uniform, his backpack rubbing against Mother's leg. "Why, aren't you the cutest. Don't stand like that. Come sit on my lap."

Mother and the woman talked a little as they waited for their respective stops. They started with the niceties. Things like, "Why, isn't our leader just the greatest in the world?" and, "We should be proud to have a leader like him." Then, as they got more used to each other, they became more disclosing. "I remember when the bus rides weren't crowded," said Mother. "There was a time when we would be the only ones sitting here. Those were the good times, indeed. Mmm." Before long the old lady way saying things like: "I certainly miss my husband. We aren't city people, actually. We come from the country. I won't say the name. You won't know it. It is too far. Our daughter lives here. We are lucky. She works as a tour guide. She has a really good life, much better than anything we know. My husband passed away two years back, the happiest man, really. But our grandson was born a few months ago. Seeing that he is alive, and my husband is dead, I don't think my husband ever knew happiness. He never got to see his grandson. Because now that I have my grandson, I know that I am the happiest woman I can be. And I know that whatever happiness my husband knew is much less than what it could have been. Oh, I am speaking too much. You have a grandson as well, and he is the most beautiful boy."

"He is in fact my nephew," Mother said. They were getting close to the city, so she was making him get up. "And he is nothing compared to our great leader. Happy Day of the Sun."

The grandmother responded in kind, then added: "Where do you stay? Is it near?"

Mother didn't answer. She was too busy negotiating a route through the crowd of bodies towards the exit. They alighted by one of the government buildings, a dark hunk of concrete with small, thin windows. From there, they would head straight on the wide and desolate avenue, then turn in through another set of buildings to the school. The ground was shaking from all of the military trucks and people marching about in Kumsusan Palace, while announcers on the speakers boomed slogans to the great leader and the Workers Party. It was in this noise and yet in this solitude that her precious little Han-jo suddenly started to pout. Mother immediately felt the change in energy. This was not the place to act out. Soldiers were in all corners of the block. She turned to him. "What's wrong?"

Han-jo looked down and didn't say a word. Mother let the sadness inside him speak for itself, and assumed it was best that nothing was said between them. Nevertheless, just as they were turning into the school, Han-jo hugged closer and said, "Auntie, why is it that someone was born like General Kim Jong-un, and then someone else was born like me?"

"Why, what are you asking? I don't understand your question at all."

Han-jo stopped walking, as if he had said the worst thing in the world. His legs were shivering, and he had trouble looking up. He said, "I want to draw well. I want to be the best at drawing North Korea has ever seen."

Mother didn't know what to say to that. She did know that if they spoke for too long they would be late, and as someone who had spoilt a son of her own, Mother knew that a lot of the wrong decisions a child made later were a direct consequence of a lack of discipline at her nephew's age. This one at least had time to reform.

"You have a good life," Mother said. "You have parents who love you. You have a roof over your head. You eat well. You have all of this because of our great leader. You should be thankful."

She smiled as widely as she could, hoping Han-jo would follow suit. Instead, he winced. She could see that his mood had changed. Han-jo confessed, "I didn't get picked to perform for him."

Mother chuckled, "That is why you are upset? You tell that to your teacher. I am sure they will be happy at how badly you want to perform for him. They will give you the right advice so that next year you will be on that stage, dancing."

Mother knew that if that was the real reason why Han-jo was upset, he would feel better the moment he went into his classroom. After all, it was the Day of the Sun. The teacher would greet him with a wide smile, and with bags of candy and cookies, and he would sniff that glazed sugary smell, and his stomach would gurgle, and his eyes would be drunk with gratitude. He would bow to the portraits of his country's great leaders and exclaim, "Thank you, Great Leader Grandfather! Thank you, Father!" It would be a genuine feeling, straight from his heart.

They reached the door of the school. Men and women were dropping off their young ones. Some of them were in their everyday wear, but a good deal of the men wore army uniforms, while many of the women wore choson-ots, the bright green and blue and red flittering like multi-coloured paper in the wind. Han-jo took one last look at her, then made his way inside. No matter who was around them, Mother kept her eyes on Han-jo. "Happy Day of the Sun," she shouted out.

Han-jo looked down at his shoes, and with the full weight of the words on his tongue, said, "Happy Day of the Sun."

CHRISTINA YIN

A 22nd Century Au Pair

Sometimes, it feels as if the day in this new Bornean World will never end. Wake up, cook breakfast, prepare the lunch boxes, wake up the children, make sure they eat and take their vitamins, wash the dishes, prepare the children for school, take them to school, come back, give the holographic chameleons a rest, check, prep and charge up the robot guard dogs, get to work - thank the good Lord she just needs her computer and internet connection - work, work, work, pick up the children, prepare dinner, help them with homework, monitor and limit their gaming and fend off any explorations in dubious websites, send them off to bed in their sleeping pods.... the rest is repetitive and boring if you've ever had kids or been an au pair before.

It is the year of our Lord 2113. Being an au pair in the 22nd century is not as grand as the job vacancy advertisements make it out to be. This is more like indentured labour or enforced parenthood when the parents are engineers on one of the teams building an artificial planet. Why have children, holographic chameleons and robot guard dogs if you aren't going to be around for them?

It is a rhetorical question. She knows the answer because it is the same for every parent in the 22nd century. The human species is critically endangered and if a couple can procreate, they should. The domes in which human populations can survive are limited and too many are dying from fear, loneliness and hunger for real companionship.

Through the dome's protective shield, the sun's rays barely penetrate to lighten up the gloom. Taking the travelator to pick the children up from their Bubble-School, Diyana has suited up – mask, face shield, full jumpsuit, gloves and boots. Other passengers are similarly kitted out, but as the travelator rumbles from the Housing Dome, a different world emerges. Through the travelator's smokey grey bubble-tube, she sees trash littering the ground, broken traffic lights and lamp posts that once created order in the old world, graffiti on crumbling buildings and as the travelator crosses the once mighty Sarawak River, dilapidated kampung houses. These she can ignore, but it is the sight of the Outliers pacing the roads or picking through the rubbish that burns in her mind.

If the news is to be believed, the Outliers are ruling the World Outside where the pandemic still rages amid Borneo's once thriving cities and towns. That tenacious virus has taken root and no vaccine can eradicate it. No matter how clever the scientists had been nor how much the philanthropists had donated, there had still been the masses of poor all over the world who could not get access the vaccines. It should have resulted in a brutally achieved herd immunity, but somehow, the virus kept on mutating several steps ahead of the most brilliant of scientists. No one could not have dreamed up a more perfect organism, though the conspiracy theorists believed someone really had in a laboratory's petri dish.

Today, the news headlines etched against the deceptively pretty blue skies and fluffy white clouds tell of a kidnapping of the only son of a high-ranked Government official. Diyana shivers. Even the high-ranked are not immune to the Outliers. As the travelator dips and swoops round the bend, Diyana sees the next headline with Mount Santubong in the background. What better backdrop for the news that six couples have married; their nuptials are being celebrated at the Talang Salang Islands. Rituals of the old world once performed in secret are now openly practised because people are desperate. Birth rates have steadily plummeted over the years. Once inhabiting every liveable habitat on Earth, the human species seems to be fading. Is it a side effect of the annual vaccinations in a desperate attempt to ward off the tenacious virus? Or the dehumanizing isolation that has triggered the infertility?

The artificial planets are the people's biggest hope. The Mayflower and Golden Dragon colonies on Mars still require supplies from Earth while the Helios spacecraft with the volunteer colonists shot out of the solar system with booster rockets has not been heard from for three years. Sometimes Diyana sees the spacecraft floating out in space, with its crew and would-be colonists themselves suspended forever, aimlessly, infinitely. What must it have felt like to realise that there was nothing out there and that there was no way back? Could there be anything worse? Perhaps never having left this doomed Earth's surface.

But today is just another day on this Earth. Although she knows it could be propaganda, she cannot help herself and looks up to catch the next headline. This time, the words pitched boldly across the sky are accompanied by a photograph of the artificial planet being constructed by the Equatorial Team. Her employers are on that construction platform. Someday there will be a Bornean rainforest thriving with orang-utans, sambar deer, sun bears and the hornbills that the land was once famed for. That someday, apparently, has been delayed yet again. Diyana wonders if the children will be adults before they meet their parents in person again.

At the Bubble-School's shielded pick-up space, the children seem genuinely happy to see her. They look like little astronauts in their protective gear, but so do all the other children. This has been a part of their uniform since the pandemic raged out of control in the year 2021. Diyana casts her government-approved identity scanner fastened on her wrist over the children's helmets. Diyana knows she would never mistake the children, Kai and Nerissa, but she cannot be too careful. Au pairs and even parents have been known to have taken the wrong children home.

The ride with the children back to the Housing Dome is happier; she feels more purposeful, more alive. And the bonus is that the children are even affectionate. Against her best instincts, Diyana has become quite fond of the charges in her care. But this is not the time to be sentimental. The homeward-bound commutes are notoriously the weakest link in keeping the children safe. She pops the token-ringgit into the payment slot to activate a Safety-Bubble and when the doors slide open, seals the children into their individual safety pods, locks the Safety-Bubble and turns away from them to face the only entry-exit point. Her Au Pair trainer had been very particular about travel safety. The daily commute to the School-Bubble is porous despite protection from the Government Guard. It is rumoured that the last two kidnappings had been enabled by unnamed Guards who had been paid handsomely or had even been recruited by the kidnappers.

Many parents have argued for remote learning from individual family quarters in the few Housing Domes left, but the Government has learned from the past. The human species needs to socialise to procreate. Human interaction, even in protective gear, must be enforced to provide the optimal conditions for young bodies to grow and mature naturally. Every milestone in a young body's progression through its natural phases is a cause for celebration; a girl's first menstruation, a boy's voice breaking, facial hair and budding breasts.

So, when the travelator makes it into the Housing Dome and the shield comes down behind it, Diyana does not relax. The Outliers have been getting very bold, recruiting comrades from within the Domes. Getting the children out of their multi-layered protection – the safety pods, Safety-Bubble, and travelator - takes time, and throughout the process, she is on high alert. Finally, the children are in the family quarters. They are still young enough to enjoy the chameleons' neon greetings and the robot guard dogs' nuzzling their hands for pats.

Diyana's previous employers' children had already been teenagers when she had been brought in as an au pair. They had preferred to keep a distance, interacting only when necessary and eschewing all physical touch. It had been Diyana's only failed assignment among the three families that she has worked for so far, but she had not been blamed when both reached 18 without exhibiting sexual maturity nor interest in family-making. She had just been the last au pair in a long series who had tried to make a difference in their lives, but it had been too late. The young adults were now working in research laboratories, being trained to find the best ways to help humans procreate, to unlock the mysteries of birth and death, to find the secret to procreation that had been lost and which had passed them by.

When Diyana finally completes another day as an au pair and the children are fast asleep in their protective sleep pods having finished their homework followed by a healthy home-made vegan stew with Bario rice topped off with authentic *pisang goreng* and yam ice-cream (the children's favourite), she can finally rest. The robot guard dogs are primed, ready, and roaming the family quarters and the chameleons are in their case camouflaged to blend in with the night's blue rays. It is the perfect time to take a nocturnal stroll.

Outside the family quarters, she walks slowly, her feet padding softly on the pavement that is cracked and uneven. Repairs need to be made, but the Government has asked the citizens to be patient. Most of the funds are going to the Equatorial team trying to build the artificial planet. As usual, the Bornean workers are directed by the team from the International Artificial Planet Agency. The North American Alliance and the European Enclave have the technology and are guarding it jealously. Security protocols are so extreme that home leave is only possible when a worker retires. It is a sacrifice that the Government rewards handsomely and those who have successfully procreated are treated like gods. But for now, space-time video calls from the platform far beyond Earth's orbit are all the parents and children can enjoy.

Slipping out of the Housing-Dome through a hole she has fixed with a patch that she can open and close at will, Diyana breathes in the unfiltered air. She knows about the warnings to stay in the dome, but she can't resist the cool night air and the real breeze that rustles the leaves of the surviving trees. While she is outside, she allows herself to dream, to think of a life beyond the dome and the artificial planets being built.

As raindrops start to fall, she gives herself up to dreams of swimming in clean tributaries upriver where the Batang Ai Dam was created in the late 1990s, flooding the longhouses and traditional homes of her ancestors. She imagines riding a longboat into the interior. Her own mother told her the story of their ancestors being born in a rudimentary Government clinic in Lubok Antu. Before that, incredibly, women had given birth in the longhouses without any modern healthcare. But what is even more extraordinary is the story that the fabled orang-utan taught women to give birth naturally.

It is told that one day, a couple was walking in the forest from their longhouse to the little field where they planted okra and yam when the woman was overcome by birthing pains. As was the custom in those dark days, the husband was about to use his parang to cut open his wife's belly to birth the child when an orang-utan came down from the trees. The orang-utan spoke to the man, telling him to put down his parang and to come up with him to his nest. With those words, the orang-utan took the labouring woman in his arms and climbed up into the forest canopy. The man followed.

There, in the orang-utan nest, the woman lay, in pain and crying. But the orang-utan rubbed wild ginger on her belly and taught the man to massage his wife. Soon, a live child was born from the woman. The parang lay on the ground below the tree untouched. The orang-utan taught the husband to care for his wife and later, he cradled the live child and mother, taking them gently down the tree. The awe-struck husband followed them to the forest ground. "We are brothers," the orang-utan told the man. "Teach your people how to birth your young and never hunt an orang-utan again." And so, he did. That is how the Iban in those longhouses learned the mysteries of natural childbirth and why they never hunted orang-utans again. Whether it really happened or not, for many generations, the orang-utan roamed free in the forests of Batang Ai and the Iban people lived without the fear of having to sacrifice their women to procreate.

Diyana loves that story. It tells of a wild Earth and a wildlife among creatures that live and breathe without domes and bubble-tubes. Few people speak of the old days; many are scornful of times when technology was limited, and life was unspeakably harsh. But Diyana longs for such times. What it must be like to live unfettered by masks and shields, protective gear and filtered air! She dreams of going to the beach and touching the sand with her toes. Her mother had whispered those stories to her although she had known that encouraging her child to dream of things long gone was against Government decrees. The Government's fear of rebellion has always been very real. What if the citizens were to rebel against life in the Domes? What would happen if they wanted to explore the Outside World? How could anyone be safe from the virus? Humanity is at stake and sacrifices have to be made. That is how human life can be sustained. The most important pillar of rule is very clear: *Ask not what your Government can do for you, ask what you can do for Humanity.*

As she slips off the road to a patch of overgrown grass and weeds, Diyana remembers her mother's stories and the pictures she drew for her when she was a child. She imagines little crabs scrambling on the fine sand of a beach and the moonlight on the waves curling onto the shore. Her mind wanders to the forests further up the shoreline and the animals that once lived there. Perhaps she might catch a glimpse of a sambar deer or a tiny caterpillar on a leaf. Listening to the patter of rain on the leaves and breathing in the smell of rain hitting the scorched earth, Diyana can almost see the orang-utan in its nest with the woman at labour, her husband learning to massage her. She can almost see a sun bear ambling along, snuffing the air, scratching its back against a tree. The earth and the wild things are alive, she knows. Somewhere here still.

Yet, she knows she has to return to the Housing-Dome and so she does. Keying in the codes of the family-quarters, the door slides open and the robot guard dogs let her back in with gentle snuffles and happy licks, though she knows they are not real at all. When she turns to her own sleeping pod, she realises that the air in the family-quarters has changed and it is not because of her own nocturnal stroll. Someone or something has entered and has not left. But then, why did the robot guard dogs not corner him-her-it? Why were they not on attack mode?

"Peace be with you, Citizen," the shadow next to her sleeping pod speaks. It is a greeting from the past that has survived, but Diyana is wary of such greetings. Humans are crafty creatures, she knows. Often, they mean the exact opposite to what they speak.

"Leave now," she says quietly. She is not ready to sound the alarm or to wake the children.

"I will leave soon," says the man who emerges from the shadows. He is about Diyana's age, about 27 or 28, but he has a face that seems to have been in the Outside World. His hands are strong, with tough skin that has seen manual labour, uncommon within the Domes. Unless, perhaps he is from one of the Farm-Domes. If so, this is strange for the nearest one is far away in Danum Valley, one of the last fertile pockets on Borneo.

"But first, I have a suggestion," the intruder says. "One that might interest you."

"Two minutes," Diyana says, surprising herself. Perhaps it is the whiff of green leaves and earth that she can still smell. It is not from herself only.

"Would you come with me and be my partner?" the intruder asks. "I know you would be a good mother. And I know your mother had three children, all of whom survived to adulthood. Your father had three wives, and all gave birth to healthy children. I myself had a brother and a sister. They both have children of their own. I know we can have children together."

"And we can bring them up together. We don't need to hire an au pair or live in a Dome. I know where we can go. My name is Lihon and my ancestors lived with your ancestors upriver of Lubok Antu. I have been following you and I know you dream of our ancestors who lived with the orang-utan and who saw the hornbills fly in the skies. That was the Land of the Hornbills and it still is. I know where to find it. Will you come with me?"

"But what about the virus?" Diyana cannot believe she is asking this question, that she has not raised the alarm or stunned the intruder with her arsenal of weapons.

"You know as well as I do that the virus has gone or is no longer dangerous. You have walked in the Outdoor World as I have. You have walked on the grasses and patches of New World forests, climbed as far as the foothills of Gunung Serapi. Have you never asked why you don't fall sick? Why you can keep on going out there and why the Outliers continue to survive without the protection of the Domes?"

Two minutes have passed but Diyana stays still, looking at the intruder.

Then she asks, "What about the children? I cannot leave Kai and Nerissa." She realises that this is her last protest, but it is a real one. She remembers Kai's broad smile when he sees her at the School-Bubble pick-up, Nerissa's hug and their chatter when they do their homework as she prepares their favourite dinner.

"We will take them with us," the intruder says. "They will eat Bario rice that they have planted themselves. And they will live with us and find their partners with other Outliers and have their own children whom they will raise with ours. We will be a real family."

"And all this? And their parents?"

"Their parents already have their rewards. The Government looks after them now on the platform. And when they retire, the Government will take care of them. You are the children's real parent; you are all they know of real love. Never mind the space-time video calls."

The forbidden word: Love.

Diyana looks at the intruder. She remembers her dreams as she takes her night walks in the Outside World.

The intruder knows and dares to speak of all the unspoken dreams and thoughts that have driven her to this Second Life when the world is asleep. The Government is right to fear the Outliers. How this man knows all this about her and her dreams, she doesn't care. He will tell her one day. She realises she has been waiting and readying herself for a trigger to wake her up from the life that she has been living in the Domed World.

"Do we go now?" she asks.

Lihon, she thinks of him now as Lihon and not as the intruder, nods. "We go now," he says.

One last question: "The Government will come after us," Diyana says.

"Yes," Lihon nods. "They will come after us. But we will lose them and then they will not be able to find us. Trust me."

He speaks of Love and now, Trust.

Diyana remembers the headline news of the six couples who got married and who are celebrating their union at the Talang Salang Islands. Could that be any more artificial than the life she lives within the Domed World?

Diyana speaks, "I will wake the children."

But first, she must put on her Au Pair mask so the children will not be frightened when she wakes them at night. She must speak to them gently and persuade them to come without their protective gear and to travel by foot and not on the travelators. She must feed them and prepare them for a new adventure. Lihon will pack what they need: the food and water they can carry, the medical kit, the tools that might help them along the way. And if the children cry and refuse to come, she must be ready.

She must be prepared to let them stay here in the Domed World. She will leave them behind and go to the world of her Second Life which will become her Only Life. It is where the orang-utans live in the trees above the great Batang Ai and its tributaries. It is where the hornbills call to each other and swoop against a blue sky that is real. It is where she can step on the pebbles at the water's edge and let the water touch her toes. Where she can feel the breeze blow back her hair and breathe in fresh air. Where there is no fear of a virus nor fear of a dying Earth and a dying species. Where life can continue where her ancestors lived. There will be other fears and other battles to overcome and survive, and the Government may pursue them, but it will be worth it. She will be alive.

This she believes as she goes to wake the children.

Diyana presses the button to unlock the sleep pods. The casings open and the children stir as they feel the change in the air. She touches them gently and speaks softly, "Wake up, children." And they do.

GANKHU SUMNYAN

Local

National Highway 37, passing through Assam and connecting eastern and western Arunachal Pradesh, had been the usual bedlam of dithering cows, strolling public, and ceaseless traffic. But a Tata Sumo, proudly bearing the "AR" registration number, worked through it with equal disdain and bravado. The six passengers had started at dawn towards Itanagar, capital of the mountainous, tribal state. Hours had passed; jagged hills ran down to the plains, the cool of the morning dissipated, and the roads became wider as they led to the mighty Brahmaputra. The endless stream of the Assamese countryside – yellow paddy fields, dark clusters of trees, and murky pools with red, white, pink lotuses – passed by and in the breeze, one's heart could expand, and one could forget past hurts and wrongs. Just that morning, the driver had been pestered to provide Techa – one of the passengers – a better seat by his entourage; they asked the burly non-tribal man to take his place at the back, Techa being supposedly old and infirm. The driver had tried to intervene, but the group had half-mollified, half-threatened him, not liking signs of protest by a non-local early in the morning. The owner of the vehicle had turned up and rebuked the driver for being so bloody rigid. The burly man watched the proceedings with his family as not-so-old Techa was helped into his seat. Everything that was asked of him, he answered in affirmative – yes, yes, no problem, I am fine, as long as the management says so, we should go, yes. His young daughter hid from the crowd, holding his hand. This scene of compliance and rebellion, right and wrong, coloured the post-lunch dreams of the passengers. They longed for home knowing everything would be alright once they had a sip of good tea in their drawing rooms. But were rudely woken up by the driver's phone ringing incessantly and the word "accident" being repeated.

Once the conversation was over the front passenger inquired what had happened.

"An accident," the driver said, distracted.

"Where?" the burly man asked from the last row.

"At Gorujan, two hours from here."

"Will there be trouble?" Techa asked.

"I don't know."

The old lady sitting to Techa's right also woke up, "This happens all the time. Now what are we going to do?"

"Keep on driving for now. We will find a way," the burly man advised.

The passenger at the front turned and nodded in agreement, which he acknowledged with a smile. The passengers imagined an accident – ugly and messy; twisted steel, broken limbs, and the pain such distortions ensued; of things not being in their places, things broken down, things fallen apart.

"How did it happen?" another lady passenger asked.

"An AR registered Scorpio hit a schoolboy and sped way. Second time this month."

"Isn't there a safe place to stop?" the old lady asked.

The driver nodded in negative.

"No point worrying now. We will find a way," the burly man said. "I think we should search our contact lists for people who can help us."

Following his example, the passengers took out their phones. They searched for anyone who could provide least bit of help – information, security, warning. The front passenger found a police officer but bad network on the Arunachal side prevented any communication. Other calls were made, but none could put concrete information on the table.

Outside of the vehicle, farmers worked their fields and children looked at the passengers with curious eyes. A sense swelled inside that if only a willing ear was found among these natives, just one, he or she would sympathize with them and help them. Instead, any kind of walking movement, towards them or away from them, spelt danger; a collection of people could mean anything, could do anything. The middle-aged passenger called the police officer again, but there was only bad news. Arunachal Pradesh Police couldn't be of help because roads had been blockaded and they were struggling to enter Assam.

"This is bad," a passenger said. "We should stop somewhere."

"Let's try again," the burly man said. "Sir, are you sure no other number?" he asked the front passenger.

"No. None."

"Can you check again?"

The man nodded in negative.

"Anybody has relatives in the towns ahead? Driver, what about you?"

The driver didn't answer.

"Stop then, driver," the old lady said. "Where are we going?"

"Stopping now might not be the solution," the front passenger said.

"What are we doing then?" the old lady muttered.

Nothing to say. They were coasting along, minds churning, infused with doubt and fear.

"It had to happen; the way these guys drive," the driver spat.

"Madam, I am sure the locals would have more contacts…" the burly man suggested.

Techa turned, "This has nothing to do with local or non-local." After some time, he turned again, "In fact, you are much safer than us."

That shut up the burly man. He blubbered about not meaning what was interpreted but his submissive, apologetic tone was even more grating.

Suddenly the driver shouted to close their windows and duck down. A group of people were on the left, gesturing for the vehicle to stop. When it didn't, they threw whatever stones or sticks were there in their hands. The pelts rang inside harsh and the passengers cried out in fear. One stone hit the window at the back but the glass held and they roared away to safety.

"I told you to stop," the old lady was near tears.

"You wanted to commit suicide you mean?" the driver retorted.

This was considered a disrespectful tone by Techa and he told the driver to mind his language. The driver turned and stared at him, forgetting for a moment he was in the middle of a busy highway. When they shouted at him to be careful, he accelerated instead, snaking through the traffic, and without a care about hitting the potholes.

"Driver!" a passenger shouted as the Sumo landed with a crashing thud.

Overtaking one truck, they nearly rammed into another, swerving at the last moment. Everyone had cried out and grasped their seats. By the time they opened their eyes, the driver had brought the vehicle to a grinding halt.

"Go wherever the hell you guys want to," he said, walking away.

As he passed Techa's side, he kicked at the door and snarled, "And guess who is the local here?"

The passengers groaned and looked around among themselves. The men kept their hands folded, signifying their helplessness. There was an awkward silence in the vehicle until the burly man offered to drive. As he took the seat, he told the front passenger to take his phone and search for a contact called Jagjit, "A veteran driver here... knew all the routes. Tell him where we are and whether there is a way out...okay, put him on speaker...I will talk."

Jagjeet, sprightly sounding, told them of a *ghat* which could still be in use, much before Gorujan; a *kuchcha* road after Kakopathar on the left and follow it for a while; there would be few villages and then the *ghat*. Once across, the border wasn't far. Yes, be careful around groups; it could be done, yes, and he had himself been in these shitty situations a few times, but that was what it was.

Following the directions, they found the road after some searching and started on it with prayers on their lips. The road was rutty, of dried mud, dusty. Rocked from side to side, the passengers looked at the man in the driver's seat and wondered.

"We should play sick, or as if we are travelling on a hospital case, that's what we should say," he turned back to suggest.

It was a precarious situation and the passengers agreed. It was further suggested the old lady should play the sick patient while everyone else would be the relatives.

"Nothing much else we can do, if we have to survive."

"The journey was cursed from the beginning," the old lady said.

This increased the sense of disquiet, of waiting in fear for the next event. Apocalyptic visions haunted them – houses ablaze, smoke rising, people running; they had to keep reassuring themselves that each sight was a common thing, of common people leading their lives. Not able to sleep, they hoped for the sight of the *ghat*. The journey felt long, and they began to doubt whether they had taken the right path, or whether the *ghat* existed, or whether Jagjit really knew. But their hearts lifted as the canopy of trees and bamboo groves opened and moist air hit their nostrils – sign of water nearby. Not far now – the drop of land at the distance and the steel grey matter filling it was the mighty Brahmaputra. The *ghat* was visible with few boats lined on the bank, but before they descended to it, they entered a crowded settlement with shops and people on both sides. They were passing slowly when they were stopped by a group of young guys.

"We have to carry her across, a heart patient," the burly man pointed his finger at the old lady. As if on cue, the other passengers rubbed their eyes, opened windows, and sat up straight. The old lady started to groan and breathe heavy.

"Did you hear about the accident?" a young man asked.

"Yes, at Gorujan. The driver was drunk it seems," the burly man offered.

Few of the passengers flinched, not wanting him to provide any chances for questioning.

"Why do they drink and drive?" this was asked to Techa.

Techa rolled his tongue to accentuate his rustic-ness and thereby, innocence, "I don't know. I always advise the young people …."

"What the hell are you wearing? What is that red coat?" a third asked.

"Village head-men wear this," Techa smiled.

"Makes you look like *paan*-spit!!"

They laughed.

"Anyway, why do you guys drink and drive? Why don't you drink at home instead of running over children in Assam?" the first guy asked, looking around.

"We do not know about the person – " the burly man said but was cut short.

"We didn't ask you. You are not a local, are you? Where are you from?"

"I have worked there for many years – "

"Shut up then!"

"Is it your culture? To drink?" the front passenger was asked.

"Sir, I cannot speak for everyone."

"*Wah!* First you mow us down and then you say 'sir!'" they broke into contemptuous laughter but waved the vehicle away.

They reached the *ghat* but were aware of the boys being just out of sight. A boat was found to take them across and when a passenger tried to bargain, he was shouted down by the others. They waited as the boat was getting readied – just a few things to do which seemed interminable. The passengers sitting on the bank couldn't keep their hands still, constantly grabbing at something or rotating by themselves, consequent with releasing sigh after sigh, and looking at the road above the *ghat*. They tried to eat but food tasted stale. Amongst them, the old lady had a puckered, irritated face, as if she hadn't slept for two days, or as if some thought was nibbling at her as the passengers conversed.

"It was a close shave."

"What a day!"

"The gall of those boys!"

"If I were younger!"

"I thought my heart would burst!"

"These people are crazy! What is our fault?"

The old lady brought it down, "He was treated wrongly in the morning."

She pointed to the burly man getting the vehicle loaded onto the boat.

"True!"

"Shouldn't have happened. But sometimes."

"Couldn't have been foreseen."

"Young people! What can you say about them?"

"I mean, can we expect good treatment if we ourselves behave in such ways?"

"Two wrongs don't make a right."

"I am being pointed out here, but it wasn't my fault," Techa said.

"Why didn't you speak out?" the old lady asked.

"What was there to say?"

The old lady looked hard at him, "It was wrong, what happened to him. Get that inside your head and say sorry. You cannot fault the faultless."

Yes, they had been wrong about him; he had been so helpful. But was nowhere to be seen now. The vehicle had been loaded and the boat's engine was getting warmed up. Getting into the boat was both an invitation and a warning – only the true and the right may cross; not those with scurrying feet, hurrying in fear, marked with guilt; the river would claim them otherwise and renew their lives. Suddenly they heard noises behind – it was the same group of boys running down towards them. The passengers clamoured for the boat, picking up what they can. They harried each other on two wooden planks leading to the boat, nearly falling into the water, until the captain asked them to not panic. The engine revved as the boat was loosened from the anchors. A passenger ran out from within a bush and a plank was kept waiting for him. Where was the burly man? He had gone to make a call; they saw him emerge from further away, amazed, halting, and then running. The mob were on the steps leading to the *ghat*.

"Let's go! Let's go!" some passengers shouted to the captain.

The old lady tried to intervene but was violently pushed away by Techa. He warned that he would throw her off the boat if she persisted. That man had died in the morning even before the journey started, Techa said, when he got into the vehicle. What else did she expect? But the old lady wanted him to be wrong; she felt for the poor man, for his family, for his life spent ducking, manoeuvring, making himself small to not become easy target. The first man was in, landing painfully upon the deck.

"Let's go now, captain," Techa shouted.

The plank was asked to be pulled, and all seemed lost for the burly man who stopped running in surprise as the boat moved, except the captain indicated at him to run alongside the boat. The mob changed direction too. The boat steered close to the bank and the burly man slowed down thinking what was to be done. The captain shouted at him to jump. The man looked behind, made up his mind, and took a leap of faith, aiming for the empty space where vehicles were loaded. The passengers watched him fly and their doubts vanished. They wanted him to make it, for he had tried his very best and was willing to shed blood to belong; they gathered around to hold him.

PARVATHI NAYAR

Rat Trap

"Hey Janu, listen to this. Rats turn aggressive in the Lockdown with restaurant closures and their usual supplies of food running out," says Ashok, reading from his mobile. "Suburban rat infestations may spike, authorities warn."

Not a coincidence, this news article on rodents. Rats have pattered through my thoughts all morning, spreading a plague of unease. Ashok speaking aloud the words have summoned their invisible presence into the room, placing me square in the middle of their baleful gaze. The nasty karma emanating from the story brushes up against me, and involuntarily, my stomach clenches.

"I think we have rats on our apartment floor, they're trying to get into my garbage," I say to Ashok. I dislike the querulous pitch of the words, in which I hear the future echoes of my old-woman voice.

No answer. Was Ashok baiting me with the news story? No, this time he was just being chatty, I think. Ashok knows I have a thing about rats, but sometimes seems to misremember my fear as interest. Anyway, Ashok has moved on, the newsworthy rats already jammed under the next headline. And the crisp, fried vadais.

With Ashok forced to work from home, mid-morning news breaks are our new routine. I make sure snacks-and-coffee are always to hand, a necessary bandage to staunch the day's flow of depressing headlines. Biting into a peppery vadai or potato bhaji invariably lifts up Ashok's spirits.

I repeat, "Rats are disturbing the garbage I put out, Ashok."

"Didn't I predict this would happen, Janu?" He continues to read, "People with depression feel trapped in the Lockdown, studies reveal, and are in danger of – What?" Finally, he catches my baleful gaze, and rearranges the patter of his thoughts around the single word of my complaint that has registered.

"Garbage. What about the garbage Janu? You're getting rather too obsessed with the garbage, don't you think? Close-to-expiry medicines in one bag, washed-out milk packets in another, chilli powder which may have bugs in yet another –"

"I was talking about rats in the apartment Ashok, not garbage," I reply, allowing middle-age's bad-tempered cadences to mask the undertones of that old woman. The one just round the corner, who's waiting for me to grow into her.

"We don't have rats in our apartment Janu," he says, giving me a long look.

"Not inside the apartment, Ashok. Outside, outside. The rubbish bags were disturbed again, when I checked this morning."

"Janu! This is what I'll never understand – when you're scared of rats, why go looking for them?"

"Ashok, I wasn't looking for rats, I was checking on–"

"– the garbage. But why?"

"To make sure that SundariAmma's collecting the bags on time."

"Does it really matter when she picks it up," he queries.

"I- Okay, yes, Ashok, I know. The apartment's so lucky to have SundariAmma still collect the garbage in these times when even the house help can't come in. All the same, someone must keep an eye on her, given half a chance she… "

*

I allow my voice to peter out – I know that deepening crease between Ashok's brows. This wrinkle in our relationship emerges whenever the conversation veers towards my involvement in Samudraa Towers Residents' Committee. I wonder, sometimes, whether he's annoyed because it offers me a level of decision-making away from his control, his particular worldview.

But no, that's just me being uncharitable, isn't it? The real reason it bothers him must be that he doesn't get it: for all his management savvy, Ashok cannot grasp how apartment battles are fought over the garbage collector's timings and car park allocations.

See, apartment living in India is War. The inherent attitude to communal life mirrors the way our politicians approach governance. Through networks and allegiances, backstabbing and bullying. There are vested interests and few loyalties. Oh, yes – I understand the dynamics of Samudraa Towers, even if I've never held a job in the political or corporate world.

Some residents refuse to listen to us, the Committee's office bearers, and view us as meddlesome pokers-of-noses in other-people's-businesses. For instance, my detailed information on how to segregate garbage fell on clogged ears. The residents' Philosophy of Garbage Disposal is to vanish it from their immediate vision. By any means possible.

Other ideas of mine in the pre-Lockdown days did work. Take the issue of the tuition children and their minders, who came to an apartment on our floor. It was an endless stream of people, but who were they, who knew their backgrounds?

We decided to ask the security guard to check the IDs of every visitor, every day, and note it down. Ashok thought we were being unfair to the widow who gave the tuitions – our neighbour Sharada – though I think he said that just to annoy me.

But yes, Sharada held me responsible for the complaints from the parents of her tuition kids about the new regulations. She got so ruffled up! A troublemaker that one, always complaining about this and that, and the expenditure of things at our Committee meetings. After our run-in over the ID registrations of her tuition tribe, Sharada grew worse. During Samudraa Towers' last annual general meeting she saw to it that my landscaping plans for the building were shelved.

That was a disappointment, still, we got through our next rule that all visitors have to park outside. It started with that young man, a tenant in the adjoining block. He seemed to be throwing parties at all times of day, with who-knows-what going on inside. Leave him be, Ashok said – but what was the result of the never-ending party guests? No parking available for any of us.

The Committee decided to take a hand, which is how we came to have designated parking spaces. My husband might call us the Morality Police, but I can tell you, when he drove home after work each day to the comfort of the same parking spot, he was a happy man. I pretended not to notice when his complaints about the overly interfering Committee quietly died down.

Of course, none of that matters now. We are all frozen in some randomly selected, insignificant frame of human history. There are no children coming for tuition, no cars being driven, no visitors, and no wild parties.

*

Anyone with a computer seems to be writing about the Lockdown, yet nothing seems to quite capture the muddied strangeness of these days, when we are willingly trapped in our homes. If I worry about my roots showing grey without trips to the beauty parlour, or dirty room corners that an aching back can't mop, or the heartbreak of not seeing my daughter – well, this litany of personal losses feels insignificant in the larger, broken landscape.

I have not been outside at all since the Lockdown. Not even to visit Meera and Amit, a couple we socialise with a little, on a lower floor. We're all so scared. We're scared of pressing lift buttons touched by others, scared of getting into an occupied lift, scared of the ephemeral air around people.

A long time ago, when our daughter left for higher studies, we had discussed moving out of Samudraa Towers.

However, I discovered that I had sunk deep roots into its pebbly grounds. Being an old construction, the apartments here are generously proportioned with high ceilings and roomy balconies. I had room to breathe. Moving to other soils held few promises of a new flowering, just the tedium of regrowing roots in bonsai-sized pots.

Luckily Ashok humoured me, and we stayed on. Yet the shape of our lives changed well before these interred times. The people we were close to gradually moved out. One day we found we had no real friends left in Samudraa Towers. The sort you could drop in on, without warning, to borrow a few onions or a cup of milk – then stay chatting forever.

This is why I decided to join the Committee. It didn't serve my original purpose of making new friends, but I discovered what you might call a specialist political ability – managing Samudraa Towers matters. Which I must admit, gave me a certain purpose.

These days Ashok frequently points out how "his" decision to stay on in Samudraa Towers has proved to be a blessing in the Lockdown. The things we took for granted have turned out to be little luxuries, such as the supermarket right across the road. Or the conveniences that the Committee organised, such as enticing a vegetable store to open just outside, or cajoling an ironing man to set up his cart here.

Ashok goes out daily to the shops across the roads, to pick up some little things. The stores would have delivered our provisions, as we are regular customers, but my husband looks forward to his little "keeps me sane" outings. Secretly I find it amusing that the person who couldn't even tell apart a yellow lentil from a red one, now lectures me on the rising prices of *thora parippu* and *kadala parippu*.

I don't laugh at him. Like most men who enjoy teasing their wives, he doesn't like to be on the receiving end. And anyway, my secret mirth is a tiny bubble of contentment that I keep close within me.

When people are dying, how can I tell anyone that a small part of me delights in the Lockdown for it has brought me closer to Ashok in a way that I have never experienced before? It's not like those Netflix programmes we watch that detail the passionate excesses of love. This is an unexpected companionship, where we read the news together, or celebrate the windfall of fresh mint leaves from the vegetable store or savour the pleasure of ironed clothes from the newly masked ironing man.

Ashok even wanders into the kitchen, sometimes, to wash up after we have eaten and stands around to help fold the laundry. For me, these moments of togetherness are no less precious than the headiness of being newly in love.

*

"Well, no chance of pest control coming round," says Ashok, startling me out of my daydreams. The news has been consumed as well its antidote – the vadais and the comforting coffee. Our mid-morning break is over.

"We'll just have to live with it for now, but I doubt that there are any rats Janu," Ashok says, not unkindly, as he gets up. The rest of his workday will be spent in the makeshift office I have set up in our daughter's old room.

It was so dreary – that cube of empty air she left behind. I like that it's being filled again.

All that's left for me to do now is confront the day's cooking, which begins with the cauliflower. It's gone brown, so I keep it aside for throwing out, and pick the cabbage instead. The key to a basic cabbage *poriyal* lies in the extra fine, symmetrical chopping. Vegetables do taste different based on how they are cut, take it from me.

When I put the waste into the – biodegradable – garbage bags, I feel it again, that queasiness associated with rats. My pleasure in the morning's cooking is also binned. Should I ask my neighbour Sharada if she's seen any vermin? No, I'm still cross about the stupid fuss she raised over my landscaping ideas, calling them "a misguided and grandiose folly". Well.

Instead, I phone Meera downstairs. Has she had any rodent-related problems? She hasn't but has no time to listen to my worries. Meera's in a flap: her mother-in-law is coming to stay out the Covid period with them, and she wants to talk about that.

"Janu, if there were rats, they'd affect the lower floors first, don't you think?" says Ashok, triumphant when I share Meera's news over dinner. "Or perhaps they know a good feast awaits them here? As our daughter loves to say, you're so 'ageist' – any vegetable even thinking about growing old is put out!" He laughs, but I'm not amused.

"We might have a hole in our wall that's allowing them to come up," I say, refusing to give in.

"Janu, d'you think that being trapped indoors is getting you depr– unhealthily caged in?" Ashok says.

"This obsession with rats ... Why don't you go downstairs tomorrow morning, walk away the cabin fever round the building."

I accept that I get fussy over certain things. Squelchy tomatoes. Beans that are blackened at the sides. Not in my curries, thank you. But for Ashok to imagine that the Lockdown is driving me round the bend, is really pushing the limits of home diagnosis. I see the effects of the article he has read this morning.

Anyway, I don't prolong the argument about the rat because I know my husband. We are now trapped in two entrenched positions of Rats - No Rats in our apartment. As I tidy up for the night, feeling disgruntled, the solution comes to me.

My day starts early at 3.45am, for I believe prayers are more efficacious at the *brahma muhurtham*. Afterwards, I have fallen into the habit of a quick clean up and putting out the trash. I could keep a vigil on the garbage bags and take pictures on my phone of the attacking rats.

Ashok will be asleep, and therefore unable to trot out his annoying lines about obsessive behaviours. But oh, it'll be hard for him or anyone else to dispute photographic evidence! Some action will have to be taken when they see my photos. I will remind everyone about how rats spread the plague – so how good is it to have them in the current pandemic? Perhaps it will force Ashok to source some rat traps, or perhaps the Committee can declare a pest control emergency.

*

The next day, in the blackness of the very early morning, I am armed and ready like a soldier preparing for war. I've made coffee and kept a packet of my favourite biscuits on the dining table, in case the wait is long. I pull up a chair to the front door and wait, phone in hand.

Will the rats come? Well, the intensive cleaning out of the fridge has translated into several bags of garbage. Between the large chunk of brown cauliflower and rancid *jalebis*, there's enough to attract even the fussiest of rats. I have deliberately put the garbage further away today, near the stairwell, so there's no chance of the rats running into my home.

Every passing second carries the weight of waiting. Just ten minutes into my vigil when I'm reaching for the sugary support of biscuits, I hear a soft sound outside. A rustle. Something's being moved. Something's moving.

Even the most prepared soldier must feel a moment of panic when heading out to war. Despite the best-laid plans, what if the rats run into my home? That little hamster of fear runs round my mind in tiny circles. But this is my moment of being proved right, away from Ashok's disbelief. I grab on to pride to move past the fear.

Before I can change my mind, I push open the door, poke my head out into the neon-lit landing, and lift up my phone to take a picture – of my neighbour Sharada rooting around the garbage, my brownish cauliflower already in her hand.

*

We grow instant roots into the ground and gape at each other, motionless. We are the only two people alive in a cone of neon trapped and encircled by the still-thick night air. I don't know who's the more horrified. But it isn't just horror on her face, it is –

"Please don't tell anyone, *Akka*!" she whispers, panic-stricken.

What I am not supposed to say, and to whom, isn't clear to me at all. A suspicion, half-formed, presents itself. Was this woman trying to trick me into believing I had rats outside my home, because she knows my fears?

Was this revenge?

"Wha- what are you doing Sharada?" I can't think of anything else to say. The words come out in the sharp, old-woman voice that raises her ugly head when I'm agitated.

In response Sharada burst into tears. A sea of saltwater courses noisily down her face. This leaves me in unchartered waters, directionless about landfall. However, enemy or not, I can't leave this sobbing woman on my doorstep.

"Please come in, Sharada, come in," I say. "Please."

She looks ready to flee.

"I've already made the decoction. Let me get you a nice cup of coffee," I say, more firmly, now on terra firma with the offer of coffee.

Leaving her in the living room to deal with the salt-stains, I go into the kitchen. There's no fear of Ashok coming to inspect. Sleep is a mistress he embraces with absolute commitment, clasping her through howling babies and thundering skies.

I return to find Sharada seated at the edge of the sofa. When her hands reach for the coffee, I notice the cauliflower still lies within the semicircle of her lap. The tear streaks have been scrubbed away, but the mixture of fear and that-something-else-that-resembles-, still lurks in her eyes.

I wait while she untangles the chokehold of emotions and words, and lays them out as sentences. "I can't lie to you, *Akka*, but don't think too badly of me…"

Is a confession about pretend-rats forthcoming, I wonder.

"These are tough times," she says, so quietly that I strain to hear the words.

I wait.

The voice decibels drop further. "I didn't know where else to look."

I don't understand.

"I was looking for food," she says on a whisper.

"In my garbage?" Luckily the etiquette of silent listening shuts me up before I can say anything more hurtful.

For a moment she looks resentful. Then shrugs in a defeated way.

"You see, you – you segregate," she replies. This is not the answer I had expected. Her hands fitfully clasp and loosen around the coffee mug. "Remember? You told us, in detail, at one meeting."

Sharada continues, "I was so desperate, then the idea came to me… when I looked through your garbage last week, I saw that nothing was stinky, or messy… And you threw away so much I could use.

"Out-of-date biscuits work alright for my daughter. And the vegetables? Oh, they're fine, *Akka,* just a bit sad looking. Chilli powder can be dried in the sun to get rid of the bugs. You see? Since then, it's been – you've been – a heaven-sent blessing for us *Akka*." She falls silent.

I feel her anguish and her strange gratitude, which I don't deserve. I'm horrified and horrified at myself for being horrified. But I push aside these feelings, as I want to understand: Why can't she buy food. Where's her money.

It's like tooth extraction, but finally I have it in my grasp. Those tuition students who can no longer come, it turns out, were her money. The apartment belongs to her, gifted by long-dead parents. But when her errant husband too died some years ago, Sharada was left with no savings, no real skills, a daughter to bring up, and mounting expenses. Part-time jobs didn't work out. Eventually, giving tuitions did.

"I could manage our living expenses, pay the monthly maintenance dues. But never had any extras to save up. Or pay for, for – totally unnecessary things," she says, a hint of her acerbic side surfacing. I translate that random sentence into "no money for your landscaping plans". But we both quash our various irritations.

The scaffolding on which she hangs her Lockdown life is revealed in difficult sentences. The gold chain's been pawned, the expenses pared down. Sharada says, "We've cut out everything we could, we only eat one meal a day now, *Akka,* just boil together some rice, *parippu* and salt."

In this world of no-safety-nets, there was nothing to catch her fall. No-one to whom she could turn for a cup of milk, let alone a loan of money. No place to go from the place she has fallen, scrabbling between black plastic bags of garbage, mine, and a white plastic bag of rice, hers, measured out in cup-fuls.

I want to weep.

She wants to talk. Now that the curtains have been forcibly parted, she wants to let her story stream in.

"What will become of us *Akka*, when will the Lockdown end?" Sharada says. I can think of no answer to give, there's no twenty-twenty vision granted to any of us in this poorly numbered year.

She continues, "But even when it ends – will my students come back, will their parents risk sending them?"

The defunct tuitions. I had almost forgotten.

"That's it! You must start online tuitions," I exclaim. "You know, download this Zoom thing that seems to work for everything from corporate meetings to weddings. The school are closed now for summer, but we read in the papers that they'll open in an online mode. Parents are fraught with anxiety – they'll jump on your offer to tutor the children online. You can email them homework, ask them to scan and..."

My enthusiasm that had taken off like a jet-propelled rocket isn't finding any landing ground. She says, "I know how to use one *Akka* – I had to learn at one of my part-time jobs – but, I don't have a computer."

Oh yes. Of course, she doesn't.

Such a tiny bit of empty space separates one point from another along any sort of Number Line. But the further away the two points in question, the opaquer that line, more like a wall shutting out even simple realities.

As we fall silent, thoughts race through my head. I could give her my daughter's old computer. Would she accept it? How about money…. Should I offer to pay her maintenance for a while?

On cue, that inner needling voice: What will Ashok say about my fairy-godmother-impulse? He isn't an unkind man. But he does usually throw cold water over my independent project proposals, especially those involving money. And when he feels I'm being meddlesome.

I can almost hear him telling me that I'm interfering in Sharada's affairs to suit my ends. To push away the irrelevance that awaits me along with that old woman voice.

No, I must follow my instincts, help her without letting Ashok know. Then it occurs to me – in terms of monetary help, I'm in a trap too. I have no money of my own, or rather, I have no money that Ashok doesn't know about, or rather, it is all "our" money as he says. I could still sneak her some vegetables every week. Will she be offended if I give her clothes?

Sharada stands up with a suddenness that switches off the plan-maker in my brain. "If my daughter wakes up and doesn't see me, she'll get very worried, I must go." She bites her lip. Pride quarrels with necessity, then she asks in a rush, "May I keep this cauliflower though, *Akka* – there really isn't anything wrong with it..."

"Let me give you some of this coffee, or maybe milk, for your daughter?" I reply, avoiding her question.

Not giving her time to answer, I rush off to grow octopus arms in the kitchen. Before Sharada lets slip the leash of politeness and runs away I want to give her something to take back. I fill one flask with milk and another with coffee, while trying to stuff a large cloth-bag with whatever fruit I can find.

As I come back, I spy my packet of biscuits on the dining table, put that in as well, and hand the bag to her.

She tries to hand it right back to me. "I-I don't want to take the things that you need and use, when I've nothing to share in return."

I'm not offended because I understand.

What I say is this: "Think of this as a ritual from a past time, Sharada. A time when neighbours knew each other, could call on each other, at any time, for a couple of onions or a cup of milk. And... and stay chatting forever."

What I really want to say is this: I'm not being charitable; I have plenty to share. Take my daughter's computer. Let me help you with food. We will pay your maintenance for the next few months...

The fairy godmother impulse still hovers over my shoulder. But there's no wave of a magic wand to free the patter of words constricted in my throat. Words unsaid by What-will-Ashok-say. Just like so many invisible rats caught in an invisible rat trap.

SMITA P MUKHERJEE

The Monstrous Hermit

The Hindu crematorium nestled in one of the quietest suburbs of Mumbai was working four shifts. Bodies hadn't stopped coming at this multi storeyed crematorium. There were options for using the wooden pyre and the electric incinerator. Most mourners were opting for the incinerator since it took 45 minutes to get the body to burn into ashes as compared to the other one taking 4-5 hours. Within 45 minutes the ashes were being collected by the relatives and taken to the nearest river to sprinkle the ashes and finish off the rituals. The pandemic scare and new regulations were forbidding a full house of mourners and except the undertakers no one was around to conduct the rituals. In the past one week though, the ashes of many bodies had gone missing. It was a peculiar case. How could the police look for ashes that were not even labelled to know who it belonged to? Who was stealing them? The Station head of RC Marg area, an earnest, lean-faced police officer Jaywant Nadkarni was bewildered with this newly found crime. Ashes gone! Relatives were pouring in by the dozens criticizing the establishment and the police for conducting unsupervised funerals. Jaywant hadn't slept in days dividing his time manning irresponsible covidiots and the pending case of the missing ashes. Even though the funerals of the infected dead were conducted under full security yet there were lapses. His staff was clearly stretched. At 55, Jaywant was feeling like an eighty-year-old. He hadn't gone home in weeks and not slept in the last 72 hours. There were whispers in the department that the recent death of his wife had made him turn to work with a vengeance.

After mulling over this peculiar case of the missing ashes Jaywant decides to take things in his hands and visits the crematorium to look for clues. While conducting interrogations with the various undertakers, his eyes fall on a middle-aged hermit with flowing beard and knotted hair. He was playing with the remnant ashes in the crematorium. On enquiring, it was found that the hermit had been a constant resident of the crematorium for nearly a decade, mostly seen meditating. Despite much resistance about interrogating the hermit who seemed a madman, Jaywant insists on interrogating him.

"There's no CCTV footage, he's the only one who could throw some light" was Jaywant's argument.

"Aye *Sadhu*, did you see anyone stealing the mud pots of ashes from here?"

"Yes"

Jaywant turns to the staff of the crematorium giving them a look of "I told you so!"

"Where is he?"

"He's right here sitting in front of you!" the hermit quips.

"What? Where are the ashes?"

"There's a story behind it — Do you want to listen?" The hermit guffaws.

Now it was the turn of the staff at the crematorium to give Jaywant those knowing looks of 'that the hermit is stoned!' Jaywant doesn't budge and insists on hearing him out. One of the undertakers hurries back with a chair so that an over-worked Jaywant could let his exhausted self sit. His team recommends, "Give him one tight slap and he'll come to his senses, *Saheb.*" Unsure, Jaywant gets up to leave but stops when he hears—

"I killed Jagtap first, the man who was using the ashes"

The hermit didn't have a speck of remorse on his face making it difficult for Jaywant to ignore his testimony. Jaywant takes a seat.

"Who Jagtap?"

"The man who uses the ashes to make mud pots!"

The hermit recalls: *Deep in the forest, he digs up a place like a mad man. His long-twisted nails run through the mud like a maniac – He's hassled not to find what he needs – only stones everywhere. He notices some women giggling away as they carry pots. They call out to him, "What are you looking for? Mud? Mud has been taken by Jagtap the potter – If you want to make pots go to him. The hermit clutches the mud in his hand, it slips – He gets up and mouths – Jagtap.*

"Where did you find Jagtap?"

"At the place where no one ever goes or visits *Saheb*, behind the ruins."

Jaywant and his team drag him and lead him to the ruins.

"What was he doing with the ashes?"

In a quaint looking pottery studio, a warm-faced and medium built senior, Jagtap makes pots. The mud that he takes from the side seems to turn black and then turns grey. He keeps aside the pots and goes in to have his food. The pots weren't pots but human bones as seen by the Hermit who's now in his visibly restless state makes a dash for him.

As Jagtap sits to eat he hears some noise outside, when he readies to look out, something goes around his neck—it was knotted hair. He yelps in fear. He almost chokes with the knotted hair. And out of nowhere the hermit steps in, in his terrifying get up and hoarse voice. "Where's ashes?" "What?" asks Jagtap, barely being able to speak. The hermit starts breaking all the pots – everything is crushed to mud, except one pot that doesn't break – Jagtap cries for help – the hermit comes close – and blows smoke at him – his tongue red with blood – "Where's ashes?" Jagtap trembles. The hermit breaks the hard pot, and a skull is in its place – In doing so, he breaks all the pots. One by one human bones are thrown off due to the breakage. Jagtap screams for help but the hermit gets ahead of him and punches him continuously with his long nails. Blood oozes. "How could you take the ashes? Why?" Jagtap argues with a quiver in his voice, "Because it's my business to do so –" Jagtap dodges the hermit from the incessant kicking and hitting but it doesn't help.

The hermit points out – "She – that's her head – and in every pot and pan made from this mud carries a body part of her – Tell me where's she?" The hermit demands. Jagtap says that he sold the pots. He names a few customers in a jiffy. The hermit before leaving tugs at the hairy lasso choking Jagtap to death. Strangled!

"What? You killed Jagtap? Where's the body? Arrest him!"

"Not so soon, arrest me after I have collected all the pots he sold"

The hermit sprints at a maddening speed catching Jaywant and his team off guard.

"And then I ran to find the remaining ashes *Saheb*. I ran"

In a random home – A lady uses her new pot and pan for preparing food. She beckons her brother asking him to join her for dinner. The hermit watches them from a distance. He eyes the pots and pans – "Jagtap's customers!" When the brother comes out to feast, the hermit hurls a lasso of his knotted hair. The brother chokes on the knotted hair. His sister comes to his help when the hermit enters. He breaks the pots and pans. The sister pleads with him asking him who was he and why was he destroying things? Terrified to see the deadly side of the hermit she runs but in time the hermit steps in and pierces her with his nails. The sister howls in pain and breathes her last. The hermit brings out all the pots and pans, and after breaking them, they convert into bony parts of a body, an arm, a leg. He laughs. His bloodied tongue salivates – Ha! Ha! He deposits all the bones in his bag.

Jaywant and his team find themselves in a room full of broken pots and pans and two bodies. Next to the pots and pans are ashes. Paramedics wheel out the bodies so that they could be sent to forensics.

Jaywant was now panting for breath because the hermit had sprinted out of this house too. His team couldn't keep up. Ambulances come in to collect the bodies, but they were losing time. The hermit was gone! Jaywant chases him. Who was this guy, leading them into all the crime scenes?

In another random home – another couple had finished eating and were cleaning up their pots and pans. They hear the sound of the door being broken. When they step out, they see, it is the monstrous hermit waiting to attack. They freeze seeing him, his eyes arresting them into an immovable object. The hermit advances towards them and strangulates them. On the way out, he takes all the pots and breaks the mud water jug. Within minutes the broken items convert into different bony parts of a body. Hands, torso, he laughs and collects them.

Jaywant is shocked at finding more bodies piled up. Yet again the place fills up with blaring sirens and paramedics rushing the bodies to the forensics. Jaywant manages to pin down the hermit to the ground demanding answers.

"Did you kill these too?"

Jaywant was staring at a heap of ash and broken pots that now resembled human bones. The serving spoons morph into bony human hands, the plates and pans morph into the human torso. Shocked to the point of insanity. Who was this criminal hermit driving him into nowhere? Jaywant struggles to balance between the real and the illusionary images ahead of him. Before he could call his team to claim the dead bones his phone slides out of his hands. The hermit wriggles out of his clutches and is now far off running like a madman. Jaywant skips a step unable to catch his breath. What kind of spell had the hermit cast on him? He wonders and after much struggle he crawls and finally gets back on his feet to give the hermit a good chase.

Jaywant reaches deeper into the wilderness of the suburbs where not far away the hermit was deep in meditation before a heap of ashes. Jaywant staggers along and reaches the spot too weak to arrest the hermit for his wrongdoings. The hermit was still in meditation. Jaywant blinks his eyes to clear his vision. Not far away sirens were blaring, his phone is buzzing somewhere but his hands aren't moving. They have frozen in the cold dark wilderness.

The hermit enquires, "Weren't you looking for the ashes of Bhavna?"

"How did you know?" asks Jaywant.

In the middle of a mud patch the hermit stares at the mound of ashes. He slowly assembles all the bones that were collected before and starts putting them in the shape of a human.

"I'll bring her back to life, Just watch! – O'Bhavna! Bhavna!"

J Jaywant stares at the unimaginable trick nature was playing with him. This hermit had assembled all the ashes to recreate his dead wife Bhavna! Really? Was that going to be possible?

The hermit lights a fire and starts chanting, "Now you'll see your wife transform into a human being—And you can remarry her"

A shot of disbelief fills up his face. Jaywant's eyes glitter with joy. He would finally be able to fulfil the promise made to his wife for their 25th marriage anniversary.

Bhavna, frail with sickness lies in a hospital bed drowned in all kinds of tubes that were feeding her body with the essential amount of medicines to keep her vitals going.

Jaywant clutches the glass window separating them by at least 6 feet. She was ensconced in the infectious diseases ward of the hospital. Her lungs had given way. Jaywant looks away in quietude as tears flow. The doctors had given their verdict. She wouldn't be living more than a week. Bhavna looks over to Jaywant, mouthing the words, 'Happy Anniversary, dear, dress me as a bride when I leave this world.'

Jaywant howls holding the glass. Being a police officer, he had been granted special permission to see his wife but from a distance. The 25th anniversary plans that had been made by Bhavna last month, a few days before she got sick, were now staring at infinity. Invites had been sent out. The caterers and decorators were briefed. Jaywant's constant warnings to keep the celebrations to a small number met with a lot of resistance. She kept arguing that a silver jubilee doesn't happen every day and that diseases come and go. The flare ups were becoming a habit between the couple. One day Jaywant returned from work feeling feverish. He was having a cold. He went back to work the next day but his wife caught on to the cold. A few home remedies gave her relief but then within a week the breathlessness hit her, and she had to be admitted. Her condition took a serious turn in a few days such that she was declared untreatable. After her death he learnt that the invite list to their anniversary celebrations only consisted of her and him accompanied by dinner cooked by her. She had deliberately put up an act of throwing a lavish party just to irritate him. Jaywant hadn't shed any tears, he was far too shattered to emote. The guilt was eating into him. Her funeral was conducted by hospital officials to avoid infection.

The hermit stares at the bones and ashes.

"You regret, don't you? For infecting her?"

Jaywant breaks down, as copious tears flow down his cheeks.

"I did enough penance to get here, Jaywant. And now I am ready to use my powers to help people like you, living their lives in hopeless grief. I am here to bring her back from the dead. To give her a new birth, a second chance."

Jaywant falls on his knees unable to believe his luck. He was going to get his wife back. Not far away, he could hear his team looking for him. He stiffens and gestures the hermit to hurry up the process.

The hermit's chanting increases in decibels as he lights a fire to the heap of ashes. The bones assemble giving form to Bhavna. The hermit is thrilled to bits. He laughs aloud, beaming in pride looking at his achievement. A human being was coming into form as he sees through the fire. Jaywant shuts his eyes crying, this was true redemption, wasn't it, he thinks. He imagines Bhavna, her smiling face, excited to be dressed as a bride on their anniversary.

The hermit lets out a cackle, "Very soon she'll be restored, and you can then remarry and fulfil her wish"

Jaywant stares into the fire hoping Bhavna would emanate from it. When her last rites were being performed the undertaker had sent him pictures and all he could see was her body sliding into the electric incinerator.

He opens his eyes, the fire is still burning and then Bhavna appears, in form.

Astounded that he was getting a second chance, he brought out a tiny box out of his pocket. He holds the box out and opens the lid, it was vermilion. He takes a pinch of it and waits for her to step out of the fire, in her original state dressed in bridal wear.

"There, I am ready to remarry you my dear, I am here to keep my promise. I am sorry, forgive me for doubting you my love, for infecting you---"

Jaywant sobs.

The hermit laughs putting more ash into the flames. Huge lumps of fire bellow into the air. Bhavna advances towards Jaywant, slowly, her eyes downcast.

The hermit inches towards Jaywant and with swift movements he takes Bhavna's sari *palloo* and ties it to Jaywant's belt that held his trousers.

"Take the *pheras* around this pious *agni*"

Bhavna takes the lead and Jaywant follows her in a trance. One, two, three, the hermit counts till seven.

"Now you are man and wife, dear"

The blaring sound of sirens makes Jaywant shudder for a moment. He had left his team at the crime scene while he was here allowing a murderer to roam around free. He shakes his head wanting to get a grip on the situation, he could hear his team members calling out to him.

"Jaywant *Saheb!* Jaywant *Saheb!*"

The hermit's eyes redden. "I helped you fulfil the promise you made to your wife, *Saheb*, you can't arrest me"

"I killed the potter who took away her ashes only to bring her back to life. You can't arrest me!"

Jaywant holds his wife's hand to run but he couldn't because the hermit had held onto his legs.

Not far away, Jaywant's team was nearing them.

"Tell them, tell them that you were the one who stole the pots of ashes every single day, ever since your wife died. Tell them!"

Jaywant freezes. What was this he was hearing, a monstrous hermit accusing him of crime.

"Tell them that you were the one who sneaked into this crematorium to steal the pots of ashes hoping one of them would be your wife's? I couldn't see your plight *Saheb*, Tell them"

Jaywant receives a jolt, the hermit was at his feet pleading with him to tell everyone that he was the one guilty of stealing the pots of ashes. He looks around. It no longer was the wilderness of the woods. It was the crematorium where he first started the interrogations with the hermit. His team weren't far off but around him trying to bring him back from his state of trance. They splash water on his face trying to bring him back to his senses. His eyes were open, he could see that he was surrounded by his team and the crematorium staff.

His wife was gone, his hands still held the tiny box of vermilion. He shakes off the feeling of illusion. He looked around, all of them were looking at him quizzically.

"*Saheb,* is it true? He says you were stealing the pot of ashes."

Jaywant looks into the deep hypnotic eyes of the hermit. How could he confess to his team that in his deep state of grief and anguish every night he walked over to the crematorium to mourn for his wife. In his state of maddening desperation, he would sneak into the room where the pots of ashes were kept and steal them. He would hold onto the pot and cry hoping he could bring his wife back to life, someone who he had infected with the deadly virus. He was seeking redemption of some kind and his mind in a way had placed him in this illusionary world where God's messenger *Yamraj*aka Jagtap was a potter making use of the ashes to create new pots as in 'new life.' Jagtap had to be killed along with his other 'customers' to have access to the ashes before they went into the assembly line of creating new life. The hermit in a way was Jaywant's imaginary medium, like a portal to make all this happen.

Jaywant stands up unable to make eye contact with his team.

"The stolen ashes are hidden behind our police station" he confesses.

The hermit lets go of him, relieved. His team wondered about this unforeseen confession.

"*Saheb* go home, you haven't slept in days. Go home and mourn for your wife, *saheb*" the head constable consoles him.

Ashamed of his crazy state of mind he saunters out of the crematorium as a group of bystanders watch him. His eyes wander to the hermit. Their eyes connect. He lets out a smile depicting he was thankful for helping him keep his promise with his wife. He drags his feet out of the crematorium and turns again, wondering if this was redemption?

SUSHEELA MENON

Kintsugi

"Are you home?"

Rani twisted her hair into a croissant and pushed a bun stick into it. Her phone was wedged between her ear and shoulder.

"Yes, babe."

She closed her eyes for a second.

"I just got off the train…heading to the mall for something…"

"Okay," he said. "Come soon."

Rani slipped her mask down to her chin and breathed in and out for a few seconds. She sat under an ancient *Pukul Lima* tree near the train station and kept her bag to a side.

Kabir was a good man. The pandemic had somehow brought them closer. He worked from her home most days and Rani liked having him around, but not today.

Her phone beeped. A barrage of emails flew into her Inbox, but she ignored all of them, and clicked on a message that was on her mind all day. It was from a former classmate.

Remember HIM?

She read the words again and again but didn't click on the image attached to the mail.

She knew who HIM was.

She threw the phone into her bag and looked up to see a streak of lightning dance on the horizon.

Singapore had little room to grow but it built and rebuilt itself — tunnels, bridges, tracks. The sea stared at it from all sides. She was terrified of the dense thunderclouds and stinging rain that the country withstood most of the year.

Kabir had smiled when she told him.

"You feel trapped?" he asked.

They stood on her balcony surveying the thousands of flats that gazed back at them. Kabir's jet black beard matched the colour of his eyes. They sparkled like lamps behind his glasses.

"Yes…it's as if the sky and the earth turn into a prison…I feel tied down by my own fears."

"Hmmm."

Rani looked away.

"What else are you afraid of?" he asked.

"You."

He squeezed her hand.

"You ever think of marriage?"

Rani could neither want him enough nor let him go.

"I don't know."

"What's stopping you?"

She hadn't replied. She envied Kabir's simplicity. He was so uncomplicated.

The *Pukul Lima* tree swayed like an elephant. Rani looked up to see a maze of branches and sullen leaves above her. She crossed her legs and rubbed her eyes.

Did she want to see HIM?

She pulled out her phone again and stared at the attachment. Her heart shrunk like the leaves of the *Pukul Lima* as her fingers hovered over it. She hurled the phone back into her bag and zipped it shut.

A milky moon sat on the sky and the wind danced around like a dervish. The air carried the smell of durians and cempaka flowers. It was the Ghost Month, a time for many families to remember the dead.

Rani saw a man with a guitar in his hands a few steps away. He wore a white shirt with full pants and fiddled with his guitar like a professional busker. The skin on his neck sagged and his lips drooped like a bow.

He opened his mouth and said something: Fook Chong.

His name was Fook Chong. The long silver hair on his head made him look like an ancient Chinese philosopher.

Rani looked around to see if anyone else had heard it but none stopped to acknowledge the old man. She felt sorry for him. Perhaps he was one of those the virus had struck hard.

He cleared his throat once, straightened his bony shoulders, and began to sing.

Lady in Red.

Fook Chong's voice rose and fell like waves in a storm. It shackled Rani to the moment and surged through her like lifeblood. She sat till the very end and walked over to where he sat with his guitar by his side.

"That was so, so divine. Could you please sing that song again?"

Fook Chong lifted his guitar. Rani noticed some dark brown stains on it. She waited for him to begin.

The sky behind them darkened, like the burnt shell of a broken coconut. A dog barked and a pigeon flapped its wings. Several people passed them by. Trains rattled into and out of the station.

Fook Chong was oblivious to the chaos around him. He closed his eyes and sang like he was all alone.

...is dancing with me...cheek to cheek
...there's nobody here...just you and me...

Rani clapped softly when the song ended and looked for his tip box, but there was none. She offered him a two-dollar note. Fook Chong ignored it.

"Do you not like to sing?" she asked.

"I don't enjoy singing English songs."

"Why?"

He rubbed his fingernails together.

"What's de Burgh before Zhou Xuan?" he asked.

Fook Chong spoke fast. His syllables jumped like frogs in tropical ponds. Rani stuffed the note back into her wallet and wondered why he didn't look at her.

"Who is Zhou Xuan?"

A muscle twitched around Fook Chong's eye.

"Zhou Xuan's *Shanghai Nights* is my absolute favourite but I rarely sing it."

"Why don't you sing what you like?" she asked.

"Would you have liked that? You don't even know who Zhou Xuan was."

He examined his guitar and spoke again.

"*Lady in Red* is my wife's favourite song. She once told me I could heal broken hearts with it…like the Japanese fix broken pots and vases…"

His hands stirred the air around him.

"… by mixing lacquer and gold," he said.

"Where is your wife now?"

"I lost her."

"I am sorry about that."

Fook Chong gazed at the moon.

"She loved to hear me sing."

"Do you observe the Ghost Month?" asked Rani.

"Yes, I do."

Rani thought a dead person turned to dust. That was that. But who was she to kill an old man's hope?

"I loved what you just sang. It reminded me of someone," she said.

"Who?"

Fook Chong hummed a melody, as if her answer didn't matter much to him.

"Oh, he left me…long ago."

He pulled a string. It made a sad, long sound.

"Was it the virus?" he asked.

"No, no. He is alive…just…not with me."

Rani felt a warm tear winding its way down her eye. She quickly wiped it.

"Why do you cry?" asked Fook Chong.

He still didn't look at her. Perhaps he was blind.

"How do you know I am crying?"

"We don't cry with our eyes alone," he said.

"You are an amazingly sensitive person, Mr Fook Chong."

A hawker stared at her as he walked past. What could an old Chinese busker have in common with a young Indian girl? Maybe that's what everyone was thinking.

"Why do you cry now?" he asked.

Rani pushed her hands into her pockets.

"Oh...I'm not sure...maybe because he left...and I could never figure out why."

She bit her lip and dug in her bag for her handkerchief. She wanted to slap herself. Why the hell was she saying all this to a stranger?

"He is a mere mortal, girl."

Fook Chong wiped all the little knobs on his guitar and spoke again.

"Think about it this way. Life is standing by you...you are full of it. Who cares if some man somewhere has left you? Life hasn't."

Rani felt a sharp pain coursing through her head.

"We were in love, Mr Fook Chong. If love can be alive at one moment and dead the next...how can I believe in love anymore?"

The old man shrugged his shoulders.

"We can be alive one moment and dead the next. You just believe, girl. Your life is as flimsy as the love that left you...but you live. You believe in life...even when so many die around you..."

Rani stared at him and hoped he wasn't a freak. Half her mind wanted to run while the other half wanted to stay.

"You must be married now?" he asked.

"No...I...I am with someone."

"The boy who left you…is he married now?"

"I think so."

"Is he happy?"

Rani kicked a stone near her.

"What about you?" he asked.

She let out a false laugh.

"Do you want to marry him…this man you are seeing?"

Damn this man and damn his song. Rani couldn't believe she was having this conversation with a busker on the street.

And yet…

"Do you really love this man?"

Rani didn't blink for a full minute.

"I do love him…but…what if he leaves too?"

She bit her tongue the moment she said this. That she was talking to a stranger, not to Kabir, about her darkest fears — it didn't feel right.

"Ah…I see. You don't trust…"

"I do."

Rani couldn't look at him.

"You are afraid of love…and of loss…they are two sides of the same coin. You can't have one and avoid the other," he said.

Rani stood next to him for a few more minutes. His eyes sought someone as he looked at the crowd crossing the signal across the mall.

"I hope you see your wife soon, Mr Fook Chong."

He didn't reply.

Not once did she turn to look at Fook Chong, but for the first time in years, she felt unburdened — as if someone had lifted a rock off her chest. Her life didn't feel like a lie anymore. Someone knew that she still grieved, that it hurt.

She fell into a dreamless sleep that night and woke up to find Kabir sleeping next to her.

The balcony door was open. Black rainclouds rolled in from everywhere. The sky flashed a warning; a piece of it shattered somewhere. Rani rubbed down the rising goosebumps on her arm and left the house.

She didn't wait for Kabir to wake up. She couldn't face him. Not today. Not now.

The lone security guard at her office took her temperature and she soon checked in to her little cubicle. There was no one in her office. She switched on the laptop.

All those who knew her believed that she was over it, as if heartbreak was a wave you surfed.

Yes, she loved Kabir, but that didn't make it any easier for her. Her sense of abandonment had turned her heart into a sieve. It could hold nothing.

She opened the browser and typed HIS name.

Her phone beeped.

"Hi."

It was Kabir.

"Hi."

"What happened?" he asked.

"Nothing."

"You slept early last night and left home early today. All okay?"

"Yes. I was tired."

"What's up, Rani?"

She closed her eyes.

"Should I worry?" he asked.

Rani broke the long silence that followed.

"I want you to know that I love you."

She pressed ENTER on her computer and waited. HIS name stared at her from the browser, as if she was a stranger to HIM.

Rani grabbed her mobile, found the email and finally clicked the attachment.

It was HIM.

HIS arms were around a woman much younger. They held an infant together.

The more she looked, the more unreal it felt…as if it was all a dream. As if HE never existed. As if they never met. As if HE never left.

The rain thumped the windowpane behind her like a maniac. A pair of mynahs screeched on the sill. She turned to see rainwater streaming down the window. Rani's legs grew cold. Her head spun like a top. She noticed her breath. It flew in and out of her nostrils.

Rani deleted the email and HIS name off her browser. She stood up and put on her raincoat.

Thick black clouds questioned her presence on the street. A bolt of lightning slashed the world in two. The wind howled in her ears. Fear shot up Rani's spine and filled her body with the urge to run, to hide.

But Rani trusted life and walked.

The empty street made a pattering sound that grew louder and louder. The rain pricked her face and washed away the salt of her tears. She took her mask off and stood with her mouth open, as if she were making love to a sea monster.

When she opened her eyes, the downpour had mellowed to a light drizzle. A sharp ray of sunshine fell on her, like an archangel's blessing. The Universe was on her side. She wasn't alone.

She clambered down the steps of the train station that evening and turned towards the mall to look for Fook Chong.

No one sat there.

There were stalls nearby where people ate their daily porridge. The smell of steaming noodles and fishballs pricked her nose. She came out to the open field and saw wish lanterns float up the sky like giant glow worms.

Fook Chong was nowhere.

She walked back to where she sat yesterday. The leaves of the *Pukul Lima* had withdrawn from the world again. Rani stood under the tree hoping he would come soon to play another song.

A familiar voice startled her.

"The Ghost Month ends tonight."

She turned to find Fook Chong standing on the other side of the beautiful *Pukul Lima*.

"Mr Fook Chong."

He straightened his shoulders and hobbled towards her.

"I wanted to see you," she said.

Rani struggled to speak.

"Mr Fook Chong…I want to thank you…for the song…for talking to me."

Fook Chong just stood there under the moonless sky.

Had he waited the whole month for his wife?

"Yes," he said. "I waited for her."

Rani was sure she hadn't spoken aloud.

"How...how did you know what I was thinking?"

Fook Chong ignored her question.

"*Kintsugi*. That's what my wife said. My songs are like *Kintsugi*, the art of mending things."

He looked at Rani for the first time.

"She said I could heal broken people with my songs... make them beautiful again...like how the Japanese mend things, with gold and lacquer."

He wasn't blind. He could see but...his eyes...and the pallor of his face...

Mr Fook Chong looked like a...a...

"You are right," he said. "I died of the virus several months ago."

Rani felt her armpits dampen. Her mouth tasted like sawdust.

"You are joking, aren't you?"

Rani knew he wasn't. She wished he were. Fook Chong's smile didn't reach his eyes. Rani took a step back. She pinched herself.

"Your heart...it folded into itself, girl...like the leaves of this old tree. It pulled me to you."

Rani stood with her mouth open. He spoke again.

"This world is full of magic. It isn't open to everyone... just to those that need to see it."

"That's…just…nonsense," she said. "No one can hold on to dead people. They are just…memories."

"Why are you holding on then?"

Rani couldn't speak.

"You are holding on to a memory, girl…your past is dead. Let it go."

Fook Chong stepped away from her and into the crawling shadow of the majestic *Pukul Lima*. He vanished like vapour.

Rani's legs trembled. She felt her heart pounding against her chest. She wanted to sit down but her phone beeped. It was Kabir.

"Where are you?" he asked. "It's late."

"I…have to do something."

She heard someone strum a guitar and walked towards the mall to find a young boy standing near the train station.

"Where is Mr Fook Chong?"

The boy blinked. She noticed the guitar in his hands and touched the dark brown stains on it.

"Where did you get this from?"

"It's a used one."

Rani went back and stood under the *Pukul Lima* tree for some time. The leaves of the tree slept like new-born babies.

She walked towards a line of shops nearby that sold wish lanterns. A big red lantern hung from a hook in one of the shops. She touched it.

"It's for spirits to find their way back," said the shopkeeper.

Rani bought it.

"You can write something on it."

She borrowed a pen from him and wrote *Kintsugi* on it.

Her phone beeped again.

"What the hell is wrong with you?"

It was Kabir. She apologized for not calling him back.

"What happened?" he asked.

"Kabir…I met someone."

Kabir spoke after a minute.

"What are you saying?"

"No, no. Kabir…it's not what you are thinking…I met a…a…"

He laughed.

"Now don't tell me you met a ghost…you have been acting really strange."

"I don't know who I met, Kabir."

"You don't believe in all this Ghost Month stuff, do you?"

"I didn't believe in life either...or love...until I met you."

Kabir said nothing. His silence irked her.

"I am at the field across the mall," she said.

"Okay."

"Will you marry me, Kabir?"

Silence again.

Rani held the lantern in her hands and stared at the vast black sky.

Why did he end the call? Did he not want her anymore? Was it too late?

Rani slipped her mask off and inhaled the night air. She would be okay...even if he left. Someone touched her shoulder just then. She turned around to find Kabir standing next to her.

"Where's your mask, you idiot?" she asked.

"I forgot to wear it because of all that you said."

She laughed and gave him a spare mask. Kabir quickly put it on and touched the letters on the lantern.

"What is *Kintsugi*?" he asked.

"It's a secret."

They released the lantern together and watched it float far, far away.

"Will you marry me, Kabir?"

He took her face in his hands, but she didn't look at him.

"You aren't my first love," she said.

"Can I be your last?"

Her eyes twinkled as she looked up at him.

"Yes."

"Do you want to marry me, Rani?"

"Yes," she said. "Yes, yes, yes."

She heard the old guitar strum on near the mall. It played a different melody.

"Hey, look," said Kabir.

He pointed at a star burning right above them.

"It looks like someone has stitched it in, to fill a hole in the sky..." she said. "...a drop of golden lacquer."

ANDREW INNES

The Short Story Collective

"Now, Haruto san. What have you got for us this week?" The professor and chair of The Short Story Collective blew cigar smoke into the air before resting his stare on the promising writer. The exclusive club they sat in hosted six esteemed members who took weekly turns introducing a short story they had worked on over the preceding six weeks. This was always interspersed with a great deal of literary talk, references to obscure Russian authors, a dash of pretension, and lots of expensive sake.

Haruto's leather armchair slightly creaked as he shifted nervously and began to read the latest of his travel diaries. He talked of his days walking across Japan in the oppressive heat of summer and studying haikus at night. He spoke about evenings spent at temples hidden deep in the misty mountains of Kyoto and the kindness of strangers when he had been lost or had trouble with the local dialects. He mentioned pacing the crowded fish markets of Tsukiji while listening to the vendors banter with one another. He expounded on the ethereal stillness of snow lined hot springs only accessible by foot in Tochigi. He recalled how soaking in them had the liminal quality of being neither in the present nor the past but somehow outside of time. He described the experience of being enveloped on all sides by a kaleidoscope of colours that seemed to burn on fire as he walked on carpets of leaves through Tohoku in autumn. He held court on the food he had eaten on the streets of Osaka: the umami richness of the ramen, the lightly charred chicken and leeks on sticks roasted on the side of the road, the depth of flavour of a cut of wagyu beef served with just a suggestion of ponzu.

The members made the right gestures as they listened. Heads cocked to the side, and eyes looked off into the distance as he described the hot springs of Kyushu. Eyes closed and heads raised to the ceiling as he painted a picture of the snow festival of Sapporo. Heads nodded slowly as he detailed the cuisine provided by the monks who had hosted his stay in Mount Koya.

A polite stillness was preserved throughout the story, save for the occasional sound of a sake cup being returned to the mahogany table, or the occasional creak of a leather chair. His words danced in the air like the dust motes in a single ray of sunlight that cut through the haze of cigar smoke. Haruto put down his notebook and raised his eyes to let the group know that his story had been told.

He had often mused on the purpose of the weekly meetings; why did he bother when he could simply sit at home and watch TV? What did he or any of the others get out of it? Calling the activity an exercise in collective backslapping and validation wasn't far off the mark, but surely, the same could be said of all social interactions when broken down to their constituent elements. Perhaps fine tailoring and the ability to hedge their words carefully merely obfuscated the basic animal fact that the collective was engaged in nothing more than a form of preening, each member serving to validate the other.

In this sense, were they nothing more than primates sat in a circle, each picking grubs out of the other's hair before consuming them as they consumed each other's stories? Had they even paid attention to what he had just said, or were they simply waiting for their turn to arrive so that they could have their own fur carefully groomed? These were the things that often played on his mind.

As he looked around the table and reached for his sake, something curious happened. It was something that took him quite by surprise and caused something of a stir. The other members started whooping loudly while jumping up and down on the tables before proceeding to smash the furniture up with their bare arms. A bowl of pistachio nuts was sent flying off the table, where it shattered into a thousand pieces on the wall. The leader of the collective swung upside down from a small chandelier hanging above him, and the club was sent into chaos.

Paintings were trashed, and food was picked up from the adjacent tables and flung at the walls. A cheese plate was trodden on and squashed into the carpet. A cafetiere being carried by a waiter in a waistcoat and bowtie was toppled over. The hot coffee spilt onto a businessman's suit as he leapt to his feet in pain.

In the ensuing fracas, the chairman's trousers had split at the back, exposing a pair of bright red cheeks that he thrust in the face of a shocked older lady sat near the bar. Several customers ran out onto the alley screaming, narrowly avoiding a merchant who happened to be riding past on his bike before he swerved and crashed into some bins. Back inside the club, two of the members jumped from table to table, and a third relieved himself into a Yukka plant in the corner. Each member wore a toothy grimace as he nodded his head in glee at hearing Haruto's story while administering hard slaps to his back. Of course, this was how Haruto replayed the scene in his imagination. In reality—and as usual—he simply received a polite round of applause.

He awoke late the following day in his small apartment and mulled over the events of the previous evening. Emerging from his futon with his head swimming slightly, he made a cup of coffee and opened a window, the warm spring air ridding the room of its fug. In the park below, cherry blossom trees stood like giant servings of candy floss as families set down tarpaulins for early hanami parties. A dog barked as a cat made its way across the blue roof tiles of the adjacent building towards a small bird. A buzz in his pocket interrupted the events. It was his friend Akiko.

"Hey, how were things last night? I hope they liked your latest story."

"Yeah, I think it went well. They looked like they enjoyed it, but I need a bit of inspiration for the next one. Writer's block, again.

"When do you have to give your next reading?"

"In six weeks, as usual."

"Well, good luck. I know how much it means to you. Say, are you free this weekend? I was thinking of going up into the mountains to get some fresh air."

"This weekend? Sure, why not. What's the plan?"

"Oh, nothing really. Head to Ikuno. A bit of walking on the Saturday, hot spring followed by a barbecue in the afternoon, then maybe visit the local town the day after and wander around the shops. Are you in?"

"Sounds great. Maybe I can get some ideas," Haruto said as he watched the bird fly away just in time.

"Yeah, it'd do you good to get some fresh air—get in touch with nature and all that."

"Sure. Okay then, I'll meet you at nine on Saturday morning."

*

The following Saturday, Akiko's car pulled up outside Haruto's apartment building with a quick beep of the horn. Just out of university, she had recently started working at an accountancy firm and was adjusting to the steep transition from university life to what seemed to be a contest to see who could put in the most overtime. After loading up the car, they set off for the small bucolic town set among the mountains of Hyogo prefecture.

"So, tell me again what Ikuno's got to offer," asked Haruto as he took a sip of coffee from his flask.

"I picked this up from tourist information yesterday. Maybe you can read it while I drive." Akiko tossed Haruto a leaflet which fell to the footwell. Picking it up and wiping away the detritus, he scanned the pictures and read the accompanying text.

"'Located just fifty minutes by train outside the Castle city of Himeji, Ikuno is a lovely town that can be visited all year round. Attractions include Black River hot spring, a natural, wooden hot spring surrounded by nature; Ikuno Silver Mine, which dates back to the 16th Century; and an abundance of nature's treasures.'" Haruto's narration trailed off as he took in the pictures.

"An abundance of nature's treasures? What does that mean?" asked Akiko, her eyes flitting between the road and her passenger.

"Hang on...here we go. 'Ikuno is home to the Japanese salamander. Considered to be a barometer of a healthy ecosystem, this nocturnal amphibian can grow to around 1.5 meters. Its brown and black mottled skin blends with the bottoms of streams and rivers, providing camouflage against predators. It has small, beady eyes with no eyelids and poor eyesight. Also known as the 'hanzaki' (literally 'half-cut), it is believed that it can survive if cut in half. Due to its broad mouth, which extends across the width of its head, it can swallow any food as wide as its body. While it generally feeds on insects, crabs, frogs, and fish, it will typically eat anything that it can fit in its mouth and can survive for several weeks without sustenance. Due to its preference for cool, clean water, the rivers and streams of Ikuno are a perfect habitat for this living fossil, the ancestors of which date back to the dinosaurs.'"

"Living fossil, eh? Sounds like my boss," interrupted Akiko. "Probably just as boring, too."

"Oh, how mean! Anyway, I'll read on. 'When it feels threatened, the Japanese giant salamander excretes a strong-smelling substance through its skin, with an odour resembling Japanese pepper and mandarin oranges. For this reason, it is also known as the giant pepper fish. While it is thought that this natural treasure can live to around eighty years old, its true lifespan remains a mystery.'"

Haruto turned the leaflet to Akiko so that she could see the picture of the hanzaki.

"*Uwa-!* It's kind of ugly, isn't it? But, kind of cute in a way with its small eyes, stubby arms, and legs. And, maybe it's just me, but how would you describe that face? It almost looks like it's smiling, have a look."

"Yeah, the inscrutable Japanese salamander. Half-cut, though? Sounds like me after a few beers."

"You should write comedy," Akiko replied as she rolled her eyes.

The scenery became increasingly rural as they made their way to Ikuno. Haruto opened a window and felt the freshness of the deep rivers, the sweetness of the rice fields, and the depth of the mountain forest pines as they carried on the warm breeze into the small Toyota. As they drove, the car hugged the side of a vast lake which—in the distance—gave way to a rugged line of mountains still dusted with the last memories of winter snow. Several fishing boats floated gently on the water, and Haruto momentarily felt as though he too were floating somewhere out there where the azure sky met the cerulean blue of the water. The lake eventually receded, and the road snaked its way along the edge of the mountains. A river rushed past to the left, behind which lay thick forest.

Signs of life were few and far between. The car shuddered as it drove over an old iron bridge and past a straw-roofed house. In the garden, a fit-looking octogenarian tended a cabbage patch while a couple of kids chased insects with a net. The car arrived at an old wooden house just down the road, and Haruto killed the engine. After walking around to stretch their legs for several minutes, the old woman strolled over while brushing soil off her hands.

"Welcome, welcome! You must be Haruto and Akiko."

The old woman had a face that had clearly weathered more seasons than the two of them combined, but she somehow looked fitter and healthier than either of them.

She handed over the key to the house, which was already unlocked and proceeded to give a quick tour.

"So, here we are," she said as they stepped inside the stone entrance hall. "It was good to talk to you on the phone the other day. Let's hope that you can get some inspiration for your next story while you're here! If you have any questions, just give us a ring at the straw-roofed house just down the road."

The pair took their shoes off and stepped up onto the tatami floor of the living room, the entire floor separated by sliding paper screens. The fact that the house was probably the same age as the old woman only added to its charm. Haruto walked into the kitchen and peered through the tiny window onto a flower garden before walking back outside again. About twenty meters from the house, the land fell away to a small river, which gurgled over rocks before running under a stone bridge. Haruto gazed down and threw a few stones into the water as he inhaled the freshness of the air. Akiko paid the old woman who tottered off back to her cabbage patch.

"So, here's the plan for today. Barbecue, go for a walk, then a hot spring. What do you think?" asked Akiko as she threw Haruto an ice-cold beer from the freezer bag.

"Sounds like a plan to me. What about the hanzaki, though?" he replied before taking a large swig of his Asahi Super Dry and unpacking the barbecue set.

"Of course. Let's go out tonight with a couple of torches and see if we can find any signs of life in the river."

Later that day, Haruto felt relaxed and refreshed after he'd spent the evening soaking in the waters of the Black

River hot spring, gazing up at the stars. His overactive imagination, having finally switched off, he was ready for nothing more than a good night's sleep. Akiko, meanwhile, was already snoring gently but deeply. Feeling himself at a loose end, Haruto ventured outside to check out the river and see if he could spot any of Ikuno's famous hanzakis. Walking down the slight incline to the river with his torch lighting the way, he heard what sounded like singing. As he moved towards the source of the merriment, he could just make out the lyrics.

One salamander in the riveeer, two salamanders in the riveeer, three salamanders in the riiiiiveeeer, doobee doobee doobee doobee dooo!

He shone his torch off to the hot spring, which lay across the narrow road on the other side of the river. Someone singing in the bath, perhaps? Maybe it was some late-night revellers having a sing-along while they staggered back from the local pub? It was certainly no song he had ever heard before.

Four salamanders in the riveeer, five salamanders in the riveeer, six salamanders in the riiiiiveeeer, doobee doobee doobee doobee dooo!

The song continued. All was silent, save for the sound of crickets and the mysterious karaoke which emanated from off in the distance. As he made his way along the grassy bank, Haruto shone his torch into the river when something glinted and caught his eye. Straining his eyes through the blur of the water rushing over the rocks, he couldn't quite make it out at first. But, like a magic eye picture, the edges of the image slowly came into focus. It was a mottled figure with a long tail, a tiny pair of mischievous eyes, and maybe it was his imagination, but, was that a hint of a smile playing about its face?

The next day, Haruto and Akiko visited the hot spring one more time. They walked around the local town and its various craft shops and headed back home, following the same route they had come. Haruto seemed a little sleepy and kept nodding off in the passenger seat.

"So, what happened to you last night?" Akiko asked.

"Oh, I had the strangest night's sleep. You're not going to believe the strange dream I had. I felt this compulsion, like something was beckoning me to get into the river. Before I knew it, I'd found myself inside the den of a drunken hanzaki that proceeded to unravel the mysteries of storytelling to me."

"Ha! that's hilarious. Go on then, how had it managed to get drunk while in a river, and how did it give you the key to storytelling?"

"Well, it explained that there was a sake brewery upstream. The manager was a perfectionist and had a habit of throwing entire casks of the stuff into the river in a rage when the current batch hadn't quite managed to meet his impossibly high standards. The hanzaki had developed a taste for the stuff and would get together with its mates for a bit of a singsong on a Saturday night when a barrel or two was flowing through the water. They took it in turns to tell stories passed on through the generations. But they had this one story that they only told once every six years as it was so powerful."

Akiko let out a sound like an asthmatic horse and slapped her knee as she convulsed with laughter.

"Haruto, you and your imagination! That's hilarious."

"Anyway, in the dream, the hanzaki was quite drunk, slurring its words and what have you. We made a deal, and it agreed to tell me one story. The Story, as it called it. But there was a condition. The Story could not pass beyond the boundary of the riverbank and be shared with others. It got quite serious when it told me this. I felt like I didn't sleep a wink last night, which is why I'm so tired."

Akiko collapsed in a fit of hysterics, her body shaking as she tried to maintain her focus on the task of keeping the small car on the winding mountain road.

"Wow, that must have been some wild dream. And you can't tell anyone this story?! Sorry, The Story. Hmm, that's convenient, isn't it! Whatever it was, you must have worked up quite a sweat as a result."

"Why's that?"

"Oh, your bedclothes were soaking wet this morning. I had to hang them out to dry before you got up."

*

Back home, life continued as usual. Akiko continued to work at her accountancy firm, coming home late and getting up early. Haruto bided his time piecing together his memories of The Story. Six weeks had passed, and the members met again at the same club in the same leafy alley. Five stories had been told, and it was Haruto's turn once again.

Like Russian chess grandmasters, each had tried to outsmart the other. Each plot was more convoluted and complicated than the last; the cant and phraseology more esoteric and impenetrable; the characters richer and more alive. The words painted pictures within the imagination and conjured up images of entire worlds. Haruto felt the weight of pressure pressing down on him. The chairman of the collective—wearing an expensive Saville Row suit—smiled broadly and asked, "So Haruto, what have you got for us this week?"

His palms sweating slightly, Haruto began to read what he had managed to piece together from The Story.

Laying his notebook down on the table to signal the end of his reading, there was an audible silence as the men looked on with solemn expressions. Panic started to rise as he absorbed the new atmosphere that had descended on the small gathering, his eyes flitting from one member to the next. Cursing the hanzaki inwardly, he was about to apologize for his latest effort when he noticed tears in the eyes of some of the men.

"Dear god. Never before have I heard such beautiful words."

"Sublime. Pure, exquisite, unfiltered joy."

"My writing career is over. Never shall I reach the vertiginous heights of the literary experience I have just witnessed, so long as I shall live."

"I feel like...like I've been born again. I feel like I'm seeing the world through a new lens."

"How can I even put into words the marvel at which I feel for my new wonder at what can be done with the written word."

The members of the collective each dabbed at their eyes, a new air of reverence hanging in the air for the newly respected master of the short story. The most expensive bottle of sake was ordered and paid for by the chairman. Flakes of gold danced and glinted in it as they caught the light. The revelry continued long into the night as they moved onto an eye-wateringly expensive Michelin restaurant. Haruto sat between two stunningly beautiful hostesses who plied him with drinks and listened with rapt attention as he was asked where his inspiration had come from.

"Oh, inspiration? Well, now, did I never tell you about the Russian authors, Dimitri Ipatov or Egor Korotkov? Or perhaps I forgot to mention the literary delights of Yekaterina Tudegesheva? Or the Japanese authors, Kono Juichi and Fujimoto Miyabanashi?"

Of course, none of the authors existed. The former were simply the names of Russian athletes he'd spotted on the back page of a newspaper, and the latter were nothing more than the names of two of his colleagues. How could he be taken seriously if he cited a dream about a salamander as his inspiration? It appeared that he was equally skilled at fabricating the truth as he had been in his recollection of The Story.

"No, I don't believe I have, I'm afraid. Do tell," asked a member as he looked at Haruto with newfound respect.

"You haven't read the selected works of Egor Korotkov? Well, never mind, there is always time. Now gentlemen, as you all know, inspiration is indeed a writer's friend. Let me tell you how it started."

As Haruto conjured up the details of his inspiration out of thin air, he drank in the attention of an audience that had hitherto been indifferent and was now hanging on his every word. As the bacchanalian merrymaking continued, he felt the room swimming as the sake rushed through his veins and coated his neurons in a viscous membrane of confidence and newfound power. The hostesses refilled his glass for him, and his phone lit up with offers of six-figure book contracts after word of his story had spread to those with the right influence. Haruto felt like a god.

It was around this point in the evening that something curious happened. It was something that took him quite by surprise and caused something of a stir. A new waiter had recently arrived from Kanto to work at the high-end bar and was somewhat unaware of the region's customs.

In order to understand what happened next, it is helpful to understand a little about the rules that determine the correct etiquette when passing people in Kansai versus Kanto. Some say that the samurai of Kanto would pass strangers on the right to free them up to draw their swords quickly. In Kansai, however, the opposite became the case after people modelled their behaviour on the streets of London. While the true origin is merely academic, the simple fact salient to this story is that this difference in crossing etiquette can cause some confusion.

As the waiter headed back into the kitchen, he collided with a staff member, each on the other's side. As a result, a tray of amuse-bouches collided with a tray of champagne glasses, which then tumbled downwards before smashing on the floor. Visually, this seemed to happen in slow motion, yet audibly, it hit the ground with such a crash that it quite shook Haruto out of his revelry.

Haruto felt as though someone had thrown a bucket of cold water over him and was gripped by a kind of instinctive fear of some intangible yet atavistic unknown variable. Senses he had been unaware of came to life, the world becoming blurry as though he were underwater. His eyes reduced to the size of one-yen coins, and his vision was superseded by tiny hair-like cells that had spread over his body to detect motion. Twisting from side to side, he searched for a predator he was aware of but couldn't see.

The corner of the bar where the group was sat was pervaded by the smell of Japanese pepper and mandarin oranges, and several guests thought the Michelin starred chef had perhaps created a new kind of ice cream. The silence was suddenly broken as a hostess' scream rang out, causing several members to cover their ears. Haruto touched his fingers to his face and recoiled in horror. His hand was covered in a slimy film that had spread over his entire body.

"Dear god. Haruto. Take a look at your face."

The chairman looked on in undisguised revulsion as a hostess, wincing as though in pain, handed him a small mirror. Holding it up to his face, Haruto took in his skin. It was mottled with liver spots and dripped with a viscous layer of something that smelled of Japanese pepper and mandarin oranges. As he looked around at the group, the hostesses could not hide their disgust and stood up to leave.

"What's happening to me?!"

As Haruto spoke, his mouth stretched open until the skin peeled back to the sides of his face in a rictus grin. His vision blurred as though underwater. He looked around at the diminishing numbers of the collective. He got up to leave the bar but could only shuffle as his legs had become fused together into a tail. At once, he was less homo sapien and more amphibian.

Haruto tripped and fell onto a table where several law firm members had been enjoying a selection of raw fish, fresh from Tsukiji market that morning. Flailing around, his stubby limbs were unable to gain purchase on the sides of the table. He raised his head and saw the horror on the faces of the assembled crowd. As though stripped of his own volition, he snapped at the elegantly presented selection of sashimi before swallowing it whole in one large, greedy gulp. For some reason, unbeknownst to him, he hadn't eaten for several weeks now but suddenly had quite the preference for raw fish and sake.

*

Six weeks had passed, and five stories had been told by the other members of The Short Story Collective. Haruto had decided to skip his turn this week, and it was no stretch of the imagination to say that he had become quite the recluse. It was as though the slightest disturbance would cause him to flinch and hide from others. He had taken to lying in the bath with the water covering him, occasionally venturing out for lunch maybe two or three times a month. He always bought fish, although he was quite partial to the insects that would crawl across the floor of his apartment now that Akiko had given up trying to contact him.

He had also developed quite a penchant for sake. He would, on occasion, think of the time he had visited Ikuno and the dream he had had of the mischievous hanzaki and its story. Meanwhile, somewhere deep in the countryside—past fields of rice plants that swayed gently in the breeze, down a long mountain road that ran past a lake where the sun danced and sparkled on the surface, over a rickety wooden bridge that carried on the sweet wind of spring—a voice, drunk on sake and free from the pressures of the city, sang out a song passed on through the generations from centuries long gone.

One salamander in the riveeer, two salamanders in the riveeer, three salamanders in the riiiiiveeeer, doobee doobee doobee doobee dooo!

VICKY CHEONG

Safe Distancing Ambassador

Anil Kumar sighs as he exits the train station, once bustling with locals and tourists, now reduced to a pathetic trickle of workers and shop owners like him, stubbornly refusing to give up the fight. Face half-masked, eyes weary, they walk at a slower pace than pre-COVID days. What's the point of rushing to open the shop when there are no customers? Yet, they must, because rent has to be paid, despite the government's generous rebate to the landlords to help retailers; employees need to earn their keep and hope has to be raised. More importantly, the two months being locked up at home during circuit breaker was more than enough for many of these Chinatown workers, who used to open 24/7 and work up to sixteen hours a day. Too much idling is bad for the physical and mental health. Better to open shop, clean the stocks, and pretend that life is somewhat back to normal.

Anil for one did not fancy being cooped up alone in his four-room HDB flat another day longer. His wife and five-year-old son had left for Nepal for a home visit early in February and had been stuck there since. He had spent CB video-calling them for hours daily until they told him they were too busy to chat. He spent the rest of the day watching Bollywood and Nepali movies until he ran out of movies to watch. He definitely cannot *tahan* another day swatting flies at home.

Two months have passed since the Circuit Breaker was lifted on 1 June 2020. Singapore is into Phase Two, with more freedom of movement but just as many restrictions as before. Gatherings are limited to five, with social distancing and wearing of masks strictly enforced. Yet Chinatown remains a ghost town, eerily quiet, more like an abandoned town in a cowboy western movie, which Anil had enjoyed watching as a child, than the buzzing tourist district it usually is. At any moment, one might expect a tumbleweed to roll into the cobbled shopping street with the wind rustling in the quietness.

Suddenly, there is a shout followed by a string of tirade. What might previously be a normal chaotic occurrence in Chinatown pre-COVID now has the impact to stop everyone on their tracks to stare at the commotion. A crowd of five has gathered in front of a Chinese Medicinal Hall. A man in red, a Safe Distancing Ambassador, is gesturing fiercely at them to keep their distance from each other but none of them wants to give up their spot. The owner exits the shop to plead with the ambassador and his customers. Anil watches in envy. Chinese Medicinal Halls are one of the few lucky retail shops to not be affected by COVID. He hopes the owner won't get a summon to shut his shop for not enforcing social distancing. Safe Distancing Ambassador was not a career choice for many until two months ago. Laid off from their last job due to the pandemic, they were hired recently for this role. He has read in the news of some being overly zealous with their newfound authority, acting more like a police officer than an ambassador.

He continues down into a deserted lane where his shop is located. The boutique on the right of Anil's shop, selling cheap cheongsams and Singapore Tee-shirts printed with the majestic MBS backdrop and Singapore's beloved tourist icon Merlion, closed shop even before the Circuit Breaker, a victim of the pandemic. The front entrance is all boarded up with wooden planks, as if preparing for an approaching typhoon or hurricane when the worst storm Singapore experiences is the year-end monsoon. On the left, the art gallery, selling cheap copies of famous oil paintings imported from China and Vietnam, disappeared one day and reopened across the lane, the rent they pay now at a whopping seventy percent less than what they were paying pre-COVID. The boss, Mr Ong, explained to Anil they could still sustain the business because they provide framing services to local artists.

Anil unlocks the door to his shop and stares at the assets — rolls and rolls of racks with colourful fabric lined the walls, with another twin rolls of racks in the middle, splitting the shop into two narrow pathways for shoppers to browse. The pathways are now blocked by four mannequins, staring blankly at him, their glazed looks seem bored yet impatient, as if they can't wait to be let out into the sunshine. For ease of identifying them to his staff, Anil has named the handsome Caucasian couple Adam and Eve and dressed them in his most popular Nepali traditional attires. The other two mannequins are headless and thus nameless, their heads replaced by a Nepali cap and hood from the jacket one was wearing. Anil rents the *Outdoor Retail Space* (ORS) in front of the shop as well, a sheltered pavilion-like space without walls. Before COVID happened, he had two staff to help remove the canvass enclosing the ORS, bring out the mannequins and other displays and tout for sales. The staff had all been let off. One returned to India; another local part-timer had been told to go too. Now, as the boss, Anil has to manage everything alone.

Opposite, the wife of the souvenir shop is dusting the curios on display. Plastic Merlions sit next to Japanese waving cats, fridge magnets, mugs and tote bags. Next to this shop, the sundry owner is also busy pulling carts of snacks into the ORS in front of his shop. As bosses, they never had to do such physical chores before. Their jobs were behind the cash registers, which had rung non-stop as soon as the shops opened at nine am until well after midnight, tending to change and passing out receipts. Now, the cash registers sit in mocking silence, the only sound coming from the radio blasting an upbeat Chinese song trying its best to stir some vibrancy into the atmosphere and spur the languid occupants.

Anil pulls a stool from under the display shelf and sits at the shop front, his chin resting on one hand on his knee. His gaze wanders around to the colourful lanterns hanging from the ceiling to the rows of patchwork cotton and viscose trousers lining one wall. Above the trousers, thick hoodies, also made from remnants of cloth into colourful patchworks, hang in rows, thick depth of inventory he has imported which had arrived for the year-end festive period and Chinese New Year sale just before COVID hits. He had expected the sales to be brisk, like in previous years since he first started business. Anil sighs. He wonders what he is going to do now if the situation doesn't improve, if the countries continue with their lockdowns, if borders remain closed, if tourists no longer come, if his landlord, Mr Singh, starts to charge rent. His head pounds with the uncertainties of the future and mounting problems piling high, a Himalaya rising in his brain.

The Himalayas, the backdrop of Nepal. He had left Nepal twelve years ago to come to Singapore on a student pass to pursue a diploma in engineering.

"Go to the USA, join your brother," his mother had urged.

His elder brother, Gahju, is now a medical doctor in Maryland, the pride of the family. Anil had defied his mother to come to Singapore instead. There was no way he was going to the USA to play second fiddle to his brother. With his diploma in engineering, he started work in a Small and Medium Enterprise (SME), while pursuing a course in public security. He had always wanted to be a Gurkha but had failed the stringent physical assessment. He looks down at his belly. He has always been overweight, even as a child, over-indulged by his mother. Now, the belly sustains its size with his nightly swipes of half a dozen cans of ice-cold Tiger beer. He needs the beer to beat the humidity, something he has yet to be comfortable with even after living in Singapore as long as he has. He had been overjoyed when he passed the security diploma examination and went on to apply for a job at Cisco, forgoing his engineering position. Still, a Cisco security guard, no matter how smart he looked in the uniform, was a poor cousin to the Nepali Gurkhas. Within a year, he started getting restless again. Yet, he stayed on the job for another year to get his permanent residency. A Gurkha can never get PR in Singapore, so this was a blessing in disguise. As soon as his PR was confirmed, he flew home to Kathmandu, married his childhood sweetheart, and borrowed money from his mother to start a business.

"Start a business? Selling Nepali clothes in Singapore?" his mother gasped. "But you know nothing about doing business.'

What his mother said was true, but he had to start somewhere. His mother needed little persuasion. She hadn't been happy about his job as a Cisco guard, not a job for his Brahmin caste. She was willing to do anything for her baby, even at the cost of a house on the outskirt of Kathmandu. The family owns at least seven houses so his mother could well afford to invest in his business.

"Don't spend all your inheritance before I die. I have invested so much money in your diplomas already, much more than Gahju," she said, but she was as excited as him at the prospect of her baby becoming an entrepreneur. "Just like his grandfather," she gushed to her friends.

She went with him to factories and cottage industries all over Nepal to source clothes and handicrafts. They visited villages around the country, to identify seamstresses and craft workers who could contribute to their merchandise. She has a talent as a curator, and soon, a 40ft container was ready to be shipped to Singapore.

Anil was lucky to locate this shophouse in Chinatown. The last tenant from PRC selling Chinese artefacts quit and Anil paid a premium for this highly sought-after location, but he was confident he had a unique selling proposition among the many Chinese souvenir shops here. His was the only Nepali boutique in Singapore.

An elderly Chinese woman enters the dark five-footway of the pre-war terrace and shuffles towards him. There are many such elderly women in Chinatown, either a resident from the nearby HDB or locals here for Chinese *sinseh* consultation, cheap toiletries, or tailors. She drags a trolley behind her and holds a walking stick. The polyester button-down floral blouse and pants she wears are ubiquitous at the market nearby, either being worn or sold. She stops in front of Anil, her eyes meeting his briefly before they rove around the displays. Anil knows nothing in the shop suits her, but he is also careful not to discriminate against potential customers.

Once, about a year ago, at almost close to midnight when all the other shops had closed except for the bars, an over-weight middle-aged lady had stopped and loitered in the ORS, looking through the racks of clothes. Anil was about to pack up to leave as well and paid little attention to her except for a glance, as she did not fit the demographic of the shop's clientele and didn't look like she would pickpocket. She would probably leave after a while. Many people are curious about his shop and need little touting to lure them to enter. After a while, that lady called out to Anil.

"Yes, can I help you?" asked Anil from behind his counter, a can of beer in his hand. He peeked out and was about to shout, "sorry Madam, no your size, too small," when the lady walked in with a stack of dresses draped over her arms like a drunkard body.

"I want 10 pieces of each of these, and these." She dumped the clothes on the counter.

Anil's mouth went wide open. She was from Indonesia. These were presents for her relatives. That sale made him two thousand dollars. And she didn't even bargain.

Anil remains on his stool and watches the elderly woman as she rubs the fabric of a dress, her fingers tracing the seam of the patchwork. He remembers the Indonesian woman and reminds himself that chance favours those who look positively at situations.

"Auntie, what are you looking for?" Anil asks in Mandarin, a phrase much used and often impresses PRC tourists, although some of them have told Anil that he looks Chinese, with his fair skin and oriental eyes.

"How much is this?" The Auntie asks back in Chinese.

"Forty-five."

"Aiyo, too expensive, too expensive." With a look of disgust, off she goes, shuffling to the other end of the terrace.

Anil forces himself to smile at her retreating back. A good start to the day. An enquiry at least, even when there is no sale, better than not having anyone enter his shop.

A Chinese man in his mid-thirties walks in the corridor next. He is about to enter the narrow staircase next to Anil's shop when he catches sight of Anil. His eyes meet and hold Anil's gaze. He lowers his mask and smiles, nods a few times as if sending Anil a silent message. He is rather good looking. Big eyes, thin lips. Fair and tall, he dresses well in a white, long-sleeved shirt and black pants. His long and slender fingers open and meet in front of his chest as if cupping a ball.

The man continues to watch Anil without speaking. He's not interested to buy any clothes, that Anil is sure. Anil blinks back at him, and a sudden realization makes him shiver. "No, no." he tells the man, waving him away.

Disappointed, the man looks away, opens the door to the staircase which leads up to *Le Spa ~ by Male Therapists*, and disappears.

Anil goes into the shop and looks at the full-length mirror. He sucks in his tummy and expands his chest. He raises his arms to check his triceps. Women find him attractive. Does he look gay? He admits he is handsome when compared to most locals, even Nepalese, with his fair skin and sharp features, a pleasant smile. Now he knows he attracts men too. His body gives another shiver at the thought. With a final glance at the mirror, he walks out of his shop. Before COVID, he has seen gay men frequent LeSpa and another spa a few doors down, but he hasn't realised spas are now allowed to operate during Phase Two.

A Caucasian couple walk past. Anil shouts, "Hello, come in and have a look." They give him a startled look and scurry away. Anil laughs aloud, amused at how comical this might look in a sitcom.

From the corner of his eye, a woman in red strolls purposely towards him. Anil's eyes light up eagerly until he spots the *Safe Distancing Ambassador* printed on the polo shirt. He sighs and is about to enter his shop when she yells.

"Hey, you!" With a hat on her head, her hands akimbo, she resembles a sheriff about to draw her gun.

Anil turns, pointing to himself questioningly.

"Yes. Where is your mask?" She roars from behind her own mask, her eyes glaring.

Anil's palms slap across his cheeks. *Oh My!* "Sorry, sorry. I forgot. I wear it now."

He digs into his pocket to produce a crumbled piece of surgical mask and hurriedly puts it on, grinning sheepishly.

"Don't let me catch you again, or the fine is $300." The Safe Distancing Ambassador's tone softens.

Without knowing why, Anil's eyes tear up at her change of attitude. She seems almost kind now, and he is grateful to her for not taking his $300.

"Hey, you okay or not?" Her voice carries an uncertain tinge of worry at the sight of his moist eyes. "Now everywhere is quiet. I know how you feel. Don't worry, this will pass soon.'

He nods gratefully.

"We're all in this together! *Jia you*!" Her eyes above the mask creases in a smile as she opens her tote bag, rambles into it, and then presses something into his palm. Anil looks down at the fortune cookie in his hand.

"That Chinese restaurant ahead passed me a bag just now. Maybe it's expiring soon. Here, take this for good fortune." She pats him gently on the arm.

Anil tears open the plastic wrapper and breaks open the cookie. A piece of paper flutters to the ground. He eats the cookie and ignores the slip on the ground.

"See what your fortune says," the lady says, pointing to the paper.

He picks up the strip and reads aloud. "Look for three blessings that will happen to you today."

He stares blankly at the lady. Three blessings? He can't even think of a single one.

The lady smiles. "I know of one. I didn't fine you."

Anil's head bobs up and down in rhythm to hers.

"Don't worry. You have until midnight for two more blessings to happen." With that, she waves and goes off.

What utter rubbish, Anil thinks. The fortune cookie says three blessings that will happen, not three bad things that will not happen. He looks at the fortune in his hands and shakes his head, and then he looks up into the distance. The Safe Distancing Ambassador is gone.

A sudden thought hits him. Where's the optimistic and jovial Anil? He's not going to let COVID beat him. He will beat this. He will *jia you*! He shall await the two more blessings that will come before the night is over.

The second blessing happens two hours later. Three young ladies in leggings walk into the shop as Anil sits dozing behind his counter. They are slim, fit, and young, just the right demography for his clothes and they look like they already have something in mind.

"Hey Ladies, can I help you?" Anil asks in his most charming manner, touching his face to ensure his mask is in place.

One of the girls takes out her mobile phone and swipes to a Facebook post. "Our friend bought a pair of skirt-pants for yoga recently. We want to buy the same for our studio's performance. Can you show us?"

"Studio performance? Now studio can hold performance already?" He walks to the racks and takes out a few hangers for them. "These are the latest fashion. Very suitable for yoga or party or just going out. Best for your performance."

"We're having a *Zoom* performance. You know *Zoom*?"

Anil doesn't but he nods all the same. They take the hangers and start discussing.

And just like that, he makes $500 for a yoga studio *Zoom* dance performance. Second blessing.

A Chinese proverb says: Better to believe in the existence of a tenet and take precaution than not. For this reason, Anil has joined the Seventh Month prayers event annually every August and contributes his monetary share to the Chinatown Merchant Association, just so he doesn't get disturbed by the Seventh Month *visitors*. This might apply to unfortunate events, but if he chooses to believe his fortune cookie, there is one more blessing coming.

By nightfall, nothing happens. No customers, no sales, not even any passing visitors. As he is closing up, the owner of the fitness studio above his shop comes down.

"Hi, how's it going?" says Anil in his best American accent.

"Bad lah. My landlord starts charging rent today, 1 August. The three-month concession from the government is up. What about yours?"

Anil thinks for a moment. The three-month rental waiver Mr Singh promised him ended yesterday too, but there is no news from his landlord. No news means no bill. "I'm not sure. I have not heard from my landlord."

"Better give him a call and negotiate for a lower rent. Even though CB is over, business is still bad."

"Thanks, I will."

Anil takes out his phone and swipes to Mr Singh's contact. Anil prides himself as a good tenant. He pays his rent promptly and maintains the shop well. But now he really can't afford to pay the existing rent. Would Mr Singh be willing to negotiate? Or would he need to terminate his business and ship his merchandise back to Nepal? Would his landlord, the elderly kind Punjabi, force him to close like how his neighbours have been treated? How could he face his mother and worse, what would his brother think of him?

Chinatown at nine pm is eerily dark and quiet. The fluorescent lighting from his shop cast a shaft of light onto the pedestrian shopping street like sun rays streaming through stormy clouds. Before he could press the call button, the phone rang, and Mr Singh's smiling display photo appears. The light from the phone illuminates Anil's face. Somehow Anil knows, the call will bring the third blessing.

DONNA ABRAHAM TIJO

Evacuation Flight

They wandered in awe and fear inside sanitized, deserted hallways. On they went, where they hadn't before, the elder one uneasy about the walkalator that rolled by on the left.

She decided to follow the instructions of her father on her mother's mobile phone, listening in, asking; her whispers echoed back, tipping her off about the silence those endless hallways possessed. Towards the gate they marched, to board the Vande Bharat evacuation flight. They were to join their father at Singapore, the approvals for which had arrived two days earlier.

"What do we take with us, what do we leave behind?" The mother had worried the day they had received the permissions.

Leave behind our yesterdays, thought the elder one, who was rarely poetic.

Goodbyes, thought Fatima the younger one.

"Ammi, the iPod we should take," said the youngest son.

In their school bags, the girls took their ID cards, a fleece jacket to snuggle into for when it would get cold in flight, a small bottle of hand sanitizer and an extra face mask. Each of the ladies also held onto a copy of the documents their father had e-mailed. Their uncle had especially sneaked in with his friend into the Internet café, which the friend owned, post-midnight, because the lockdown had caused shops to shut shop during the day. They had to get the documents printed—approval letters to travel, after all.

The eldest one also secured a tenth-grade Math textbook and a pencil in her backpack to complete the trigonometry homework during the five-hour flight. Who knew whether she would have to continue school online via India—school fees and all at the foreign country. Plus, anything to keep her mind off using the toilet in the airplane. Airplane toilets were listed as risk grade 6 to catch the virus. In her bag, she also carried an extra jacket for her seven-year-old brother.

The younger sister had lugged in her brown checkered backpack one book by Sudha Murthy, something her English teacher in school had encouraged to read to improve spoken English. And the iPod, which their father had brought home when he'd flown down on leave the previous year. Pihu had downloaded songs from *Student of the Year 2* into the iPod, from her brother's laptop. There was also the chicklet Pihu had given her as a parting gift through the grill of her bedroom window that morning. Fatima hadn't known then that chewing gums were not allowed in her new country, and she did not know that she would hide the only one she possessed in an old geometry box, unable to chew on it, remembering her best friend for years to come.

Fatima had let out her hand through the grill of the window that morning, a stream of grey mucky water from the open drain of the house behind theirs trickled below them. On her palm, Fatima had written over and over with a blue ball-point pen what all the girls in their government school were doodling on each other's textbooks those days, BFF. When the girls shook hands one final time through the grills, the abbreviation from Fatima's palm left an imprint on Pihu's palm. Pihu, in turn had passed Fatima the chicklet. It was the kind Fatima liked, spicy guava flavor, and then Fatima had shut the window to her room for God knows how long.

Pihu could only hope her best friend would return for the annual exams at the end of the school year in 2021.

Fatima's seven-year-old brother took with him to the foreign land nothing except the knowledge that he held the power to his sisters' and mother's passage to their father. The mother held onto this son, who in a face mask, face shield, gloves, and later a pair of headphones, bobbed his head to his favourite music of *Student of the Year 2*, which he got Fatima to download for him onto the iPod.

The girls lead their mother till the gate. She held onto the precious son for whose safety the family was being flown to the land of their father's work assignments after years. The virus threatened to speckle the jewel during the trying times that had enveloped the world. The girls wore as badges their proximity to their little brother, for even if the father disowned them at landing, he wouldn't disown the son, who was born ten years late into the marriage.

And if you'd been at the exit gate of the hotel when the family completed their 14-day Stay Home Notice and stepped out of the glass doors of the plush government-designated five-star hotel you would have seen the father there waiting eagerly for his son.

There you would also have seen the girls carry each other. They stood back and looked on when the father kissed the wife over the dupatta that covered her head and picked up the son and hugged him as if he'd never hugged him before. The girls looked on, much like the doorman and the bellboy of the hotel had looked on. Like the Grab driver waiting for his passengers had looked on. The girls looked on for if the father accepted the son and his mother, and refused to accept the two, they would have each other in a foreign land.

*

Into the Vande Bharat flight, Mr. Bannerjee pushed a wheelchair in which he was taking Purabi to their son. Mrs. Purabi Bannerjee's right foot dangled by the footplate because her knee was in a cast and could not be folded enough to rest the foot on the plate. Hmm… soon, she told herself. She only wished for the land of her son and daughter-in-law to allow an x-ray. Non-essential medical services were cancelled in Delhi. Non-essential for them! But for Purabi wasn't it very essential to alleviate the pain?

That is how, in her heart Purabi knew that something was not joining right in there and she took this knowledge with her all the way to her daughter-in-law.

In the breast pocket of his brown checkered shirt hanging lose over his brown cotton pants, Aubhijit kept both their passports, with corresponding boarding passes in each. Ever so often, he would check on them with a touch. And, in the pockets of his pants Purabi had slipped in a small bottle of hand sanitizer, which he used frequently, pouring a drop or two onto Purabi's palms as well, every time he pressed an elevator button, or held back the elevator door from closing in on her, or after handing her the Bisleri bottle and tucking her face shield under his armpit while she drank water. Purabi held onto the blue inflight duffel bag on her lap all the way until Aubhijit pushed it into the overhead cabin of the front row Business Class seats. Their son had reserved it under the wheelchair-assistance category.

Purabi also had a bigger bottle of sanitizer in her Hidesign leather handbag. Before being helped to the seat, she insisted Aubhijit pour some sanitizer on the wet wipes she had carried and rub down the arms of the seats and the seat belts as well. Then she handed him a double bed sheet in khadi with faded red Madhubani art painted in the centre, which she had packed into the duffle bag, so he could spread it over their two seats. Only then, did Purabi allow the cabin crew to help her to her seat. Of course, the damn armrests would not move and eventually, poor Aubhijit only had to carry her and put her into the seat. Aubhijit had always been lean. Well, she had gained some in the past six months since the fracture.

At home also, Aubhijit had helped her into an isolation gown, after she had hobbled into adult diapers—it was so she would not have to use the airplane toilets. Fomites the world was screaming, and whoever knew anything about how the strange new virus behaved.

The cabin crew handed Aubhijit also a hazmat suit because he wished to sit by the aisle. Social distancing required passengers on alternate seats to wear hazmat suits.

Face shields and white disposable packets of food had been left on each seat before the passengers had boarded, which Aubhijit had thankfully pushed into the overhead cabins and also sanitized his hands. Some of the children in the flight, though, had pulled open the packets of potato chips causing the captive smell of spices to permeate the compressed air within the carrier.

Although Purabi was beyond the years in which she could tolerate the ruckus that children created, she could not help but heave in relief that day at the sounds of normality that ripped through the otherwise ominous silence which had sat beady eyed in the evacuation flight when they had boarded.

So, while she leaned back pretending to dislike the mix of smells—spices, alcoholic sanitizers, cardamom which her husband chewed because of a problem of bad breath that he could not get rectified before his travel due to the lockdown—she looked into her handbag one more time to check off: the Strip File folder with the approvals, e-tickets, Dependant's Pass documents, medical records of her fracture and other medical declarations. She handed a packet of masala peanuts to Aubhijit in case he was hungry and way down in her handbag she noticed a booklet of paper soap. Aubhijit must have thrown it in for when he wanted to visit the toilet. Soap was always better than sanitizer, Purabi agreed. "Wherever had been this alcoholic cleanser a few years ago?'

What Purabi did not check on was the copy of the Hanuman Chalisa she was taking to the new country in a secret pocket in her bag. Although, she had been reciting the Lokkhi Panchali since the day the approval to travel had arrived, she could not find an English translation for her Pilipino daughter-in-law. So Purabi had packed in her bag the Hanuman Chalisa that Mr. Bannerjee had managed to acquire from the owner of the bookshop at the corner of their street. He was a friend of Aubhijit's.

After all, Purabi often attended Buddhist chanting sessions in her colony. Their Buddhist daughter-in-law could also pick up a few Hindu mantras.

"Hopefully, Rosa will welcome us into her home," during these times of the virus, Mrs. Bannerjee could be heard whishing.

And if you were close by, you would hear Mr. Bannerjee reply as softly as a heartbeat, "She'd better, she stays in our son's house after all."

*

Jasmine encouraged little Elsa into a diaper. She had considered it herself, then hadn't been convinced it would hold all in. In her bag, she had taken the essentials—fruits and jam sandwiches for little Elsa, also cucumber and bacon sandwiches for Baiju and herself. She hated bacon, so she had taken them off hers. She wouldn't touch the food the crew would serve with their hands, to every passenger on board.

Why did Baiju have to sign the overseas deal this past December? Jasmine fretted, while she packed in her cabin baggage medicines for six months at least. Who knew when they'd be able to locate a doctor for all their medical needs in the new country? She had also slipped in the lot a strip of hydroxychloroquine which their neighbour, who ran a pharma company, had stocked up for the residents of their entire condo; if it ever came to that, that is. There also lived the owner of a lab and a few family physicians in their condo, thereby making Covid quite manageable for the residents.

She also placed in her handbag two sets of diamonds camouflaged within crumpled brown paper packets. One, Baiju had gifted Jasmine on their anniversary. It was worth Rs. 20 lacs. Baiju's partner, it seems, had also surprised his wife with a watch worth Rs. 20 lacs that year. The other was a set that Baiju had presented to Jasmine on her birthday.

When Jasmine and Baiju had visited the Gold Souk to buy a gold bangle for Baiju's new born niece, Jasmine had stood admiring a piece on display—a string of uncut diamonds. Baiju had taken note and bought a set with two more rows of uncut diamonds arranged in interleaved netting.

"It is double the amount," Baiju had said to her.

"Plus, its design will suit the saree I bought you for the Kumar wedding."

Mr. Kumar was Baiju's business associate from Hyderabad. His sister's wedding was being put-together at Dubai.

Every other piece of jewel, including the *thali mala* Baiju had placed in the bank locker at the first working hour the morning before their departure to Singapore; every diamond he'd ever bought Jasmine since their wedding day years back, and he'd bought her one on every occasion. Baiju's family and friends were witnesses. Jasmine's colleagues had noticed them too.

In the new country, Jasmine hauled the weight of those diamonds following Baiju and little Elsa around at the beach and at the office of the government's ministry when she was there for her Dependant's pass.

If you were around, you would notice her wearing them when she'd meet Baiju's work acquaintances and their housewives. She would fidget with them around her neck, and stutter in on conversations, because no one had introduced her as the programmer she had always known herself to be.

*

Meanwhile, in the airplane little Elsa who'd recently mastered the art of using the toilet, insisted on saving the diaper for emergency use. So, she squatted up on the seat and revealed to Baiju that it was impossible for her to unlearn what she had finally learned and simply had to be taken to the toilet.

"The business class toilets are reserved only for the crew," whispered the attendant.

"How can that be?" said Mr. Bannerjee, who was seated on the first seat and overheard the flight attendant's unconstitutional argument. "The Business Class toilets are for the Business Class passengers."

"Sir, the rule applies to this Emergency Covid Flight."

"We've paid for it, plus we are not Covid patients. What is this segregation?" Baiju said.

But little Elsa who had plugged a hand between her legs and had been bouncing on her toes for a while now, nudged and voiced a concerned call, "Papa."

"Sorry Sir, but those are the rules," said the flight attendant.

"What kind of unheard of rule is that?" Baiju argued.

"Sir, we have risked our lives to run this evacuation flight. The crew deserves a little respect," the attendant argued and moved a step back as if in aversion.

"But my wife can't be taken to the toilet at the other end of the carrier, you know she can't walk all the way there," said Mr. Bannerjee.

"I have paid extra for these business class seats, only so I don't have to share a toilet with so many people," Baiju argued.

"Papa," Elsa said, louder this time.

"My wife availed your wheelchair service and you want her to limp till the end of this carrier?" Mr. Bannerjee accosted.

"I'm sorry Sir, these are the flight rules."

"Papaaa!"

Baiju couldn't continue to argue against the illegitimate requirements of the crew and mumbled back to Jasmine. A happy Elsa skipped away towards the other end of the flight holding onto Jasmine's fingers.

On the way, Elsa envied the boy who bobbed his head under headphones. Red in colour they were, shiny. He had a mobile phone in his hands, silver. She touched it as she went. The boy was on the first seat behind the curtain.

The boy envied the pink, white and golden unicorn hairband on the girl's head as she passed by holding her mother's hand. It had a fluff of soft pink feathers at the centre, behind which rose up a golden horn.

The boy's sister Fatima managed to peek at the Business Class when the curtain had parted and saw a captain sitting on the seat diagonally opposite hers. White shirt with so many golden stripes on the shoulder. He was eating a spoonful of hot cup-noodles. How had he got hot food, when all the passengers in her section had had a white plastic packet kept on their seats. The packet had contained a pack of Classic Salted potato chips, a half-litre bottle of water, and a pastry box with a cold sandwich, a samosa, an apple, a brownie and a pack of Frooti.

Why was captain not driving the airplane, anyway? she wondered.

*

Captain Amar Gaur had been unlucky to have been rostered the return flight. He knew he had enjoyed an immoral number of leaves that December, spilling over to January as well for his brother's wedding. He was obviously going to be netted back from the escape exit—to serve duty. Risk the virus or risk losing a job!

"Healthy passengers Vaibhu, merely trying to return home from a distant land. I'm not flying back Covid patients!" he reassured his wife when she chewed into her fake nail extensions in worry. Most of her nails had fallen off because the beauty parlours had been locked for months now. The last few, though, now dangled at the precipice of her long fingers desperately waiting to be let go.

They were a sight, and although Amar had fancied them when Vaibhavi had shown him little red flowers on her glossy white-tipped nails one night, even wondering how someone had managed to hold down the miniature beauties to those smooth edges, these days he tended to rub extra lotion on them as part of foreplay. The flowers had toppled off chipping along the base, and the smooth edges now lay serrated. They would scratch.

That moment, as she packed the suitcase Captain Gaur had the urge to rub some lotion on Vaibhavi's fingers. *Abey*! because the cracked edge was threatening to pull the thread of the new Lacoste T-shirts she was pressing down on a pile man, what else? She had bought a couple that January during the sale season in shades of red for their fair son Vihaan.

If only she hadn't insisted on sending their son to UWC last year. The most prestigious school in that foreign land, the most expensive too, Captain Gaur rued as he sipped hot tomato soup the crew had served him in the Vande Bharat flight. He too was part of the crew, you see. Not this flight, another one; same carrier at least.

"Film actress Kajol's daughter studies at UWC," Vaibhavi had said one day after returning from a Higher Education seminar at their son's then most modern school in Gurugram. He had relented for his son, one and only, after all.

A wedding, a pandemic and a starry campus, where was the money for all this? He had stowed in a wad of SGD 5000 in his hand baggage, though. He wasn't planning on giving it to his son, but in case he needed to. Boys, after all, will be boys!

He had also packed the Tumi backpack he'd bought at duty free in Macau that December, and the basketball Vihaan had requested from the local store near their house in Gurugram. Of course, Vaibhavi had packed notebooks, pens, markers, highlighters for her son's academic enlightenment. How much of it was requested and how much the mother was piling on in hope of an Einstein *saala kisko pata*? The boy had only requested for some packets of Ratlami sev and aam ka achar.

Anyway, everything was at least five times the cost there. Indian snacks, though available, tasted of naphthalene balls and were invariable edging close to the expiry date Vihaan often wailed to his mother on the phone. All imported from India anyway, Captain Gaur reminisced biting into a cold samosa provided in the pre-packaged in-flight meal packet left on his seat. Especially then Vihaan's voice would definitely squeak to a wail, Captain Gaur thought. The other times it was indifference muffled within a sneeze whenever Captain Gaur enquired about his grades.

Anyway, it was possible the school would switch to online classes much like the schools in India, and Vihaan could travel back in Captain Gaur's return flight, the captain thought as he pulled up his zip in the business class toilet reserved for the crew. He could hear some commotion outside.

"How can you expect my wife who has taken your wheelchair service to limp till the end of the flight to use the Economy class toilet?" the silky grey-haired man from the first seat was asking the flight attendant. Oho! The man had started the fight again? wondered Captain Gaur.

Phaltu ki baatein. Not my flight; not my fight, Captain Gaur thought while picking up from the galley the samosa the flight attendant had heated up for the

Captain. Captain Amar Gaur, since he was not the captain of this flight, walked away to his seat on the third and last row of the Business Class.

The fight continued for a while. Captain Gaur saw the flight attendant head into the cockpit and eventually come out to allow the crippled lady and the husband use of the Business Class toilet. The only other family in the reasonably occupied Business Class had gone to use the Economy toilets at the other end of the carrier anyway. Captain Gaur did not see the lady limp to the toilet, though. The man was seen chewing on something, gutka or cardamom or clove, heading to the toilet a couple of times, paper soap in hand.

*

At the destination, Captain Gaur of course proceeded towards his special gateway, pulling behind him the suitcase that contained all that his son desired.

Everyone else queued up for immigration checks in one queue, with their hazmat suits, face shields, face masks and gloves, looking much like astronauts. The local immigration officers wore only face masks.

Jasmine decided to take off her face shield and gloves, how funny they seemed now. And when she looked around, she saw most passengers untie their hazmat suits too.

Purabi noticed, as well, that she was oddly confined to her isolation gown. She fidgeted within the confines of her wheelchair, hoping the gown would slide off, but then sighed and made do by taking off her face shield and gloves.

Little Elsa twirled around happy to be free of the face shield and gloves.

The little boy with the iPod she'd seen earlier in the flight, was standing inside a box outlined with yellow tape in front of her. He looked at her. She looked at him, standing there in the box behind his mother and sisters. He was looking at her.

The boy noticed that the girl still had her unicorn hairband on. Well, the girl also had a big black mole right where her right eye ended. *Chee*, he didn't want to squeeze it.

When he was walking out, the girl was still in queue waiting her turn after his mother. His mother and sister were at the counter clearing their papers while he waited with Fatima at the immigrated side of the turnstile. Here everyone was, he thought, evacuated at last to a new country. He handed over to Fatima his face shield, gloves and the hazmat suit he had been holding on to.

Free.

There he waited, holding onto the only thing he had taken to his new home, the iPod. He looked over at his mother and saw an immigration officer nodding his head in approval, ticking off something, stamping another thing and speaking with his mother. And it felt to the boy that the man spoke to his mother like she mattered.

NAMRATA SINGH

Hiraeth

I have a lot of dead people in my family now. They inhabited the stories my father regaled us (my sister and I) with as we went about not minding our own business. Stories of uncles and aunts far and near, stories of childhood squabbles and village life, stories of growing up, marriage, and becoming distant, stories of give and take, property disputes, and stories of gold jewellery and silk sarees during nieces' weddings. Then many of them died and I let them die in my thoughts too. But you won't find *him* here. Imagine a 12-inch pizza, a Neapolitan crust with your favourite toppings (you could choose jalapenos, basil, olives, or bell pepper) divided into eight slices, four sides loaded with fresh mozzarella, hot, and lip-smacking. For me, he represented the four slices: the richest, the creamiest, and umami.

The day he died, I made love to my husband, the newlywed groom. Frightened by his death, though I knew it was coming any time, I found solace on a beige-coloured darbha meditation mat on a marble floor with my husband. Clear as the Maldives water where we honeymooned, the day comes to haunt me now and then, precisely because I lost someone so important and yet handled it with carnal disgrace. It was 9:00 am, I am not too sure about the weather, inside the tall glass buildings, the only light you know is a white LED light over your head until you step out in the deepening dusk and stand under the tawny light beneath the roadside lamp looking for an auto to ride back home. Busy shuffling resumes for the post of territory sales manager, I peered through the glass window at my pot-bellied boss with a weird dislike for women donning jeans on any day other than Friday, sipping lemon tea in his cabin, when my maternal cousin called and broke the news- *Di, he is no more.* Stunned, I let the news travel my auditory senses and lodge itself with a big thump inside the cardiovascular organ. I felt nauseous and my vision blurred with water and sodium ready to slip on the carpet tiles with cubes of grey and dark grey. Awakened by a recruitment consultant call, I let my bandhani dupatta soak the rivers flowing from my eyes and rushed to the restroom for some peace. That was a big mistake because a ladies' restroom is never in peace. Minutes later, I slid out of the glass building, the sun shining gold but somehow all I could see was grey. This man who passed away at 84 was my maternal grandfather, a self-made man from an obscure village in India, raised by a single mother, a freedom fighter who had experienced the joy of being imprisoned for his motherland, Delhi School of Economics alumni who slept on the classroom benches at night and had two sets of clothes throughout his graduation years, he was nothing less than sterling inspiration. Later, a bureaucrat, a Bhagavatam scholar, a lawyer, an author, Dr Ramashish Sinha's name was truly akin to what it meant- someone who has the blessings of Lord Rama. Behind all the accolades, was a man tall, frail, and fastidious about his grooming and daily routine. Summer vacation at my grandmother's place was filled with what any other grandchild does: gormandize the Alphonse, burst open the hot pooris with mango pickles, wander in carefree abandonment circling the pond crowded with frogbit, water hyacinths, and water lettuce. That left us with little time to interact with him, partially because we thought he was boring and dull and partially because he found us frisky and noisy. He maintained a strict regime of pranayam and bhujangasana, reading and writing interrupted only by lunch and dinner. That flouted the holiday theme and most of the cousins didn't care much. Talking to him was more like a philosophy professor's lecture whose class many students invariably love to bunk.

How it all changed is still a mystery to me, however, I am glad it did because, by adolescence, my vacations were more about him and less about what's cooking in the kitchen. I looked forward to being in his bedroom, seated next to his feet, accoutrements spread on his desk as he scribbled on white sheets of paper, his ballpoint Reynolds furiously racing from end to end. By then, it was an open secret that I was the proud bearer of his genes. My academic success at school, my oratorship, sincerity, and my poignant poems were testimonials of the treasure I had inherited, and that made me feel tall, taller than I was, and proud. The stars be thanked because no one in the extended family far and wide possessed what I had inherited, also in terms of the spiritual inclination and most importantly- words. My academic grades were important to him and I never let him down. Did he have a similar curiosity for other grandchildren? What is it that he saw in me that he didn't see in them? Not overly loud or exaggerated with praise, my Nanaji was a man of few words, spoken in a muffled voice which grew softer with age, discipline, and loss of teeth, all of them. There was a time in life when he had to give up on everyday food and sustain himself on boiled lentils, boiled papaya, and parboiled rice with a dollop of pure ghee. Just before the last few morsels, he would suddenly look at me and ask, "Mamoni, have you written anything new?" That was when I was 14. That was when I more or less recognized myself.

A few years later, I moved to Delhi, then to various other places, footloose yet desperate, exploring life in expansive and intimate ways. The risky lure of the open road kept me wild and aloof and I forgot to nurture the relationship from a distance. Vacations were the time to make a U-turn and I would pay a visit (read homage, a personal one) and find him exactly how I had left him the previous vacation, in the rightmost corner room on the second floor of his three-storeyed house. Slumping on the bed while writing happened gradually over the years for him, reflecting erosion, the kind that leaves one with just the basic structure. Though I never saw a writer's table and a chair in his room which makes me believe he was more austere in his ways than he should have been. A plain quartz HMT watch with stainless steel buckle and brush folding clasp lay next to his single-size bed with a thin cotton mattress and floral pink bedsheet. Hanging onto an aluminium rod, hung two pairs of shirt and trousers (did he ever get over the two pairs, I wonder?), and next to it was an old wooden table in caramel honeyed hues and scratches on the legs, each scratch a symbol of the creative messes the family had put it through. Now, it stood in peace, holding his bare essentials and covered with an elephant applique patch bedsheet in white and red. Is it for some reason that we find unique ways to recycle our old, faded, and worn out? I am sure there is, though, my generation is more interested in the online and the new. On it stood an aluminium trunk that housed his other necessities neatly stacked. Other than that, the small bedroom housed a pair of Hawaii chappals in white and blue, a rack full of medicines, oils, and balms (The room itself had a strong smell of Zandu balm which greeted me year after year), and a soul who kept himself alive on boiled food and words. That is the sharpest memory I have of my grandfather: his writing, so you can imagine how much it occupied a space in his existence.

One year, I also saw a spitting pan next to his bed and was informed that he was suffering from tuberculosis. When I would unbutton his shirt and take off his white vest to apply warm mustard oil with burnt garlic on his sore body, I could see surgery scars all over his chest and abdomen. Sometimes my hands trembled on his pencil-thin arms, other times it continued in a swift circular motion trying to find some flesh to grasp and let the oil seep. One couldn't find much difference between the shirt on a hanger or his body, it was pretty much the same. Even then, he never forgot to ask, "Mamoni, do you still write?" Even then he never forgot to show his pride over my accolades: a premier college, a business school, a campus placement. Everything about me was important to him, and I wonder if it had anything to do with his accomplishments in life. Around him, I felt decompressed and much closer to myself. Surprisingly, such an investment never came from my parents who were peripherally aware of my love for words. Being binary, they grasped scores and the concept of 1st, 2nd, and 3rd. What they overlooked for many years was the person I was growing up to be and the unconventional path that I set my heart upon. For people in the state of Bihar and UP, you can either be an IAS or you can be nothing; in between there is a deep chasm. An MBA from a premier institute saved my skin but drowned my soul.

Back to my grandfather, over the years, nothing changed in his room except his age which ensured the decaying process continued uninterrupted until one day he fell sick, so sick that he was finally brain dead. He died in two parts: first, brain dead, then body dead.

In my late twenties, I had moved on with my life, seeking soulmates that Shahrukh Khan had so ardently and earnestly beseeched the young blood to. - *Someone somewhere is made for you.* Work took its toll and my visit back home became shorter, predominantly spent on the phone with friends and promising soulmates. And when you do that, a heartbreak or two is inevitable, a kind where you have to teach yourself to do the basic things again: to think for yourself, to walk properly, to hold yourself upright, to sleep, and to breathe. What made me not visit him is still a question to me. Burgeoning hormones change priorities and I succumbed to them in not so graceful ways. I didn't plan to go astray in ways that the agonizing last five years of his life is something for which I have absolutely no account. Transgression of such kind appals me. I put my needs ahead of everyone else's and indulged in my independence. The only thing that still tied me to him was: my writing. "He was asking why you don't write to him," I heard, standing inside a yellow STD booth, my mother apprising me of his deteriorating health. Words kept slipping out of my hands until he breathed no more and I wrote no more. It was a betrayal on my part.

Coming back to the day when he passed away, I hastened back home and informed my husband too. I was a newlywed bride who had joined back work after three weeks of hiatus. Unwrapping wedding gifts of Corelle dinner set and electric pressure cooker, bed sheet sets and envelopes stashed with cash occupied much of my evening. That night amidst tears and muted pain, I hastened to make love, peaked twice, and collapsed in my husband's arms unaware of the new brand of anguish that had lodged in my heart that night. Settling into noisy domesticity, I almost forgot about him just the way I forgot to write. Two months later, I resigned from my job to accompany my husband to an alien land. It mattered so much to me or maybe to my hormones. Isn't it strange how ambitious and talented young women do not give a thought before dumping their job just to be with their husband in an alien land? It does not take long for lovemaking to be reduced to sex, the soft whispers and 'bombshell' fragrance of a newlywed to transform into a clatter of unwashed dishes, and the fishy odour of unwashed underwear. Eight months down, I started working in a recruitment consultancy and delivered a baby for lack of anything better. Years rolled by and under the blistering exposure to life, the Fuchsia paint on its wall started to peel leaving splotchy and hideous spots.

Corporate life on the other hand has a way of reducing you to a file existence, stifling and impairing, something that my entire being shuddered at each morning I stepped into the office. I abhorred the crazy exchange of emails and con calls, loathed the coffee machine next to the restroom, and resented the campus placement agog with fresh graduates who would soon acquiesce to the tedium of the giant organization. However hard I tried to mask myself in Chanel, black turtleneck, and fitted houndstooth pants, the feeling refused to purge. Time passed and my reason to stay in the corporate became increasingly unclear and right then the pandemic struck. A watershed moment that stretched into months, life got upended, similar to the way black resin chairs at most restaurants. Suddenly, it felt hollow like wood with a termite infestation. It's when the hollowness echoed through that I realized the pandemic simmering in my own life, my relationship. Honestly, I had felt the tremors before, several times, but sex and grocery, cooking and cleaning, Ajax and Lysol, and a nine-year-old had held me from being wobbly and off-balance. And then the biggest stabilizing factor was work- it kept us occupied and distant in a nice sort of way, intersecting for needs and updates and then crawling back to our holes. We coexisted nicely until the virus gnawed at the outer membrane and evinced the ugliness beneath.

In March the 9-year-old got homebound. By April, the husband was working from home. That's when it hit me like a bullet- we **cannot** stay **together** under the same roof **24 hours** of the day, seven days in a week with no end in sight in a virus ravaged city. A month-long furlough in August evinced the deep chasm between us. We had nothing to share, to watch, to laugh at and a week later he resumed working without work. Time and proximity hung in the house like artificial vines, nice to look at but of no use. Our nine-year-old played the cement as I continued to search for something, anything to hang on to. Is this what happens to a marriage when hormones dry up? Did we not do the proper legwork to keep some joy alive? Each waking moment life stung me like a bullet ant, erupting in my head like a Krakatoa volcano, ripping me away from my mooring (I wonder if the self-indulgence seems frivolous, is it okay to feel the loneliness and alienation when you have a home, a job, and health?) I drowned while he indulged in ROFL moments watching The Kapil Sharma Show. What a *schadenfreude to indulge in, I would muse.*

Around Thanksgiving, under a dose of Lexapro, I rediscovered it. Clutching at the straws, to dull the pain and bolster my sanity, I opened the dusty gray American Tourister under the white oak queen bed and found my diary. The last entry, a mere two lines, was dated October 2011.

Since then, I haven't stopped writing. In a span of six months, I have even won a contest at Women's Web earning a Rs.250 Amazon voucher. The topic for the contest was - No Regrets. It was an easy write: slit open the heart and bleed, let the world know under a fictional name that I do have regrets, regrets that feel like inhaling sand and chewing asphalt, however, what I don't have is being regretful about having regrets. I accept my deficiencies and admit - I might not have lived as graciously as I should have, notwithstanding, I am glad it happened. Once the fog started to lift, in the rear-view mirror of my life, I saw the detours and the bypasses I had taken and lost myself on the way.

Words helped clear the smoke, reinvent myself and find a purpose. With each word, I have felt determined to build life back, forgive myself for foolish mistakes, and reckless choices. Each word has impressed upon me that it is important to stay close to who you are and with each word I am winding myself back to *him*, my grandfather. To me these months have been like a personal funeral I engage in each day. It took me ten years to comprehend my loss. Life pivots unexpectedly; when my grandfather passed away, I lost a link that held me close to myself. There is a lot of love that went unexpressed. Some words now need to be exhumed. In my meditative moment, my heart usually wanders to this person whose genes have made me who I am and what is the calling of my life. Some days, I lay on the cool tile of the bathroom, my hand to my mouth so the family doesn't hear me cry. Other days, I feel a rock in my artery and deep remorse sucks the air out of me. Now that I am the closest to him, I am processing grief, my disappointment with myself, my marriage, and my secret shame, all of it together. Sadness, you see, is not linear; grief comes in waves sometimes years later, but it does because we all need closure. I read somewhere that the Toraja people of southern Sulawesi, one of Indonesia's largest islands perform a ritual called ma'nene', during which the bodies of deceased family members — long after their elaborate funerals were held — are exhumed, cleaned, and left in the sun to dry before being dressed in new clothes and reburied. Torajan people believe the spirit of the dead will continue protecting their families. And so, too, do Balinese. The dead never leave us. For both peoples, this way of thinking helps when coping with grief.

Regretfully, in Hindu culture, you don't have the choice of digging up the grave, rather, his body was carried on bamboo poles and cremated near the holy Ganges. The pulverized self was later strewn over the Ganges to free the soul from the cycle of reincarnation. If he was buried, I might have dug him out and lived what I couldn't for nine years in-between. His stories, his writing lay in deep slumber punctuated with commas…I should have taken it upon myself to finish his stories and carry forth his legacy, his books but I disastrously failed and this crashes me from within. I am the carrier of his genes. Emissary of words. Do you think there could be a particle of his ash still floating somewhere? Fire truly brings a fiery end. In a country and a household where the father's genes are to be carried forward, I intend to carry my mother's, I guess not even hers. It's my maternal grandfather's.

I always had hopes and dreams to make it big in this world and get written about each time a teacher assigned informative writing on- Trailblazers of the 21st century. But as I write, I think I am fine living my truth, my life without the applause from the world. I may not be able to bend the whole world, however, I may do enough to die peacefully. This virus started a pandemic and ended one. The road I travelled on was twisting and bumpy; little did I know it would get me back to where I started from.

JOSE VARGHESE

Tiger Caves and Temple Monkeys

The hills are dipped in pastel shades of gold and indigo. The wind surrounds me in playful whistles, beating against my shirt in occasional outbursts. I was troubled by a persistent joint-ache as I climbed up the rock, but that seems to have vanished once I reached the plateau and found this spot. The fragrance of jasmine garlands wafts in from the nearby flower stalls, reminding me that it's no more the deserted place I knew in my childhood. Standing here on the summit, I can spy on the whole village and figure out the way things have changed.

Right below in the valley, the natural garden around the pond is undergoing a transformation. Except for a few nutmeg trees and a line of green palms, all the big trees are uprooted, the ground is cleared for geometrical flowerbeds, and the corners are filled with flowering plants and creepers on frames to create alluring alcoves. The streams are being redirected, with several artificial fountains sprouting at regular distances. This gives a Mughal touch to the garden. Swimming pools and artificial lakes are in the making too, next to the new hotels. Walls of extraordinary height enclose all these, as if even a glimpse of this world is prohibited to those who can't afford to pay an entry fee.

The temple on the top here has been constructed recently. It's a strategic addition, aimed at the pilgrimage segment that goes with most of the tourist packages in Kerala. A lot of work seems to have gone into modelling the mighty pillars from rock and the detailed carvings, crevices, and hallways that lead to the sanctum sanctorum. I must confess that the whole aesthetic concept looks compelling from certain angles. But I won't consider that a good enough excuse for ruining a natural phenomenon for the sake of a spirituality-business spot.

*

Thirty years ago, when there were no man-made monstrosities or crowds seeking the expensive kind of spiritual fulfilment, I used to spend whole afternoons here arguing with my best friend Venu. The occasional gush of wind kept us company. We were high school students who liked to bunk the last couple of classes on certain days, when boredom defeated us. We would burn our student-life miseries hiking aimlessly, chasing birds and little animals, and then gasping for breath, once we reached here. We would raise our hands and bend forwards to touch our knees and ankles, and then turn to the other rocks to shout our own names a few times, testing which one echoed more.

We would feed the monkeys that kept jumping to the rock from the tall trees lining the hill. They seemed to be looking for friendship at first, but then a ritual of sorts started, from the day we decided to feed them our packed lunch. We were left with no choice after that, as we had to carry something with us each time - peanuts, fruit, or a proper lunch. Otherwise, they would threaten us with angry shrieks and weird gestures. But once they made sure that the last bits of food that we had were offered to them, they would retreat to the treetops and stay engrossed in the daily activities of feeding the young ones or picking lice from one another's bodies to put them in their mouths and chew on with no second thoughts. As their mischief died out in due course, a sleepy peace would descend to their eyes. We too must have enjoyed their company and the calming effect their silly acts had on our agitated neurons. We would end up stretching our backs on the rock's plateau, letting the breeze absorb our fears and frustrations about unending schoolwork that awaited us once we descended to the banal world below.

We would take the longer route here and navigate through the dense vegetation if we wanted to explore the valley and the pond as well. We were drawn to the greenery around the streams and a natural fountain that gurgled nonstop. Birdsongs and calls of animals would fill the background as we walked along. I wasn't surprised if we came across an alarmed mongoose or a nonchalant squirrel. There were water snakes too. We carried sturdy sticks for self-protection and to support ourselves as we hiked up the path. On a few occasions, we would find the poisonous kind of snakes in the thickets. Venu would run off screaming when he saw one, foolishly throwing away his stick in a reflex action. I would have to find it as I walked to him, after guiding away the snake by tapping with my stick on the shrubs and the ground. I wouldn't miss a chance to make fun of him when he began searching for me, once he felt he was at a safe distance from the snake.

"We can't take chances with them," he would say. "You know how dangerous they are. Just one bite, and you are gone!"

"Oh well, then throw away your stick, run with your eyes closed, mouth open, and step on another snake," I would say. "And tell me, wise old man, whose idea was this anyway? It was you who wanted to take this trail. And who do you think I am – your bodyguard?"

He would give me one of those helpless smiles.

On the days when we reached the pond without encountering any such danger, Venu would roll up his trouser legs and walk to its shallow portions and touch the waterlilies. Small fish would swim around his ankles, tickling him at times as they brushed past the skin. I found the flowers irresistible and would end up breaking off a couple of them despite his mild protest.

"It's better to let them stay alive in the water. See how they fit in there one next to the other in a perfect pattern! Why take them with us and leave them to a premature death on the rock? I hate to see them wilt."

"Nothing dies for no reason, Venu. Everything returns to Nature," I would imitate the philosophical tone of one of our teachers. "It doesn't matter whether they cease to exist half-way or full-way, in one form or the other. They, we, everything around us, become something else once dead."

"Thank you, but no biology lessons please," he would say. "I thought we were running away from them in search of some blissful ignorance. Give me some peace, you idiot!"

I knew he was right, at least about one thing. The place kept us calm, away from the disturbing noises of the world outside.

*

A coolness falls on me like a drizzle as I walk inside the temple area that was once the rock's plateau. I let my eyes adjust to the dim lights and shadows before treading on the narrow paths circling enigmatic contours. I stop beside a bunch of teenage school kids and a teacher talking to them in her laboured Queen's English about slaty and schistose rocks. Boys take notes and jeer at the girls who can't do anything else while struggling with their skirts that flutter in the harsh wind. A young man next to me fumbles with his rucksack. He scratches his beard as he argues with a middle-aged man in charge of the temple property. His face reddens when he's reminded, in a threatening voice by the older man, that he can't use a camcorder or mobile phone inside the temple.

"Get out of here if you can't follow our rules," The man says. "If you make a scene, you won't get back home on those two legs."

This violence from a sage-like face jolts everyone, but after an uncomfortable moment of silence, they act as if they haven't heard anything.

"Your rules?" the young man says, as he slides his phone into his pocket. "See, I haven't even clicked once. The camera just happened to be in my hand as I walked in, and I'm switching it off as well. Why do you have to be so rude?"

"So, this kid thinks I'm the one who is rude. Get out of the temple now! Or shall I call them in?" He turns his eyes to the group of young men in white-and-khaki uniforms practicing martial arts outside the temple. I move a little towards the young man, worried that he's going to get in some trouble.

"Come on, you think I'm here for a fight with them?" he says, pointing his thumbs at his skinny ribs. "Me, against the twenty of them! You said there's a rule that I can't record anything here, and I was just asking why it's not written anywhere near the temple's entrance. Anyway, you know that I didn't break your rules. But what sense does it make when you say that I can't stay here and see what's in the temple, like these people?"

"Get out, I say! I know your types. Long hair, beards, backpacks, and those bloody cameras. Heads filled with your ganja dreams of revolution. Only those who worship our deity can stay here."

"See, how many false notions you spit out in ten seconds," the young man says. "And you people act as if the whole Nature belongs to you… only you. That's how secular places end up being private properties. Fascism rules, eh?"

He raises his thick eyebrows in search of someone to side with him. No one makes eye-contact, except me. The angry old man looks around, senses the discontent in my eyes, and then turns his face away, unable to carry on speaking the way he did earlier. I am intrigued by the young man's vocabulary. Any other person his age would have lost their cool and shouted something more provocative.

His hands shake as he puts his camcorder back in his rucksack. His mumbling seems an attempt to hide the quivering lips. I see a bit of my younger self in him. I know how you feel defeated when everyone around acts as if you, and your thoughts, don't even exist. He walks away quietly, trying his best to not disturb the schoolkids.

I find my way across and catch up with the young man. He's in the open space outside the temple, still fidgeting with his rucksack, taking out his video camera and then putting it back. My faint smile and pat on his shoulder seem to calm him down. I make some senseless remark about the weather to distract him and then ask him about his work.

"I'm a vlogger," he says. "I don't know if vlogging can be considered a job, but it lets me do what I like. I earn from it all the money I need as well."

We sit in an elevated part of the rock, away from the noise of the crowds. There are several maps and signboards, all with a logo which reveals that this place is now owned by a communal outfit that smuggles divisionary politics and violence against minorities. The indisputable nature of religious faith has always been used as an effective camouflage for these foul intentions.

He talks passionately about his solo trips to distant places on public transport or on his motorcycle. It surprises me that he had been on the move the whole year during the pandemic, whenever there was no lockdown or curfews. He stresses the fact that he followed proper social distancing and took all the safety measures. He even produced some awareness videos and joined an organization that supplied food and water to the migrant workers who had to walk back to their villages, hundreds of miles from the unkind cities, in the height of Indian summer.

I tell him that the whole year I had spent in isolation was filled with hopes for a better world, but my decision to visit this dream of a place from my past seems like a mistake now. We agree with each other that even though the masks and the visible fear of proximity with our own species are gradually disappearing, it doesn't seem to be enough to erase the boundaries which were in place before the virus-induced toppling of the world order. People like us, who weren't happy with the old normal and were keen to see some positive changes are in for a major disappointment.

Then he tells me what it means to be a travel vlogger. It's a compromise of sorts to see scenes that matter through a camera when your eyes long to indulge eternally in them. There's a creative side to imagining what his viewers might be interested in, but those are seldom his own interests.

"They are concerned with the practical aspects. Reachability, hotels nearby, food choices, weather conditions, facilities on the spot, demographics, safety issues, and so on. For them, the whole experience is something they plan to purchase at some point. Value for money, you see."

"Oh, that sounds so dull! But I've never understood the whole idea of impressing others with things that can be bought."

He says he values his memories more than what he records and releases for others.

"Our most valuable experiences don't ever pass beyond the moments in which they take place," he says. "These documents just end up being unsuccessful alternatives."

I tell him a bit about my technophobia. He lets out a sigh and says that the fascinating world all this technology provides is designed to delude us after a certain point. Then he tells me that he's content anyway, that he is his own boss.

"At times, this digital documenting I do gives me a sense of purpose as well," he says. "There was a time when I was desperate to get a day job. But now I've figured out that I don't fit in the scheme of other people's visions."

"Oh, that sounds good," I say. "But forgive me if I sound too naïve. Are you able to support yourself with your vlogging alone?"

"Yes, I guess. It's not all that easy, but I get enough to feed myself and to find a roof over my head, on most days."

"Aha! What about the other days, when you fail?"

"I don't mind going to sleep with an empty stomach, and having just the sky above me for a roof, if that's how things turn out."

His chuckle relieves me. I know he's exaggerating it. A few minutes ago, he was a troubled being with too much ideological burden on his frail shoulders. Now he's a regular youth, breathing normally and letting the breeze and the panoramic vision work their magic on him.

He takes out his visual journal from his rucksack and shows me a more valuable way of recording his experiences. The thick book contains poems, sketches, hyper realistic drawings in coloured pencils, and some watercolours and pastels too.

"This is where I try to be original," he says. "I refuse to go digital with my art. The brain remembers what the hand does with real pencils and brushes on paper or canvas. It's not the result, but the process that transforms an artist's life."

"You sound like a philosopher. Art teacher stuff, I would say!"

"The funny thing is that I got into all this after I learned digital art and designing…some kind of a reverse process. Upskill gone awry, and see how doomed I am now!"

He says he had to quit his job in marketing when he fell so much in love with coloured pencils that he found it difficult to squeeze in office hours on the days in which he was working on some art project. He thinks each pencil has a soul within, waiting for the right hands to gift it the right physical forms to spread on, to reside in.

His sketches feature glimpses from his daily experiences. They are unique creations focusing on realistic human figures standing in stark contrast with landscapes or monuments that acquire a hazy, dreamlike quality in crosshatches and blurred edges. A lot of white space encircle the figures. The focal points are strong in each of them, in that they draw you in quickly to intriguing stories. The buildings in some of the works fade and merge to the trees or other natural objects in the background. I notice how good he's with his craft, particularly with the unique postures of humans and animals he achieves in minimal lines and strokes. At the same time, he captures facial expressions in minute details too.

"These look so professional. You haven't thought of selling some?"

"No way!" he says. "This is for my soul. I have gifted a couple of the finished works, oil on canvas, to friends. This is something that keeps shaping me, even as I float. Perhaps a good way to pickle my memories, as the historiographers say."

"No wonder my memories are so badly pickled! I wish I were half as talented."

He laughs again.

I point out the other rocks and areas that aren't part of the temple property and tell him about the views from there, hinting that he should try them and see what his camera can capture there for his viewers.

"You may get lucky with something for your soul too," I say. "I wish I had enough energy to go with you, but I have to restrict myself to this rock today. I'll take a walk around the temple and see how much of it still belongs to the old times."

"I keep coming back to places," he says. "The first visit is for testing the waters. It's when I go back again that I see how I'd missed what was meant for me. Most of my sketches happen then."

"I'm afraid this is going to be my last visit to this place," I say.

He looks puzzled, but doesn't ask anything and leaves reluctantly, saying how all the best spots on earth are taken over by brainless tyrants.

He's right. Entry to the temple isn't restricted for people from other religions yet, but that could happen in the foreseeable future. There's already a metal fencing that marks out the tourism counter, another recent addition, from the temple. Anything in the coming years would depend on what the priests think their gods are capable of fancying. There's a lot of trouble involved in installing a deity in a place like this, and then convincing the local people of its power. But once it's done, those who are in control of the whole project are apt to act like difficult parents. That leads to myths upon myths which misrepresent the truth, and an inevitable abuse of power. Gods end up being mere playthings in the hands of their creators.

A bunch of devotees are already in line. Bells clang in what sounds at first like a musical note, but their cacophonous echoes interfere and spoil the effect in no time. One of the devotees recognizes me from my previous life here and comes to me for a quick chat. Seeing how fascinated I am with the monkeys moving around freely, he says they had split into two groups after the temple came up.

"These are the temple-monkeys. They stay near the rock on the few trees that are left, and rely on the food offered by the devotees. They even get feasts on special occasions."

"Are they a manageable lot these days?" I've noticed a change in their behaviour.

"Yes, these are the relatively peaceful ones. They are well fed, as you can see. But they turn violent if members of the other unruly group, the 'market-monkeys', enter their territory."

"Market-monkeys? What the..."

"Yes, they live downhill, near the market. They fight among themselves to get their share of rotten vegetables and fruit."

Oh, dear. That's how the gods divide us!

I bite my tongue and maintain my serene smile, as the man walks back to the temple.

I see the vlogger climbing up the next rock. He hasn't taken out his camera yet, but I'm sure that he'll be tempted to shoot something once he sees how beautiful the sight from the top is.

*

Venu was a strong believer. Well, I can say that he was so thirty years ago. I guess there's a chip in certain people that makes them remain believers forever, and Venu must have had one of those installed at birth.

During one of our visits, he told me – "People say that the cave beneath has a tiger-couple living there, with their cubs."

"One day, we should go to the cave and kill that myth," I said.

I loved to watch the painful expression on his face when I made fun of such hearsay.

"Or kill ourselves," he responded with his lips spread in an effort to smile. He stood up and tried in vain to straighten the creases of his uniform. "When the tigers see us, they're going to think of nothing but 'lunch'!"

He walked away from me.

"It doesn't take a tiger to finish you off," I shouted in one of those moments when words came in a torrent from nowhere. "A breeze turned harsh could uproot you if you walk so close to the edges. Better still, a monkey could jump on you and you could go rolling sixty feet down from the sheer shock of it, sliding through the smooth, steep rock, and split your skull open when your head hits that blade-like protrusion."

"We shouldn't joke about such things," he said.

He walked downwards, hiding his face from me. He was pious to the extent that he believed in the spell words can cast on our lives. I knew that words cast no such spell, though I had strong faith in their power to fight ignorance.

What took his life was his bloody car, twelve years later. He would have slid from the edges of his consciousness to the hands of an all-powerful sleep in the early hours. Or a deeply disturbing memory would have gashed his senses. Or he would have been numbed by the fear of what was to come to him when it was the least bit expected, demanding something he couldn't afford to give. The magnetic fields of fate he believed in would have sucked him, his car, and the tree on which it crashed, to a vortex of oblivion.

He had called me a week before that accident to say that his parents were about to arrange a marriage for him. Like in everything else, he would have trusted their selection of a bride for him, relying more on astrology and horoscope-matching than seeing if he was going to be compatible with his future partner. What would he have made of it, if it were to fail? Life was kind enough to spare him of any such tests.

Did he know about the pleasure I derived from popping his faith bubbles one by one? I know I didn't really have to be so cynical about his belief in the physical existence of tigers in the cave. I could have stretched my imagination to accommodate a bit more of his world.

He was my only friend in those days when everyone else kept a distance from me. My parents were from two different religions and became atheists in the years before they got married. That was an unthinkable crime those days, and though there were no laws in the region to punish them, the people around us made sure that their judgmental gazes and words compensated for it.

I was raised in a way that others found it hard to make sense of my thoughts. I used that to good effect, as my self-defence. Venu knew that I didn't care two straws for the beliefs and traditions that defined his life, but that was never a reason to cut me off from his world, like all the others did. And he never got tired of arguing with me. We knew that we weren't going to change, but we enjoyed our differences as much as the things we enjoyed doing together, the way children could.

If he were me, he would have blamed himself for the careless words that had cast a spell. Such small lives we have, with beliefs and fears of something or the other. Why do I keep ruffling them? It's hard for me to keep my mouth shut and give the impression that I'm amused by everything. I know I am the same person even now, and wouldn't change for any reward in this world. But it seems this long period I had spent looking inwards has taught me to not use words to hurt others, where they can heal.

I doubt whether my friendship with him would have survived in this noisy world. Would he also have bought the arguments of these bullies who misappropriate religious faith to attack anyone they hate for no reason? I like to believe that his faith knew better. But that doesn't matter anymore. Death, after all, had put a full-stop to our debates, defeating the purpose of them all too soon.

I know it's impossible, but at times I wish I were like Venu, looking for simple answers to the biggest mysteries of life even in blind faith.

*

A monkey jumps to the rock and stares at me as it climbs over the metal fence. It shows off its ability to walk, spine up, on the narrow top and then jumps to the edges of the rock that extend a little beyond it. The scary sixty-foot drop is a blur to my middle-aged eyes now.

There is a signboard on the fence that warns visitors against going near the Tiger Cave, because it's home to venomous snakes now. It also mentions how a tourist from the West, who had gone inside the cave a hundred years ago to explore a secret tunnel leading to a jungle, was never found again. That's the story Venu was fond of, with more details about folks coming across the skeleton of someone, who they assumed to be the explorer, on the other end of the tunnel from the cave. At last, his story is immortalized on a signboard in which the foggy realms of folklore and myth are claimed by half-cooked touristy history. There's no mention of what happened to the tigers, when in the past seventy or so years there was no threat from or damage caused by them at all, to people or livestock. For Venu, a tiger was not just a tiger but a metaphor from the myths associated with the gods he worshipped. The stories I didn't allow him to tell me must have mattered a lot to him.

The name of a god must have lingered on Venu's lips, I like to believe, as he fell out of consciousness. He must have seen, in a split-second, what was coming to him. There was no way he could walk away from it. He must have loosened his grip on life in full submission to the power that controls everything. He's sure to have seen it as the inevitable completion of a phase in the unending circle of existence that he always believed in.

I have no idea why I keep drawing, erasing, and redrawing the images in my mind, in a desperate attempt to convince myself that his was a peaceful departure from this world, at least in his own terms. I wish I had the talent to draw a picture with lines that are confident and sure of themselves. I make a decision to buy a writer's journal. It's never too late to invest in words, as I retreat to my much-cherished quietude.

Dusk spreads its wings around me as I leave the place. I slip and jerk my ankle on my descent, and the vlogger runs to my side. It was just an absent-minded misstep and it's in fact easier now to climb down, with the carved rock steps and proper lighting. But I allow him to hold my hand and guide me.

"My vision is blurred these days, and it's harder for me once it gets dark," I say.

The breeze dries my moist eyes.

"My father had the same problem," he says. "And he never ventured out after the sun set."

He tells me that his father died last year, all alone in his ancestral home in a rural village. He was away on a long-stay trip in Sikkim which he cut short, to travel all the way back to Kerala. Then he tells me about his Instagram posts and YouTube videos featuring that unfinished trip.

"I had made a few empty promises to my viewers in those posts. Now I know that the journeys that had to be cut short keep haunting you. The journey back home to my father keeps haunting me too. It was perhaps the one that I started too late."

He says he had to make the biggest compromise in his life to take a journey for a religious reason when he took the ashes of his father to Varanasi, to immerse it in the holy river.

"That was his wish, and I was so bad at fulfilling his wishes when he was alive. But I ended up loving the place and stayed there for another month, recovering slowly from grief and getting back to my vagabond elements!" He tries to smile.

"You must go to Sikkim again. Perhaps you'll find an old friend there, or a new one for that matter."

"I don't know. But I hope it's destined to happen before my vision blurs and knees begin to ache," he says.

I laugh and assure him that I'll follow him on social media once I access my phone, which I'd left in my car. He saves my number and tears out a whole paper from his journal and jots down his number and Instagram profile, which reads 'Quester's Dilemma'. I ask him to have trust in himself and to continue his life's journey with true conviction. He thanks me for the good conversation.

As I walk towards the well-lit car park, I see that there's a sketch on the other side of the paper. It's a view from the adjacent rock to the temple. And it shows me, unmistakable from the attire and posture, bending towards the metal fence and offering a fruit to a monkey that approaches me gingerly, spine up and tail sideways. I wonder how visions come in search of artists. The last time I had fed a monkey was thirty years back, with Venu.

There is a note above the artist's sign, which reads, 'Words count, but only when they're from the heart. Thank you for your words, and the mystical silence that framed them!'

Once I am in the car, I make it a point to find him on Instagram and follow him. On my way out of the car park, I see a couple of school kids approaching him near the road circling the huge banyan tree next to the rock. He walks to the whole group of them, posing under the tree with their teacher, and begins to click several group photos on all the cameras and mobile phones they hand him.

I honk the car horn once and roll down the window to shout a 'Thank you!', waving the sketch. He's all smiles, as he looks at me. The schoolkids join him too, when he waves at me.

THE EDITORS

Malachi Edwin Vethamani (Editor) is a writer, poet, editor, critic and academic. He is Emeritus Professor at University of Nottingham. His publications include: *Coitus Interruptus and Other Stories* (2018), two collections of poems, *Life Happens* (2017) and *Complicated Lives* (2016). His latest publication is an edited volume of Malaysian poems entitled, *Malaysian Millennial Voices* (2021). He has edited two volumes of Malaysian writings which cover a period of over 60 years, *Malchin Testament: Malaysian Poems* (2018) and *Ronggeng-Ronggeng: Malaysian Short Stories* (Maya Press, 2020). The former won the best book award while the the latter was shortlisted for the best book in the English language category for the Malaysian Best Book Award 2020 by the Malaysian Publishers Association. His writings appear in various international publications. He is Founding Editor of *Men Matters Online Journal (www.menmattersonlinejournal.com).* Visit his website at www.malachiedinvethamani.com for more details.

Zafar Anjum (Series Editor) is a Singapore-based writer, publisher and filmmaker. He is the author of *The Resurgence of Satyam, Startup Capitals: Discovering the Global Hotspots of Innovation,* and *Iqbal: The Life of a Poet, Philosopher and Politician*. His short story collections include *The Singapore Decalogue* and *Kafka in Ayodhya and Other Stories*. He is also the founder of Kitaab and Filmwallas.

THE CONTRIBUTORS

Andrew Innes has lived and worked in Himeji, Japan since April, 2002. He has written on themes such as online misrepresentation, the consequences of the pandemic for the younger generation, the implications of online translation for the future of language learning, teaching in Japan, and how to mediate the student experience through video during lockdown. He has degrees in psychology, and applied linguistics, level one of the Japanese Language Proficiency Test, and teaches three separate universities in Kansai. In his free time he likes hiking, reading and keeping fit.

Bela Negi is a film maker and writer based in Mumbai. While she has been working as a screenplay writer for the last one and half decades, her first venture into literature is a collection of short stories. Her debut feature film 'Daayen ya Baayen' (2010, Hindi) as well as her subsequent work explores the contemporary reality of the Himalayan region, the landscape of her childhood. She also runs a production house Nitric Films, that creates content for films and web series and is the founder of Leafbird Foundation, a trust that runs educational and environmental awareness programs in remote Himalayan areas.

Bhaswati Ghosh writes and translates fiction and non-fiction. Her first book of fiction is 'Victory Colony, 1950'. Her first work of translation from Bengali into English, 'My Days with Ramkinkar Baij' won her the Charles Wallace (India) Trust Fellowship for translation. Bhaswati's writing has appeared in several literary journals, including Scroll, The Wire, Cargo Literary, Cafe Dissensus Everyday, Pithead Chapel, Warscapes, and The Maynard. Bhaswati lives in Ontario, Canada. Visit her at https://bhaswatighosh.com/

Christina Yin is a former news anchor, broadcast journalist, columnist and communications executive for an international conservation organisation. She is a writer and educator living in Sarawak, Malaysia. A Senior Lecturer at Swinburne University of Technology, Sarawak Campus, Christina's PhD is the culmination of her love for creative writing and conservation. Her thesis, Creative Nonfiction: True Stories of People involved in Fifty Years of Conservation of the Orang-utan in Sarawak, Malaysia, is part scholarly and part creative, a first for the University of Nottingham Malaysia. Her fiction and nonfiction writing have appeared in eTropic, TEXT, New Writing and Anak Sastra, among others.

Cyril Wong is a poet and fictionist in Singapore. His most recent book is *Infinity Diary*, published by Seagull Books in 2020. A past recipient of the National Arts Council's Young Artist Award and two Singapore Literature Prizes, he completed a doctoral degree in English Literature at the National University of Singapore in 2012. His writings have appeared in international magazines as well as anthologies by W. W. Norton and Everyman's Library.

Danton Remoto has published a novel called *Riverrun* (Penguin Books, 2020), which allowed him entry to the highly competitive Bread Loaf Writers' Conference in Middlebury College, Vermont. He has also published three collections of poems, which were honored with a National Achievement Award in Poetry by the Writers' Union of the Philippines [Gawad Balagtas Award]. He has been writing a column called "Lodestar" in the last 20 years for the *Philippine Star* and has worked for TV5 and Radyo 5. He hosted a daily radio show called "Remoto Control" for seven years at Radyo 5. His last posting was as a Professor of Creative Writing and Head of School, English, at the University of Nottingham Malaysia.

Donna Abraham Tijo is the author of 'Or Forever Hold Your Peace' (AuthorsUpfront, 2014). Her short stories have been published in 'Chicken Soup for the Soul, Indian College Students' (westland ltd, 2011) and 'Escape Velocity' (Write&Beyond, 2018). Her stories have also been published online.

Elaine Chiew is the author of *The Heartsick Diaspora* and editor/compiler of *Cooked Up: Food Fiction From Around the World.* A two-time winner of the Bridport Short Story Prize, she has been longlisted and shortlisted in numerous competitions (most recently, shortlisted in Cambridge Short Story Prize; longlisted twice for the Mogford International Food and Drink Prize; shortlisted for the Manchester Short Story Prize; and longlisted for the Fish Short Story Prize). Her story "The Seductive Properties of Chiffon Cake" aired on BBC Radio 4 in 2020. Her stories appeared in numerous anthologies in the U.S, UK and Singapore, most recently in *A View of Love.* She can be contacted through her website www.epchiew.com.

Gankhu Sumnyan teaches English at a government college in Arunachal Pradesh. His poetry book *Old Friends' Parade* was shortlisted for Satish Verma Young Writers' Award 2015. His short stories 'Caring' and 'Son of the Soil' have appeared in Cafe Dissensus and East India Story magazines respectively.

Ivy Ngeow was born and raised in Johor Bahru. She has been writing since she could hold a pencil, but turned serious after graduating from Middlesex University with MA in Writing, as it was here that she won her first international competition, the 2005 Middlesex University Literary Press Prize out of almost 1500 entrants worldwide. In 2016, she was awarded the International Proverse Prize in Hong Kong for her debut Cry of the Flying Rhino (2017). Author of 4 novels, numerous short stories and 4 lifestyle how-to mini guides, she lives in London.

Jose Varghese is the author of 'Silver Painted Gandhi and Other Poems' and his short story manuscript 'In/Sane' was a finalist in the 2018 Beverly International Prize. His second collection of poems will be published in 2022 by Black Spring Press Group. He was a finalist in the London Independent Story Prize, a runner up in the Salt Prize, and was commended in the Gregory O'Donoghue International Poetry Prize. His works are widely published in many literary publications.

Kiran Bhat is a global citizen formed in a suburb of Atlanta, Georgia, to parents from Southern Karnataka, in India. He has currently travelled to over 130 countries, lived in 18 different places, and speaks 12 languages. He is primarily known as the author of *we of the forsaken world...* (Iguana Books, 2020), but he has authored books in four foreign languages, and has had his writing published in *The Kenyon review, The Brooklyn Rail, The Colorado Review, Eclectica, 3AM Magazine, The Radical Art Review, Cha, The Chakkar, Mascara Literary Review,* and several other places. His list of homes is vast, but his heart and spirit always remains in Mumbai, somehow.

Namrata Singh is a multiple award-winning blogger, an author, a creative writing coach, and a life coach. She has four books to her credit - *No Apologies* by Women›s Web, *Lovers and Losers* by Momspresso, *Immortality* by Chinmaya Publications, and *I am what I am* again by Chinmaya Publications. Namrata has penned over a hundred short stories in a variety of genres with complex characters, showcasing women navigating a milieu that militates against their quest for independence, identity, equality, and dignity. Exposing the fragility of the human condition, Namrata's stories strike an instant chord because it strings together relatable, rooted characters.

Parvathi Nayar is a multidisciplinary visual artist, writer and poet based in Chennai, South India. Her complex drawings, videos, photography and installations have been presented at venues such as the Kochi-Muziris Biennale, Mumbai International Airport and Singapore Art Museum. Water, the environment and sustainability are through-threads in her work. A TEDx speaker, her talks include 'Seeing the World through Different Lenses'. As a writer she wears multiple hats: poet (photopoetry presented at HELD by Goethe Institut Chennai, featured in *Yearbook of Indian Poetry in English 2020-21*); arts writer for publications such as *National Geographic, The Hindu, The Jakarta Post* and *The Business Times,* Singapore; fiction writer (shortlisted in 2021 for *The Bombay Review*'s Creative Writing Awards Fiction).

Roy Tristan B. Agustin is a writer and a teacher in Ateneo de Manila University in the Philippines, specializing in popular culture and literature. He has written a textbook on 21st Century Literature and has written articles on science fiction stories by Filipino authors. An avid scholar of popular culture, he continues to pursue studies in graphic literature and speculative fiction, as well as practicing Aikido.

Smita P Mukherjee is an author and screenwriter. She authored collection of short stories entitled 'Table No 10'. Her work as a screenwriter spans from TV to webseries. In 2017, Smita was judged as the best screenwriter in an internal survey conducted by the Star Network for her story-telling and screenwriting work for a social crime based show called SAVDHAAN INDIA.

Sudeep Sen's prize-winning books include *Postmarked India: New & Selected Poems* (HarperCollins), *Rain, Ladakh, Aria* (A. K. Ramanujan Translation Award), *The HarperCollins Book of English Poetry* (editor), *Fractals: New & Selected Poems | Translations 1980-2015* (London Magazine Editions), *EroText* (Vintage: Penguin Random House), *Kaifi Azmi: Poems | Nazms* (Bloomsbury), and *Anthropocene: Climate Change, Contagion, Consolation* (Pippa Rann). *The Whispering Anklets* and *Blue Nude: Ekphrasis & New Poems* (Jorge Zalamea International Poetry Prize) are forthcoming. He is the editorial director of AARK ARTS, editor of *Atlas*. Sen is the first Asian honoured to deliver the Derek Walcott Lecture and read his poetry at the Nobel Laureate Festival. The Government of India awarded him the senior fellowship for "outstanding persons in the field of culture/literature." [http://www.sudeepsen.org]

Susheela Menon has written for several websites and magazines. One of her latest short stories was published in Out of Print magazine. Her travel stories, flash fiction, and personal essays can be found online. She grew up in India and lives in Singapore.

Terence Toh is a freelance writer and copywriter from Kuala Lumpur, Malaysia. He was a journalist in the arts and culture section of a major English newspaper for over seven years. His short stories have been published in anthologies such as 'KL Noir: White', 'Lost in Putrajaya', 'Remang' and '2020: An Anthology'. He was the editor of the anthology 'PJ Confidential' (published by Fixi Novo). He has written two musicals, 'Euphrasia: The Musical' and 'The Working Dead', which won Boh Cameronian Arts Awards. His first novel, 'Toyols 'R' Us', won the first Fixi Novo Malaysian Novel competition.

Vicky Chong graduated with a Master of Arts - Creative Writing from Goldsmiths' College, University of London. Her creative non-fiction stories were published in two anthologies by Singapore's National Library Board. Her short story *The Uber Driver* won third prize in the 2018 Nick Joaquin Literary Awards Asia-Pacific. She had three short stories published in the Business Mirror, Philippines. Two short stories were published separately in the anthologies *Letter to my Son* and *A View of Stars.* Her first book, *Racket and Other Stories* is published by Penguin Random House.

THE B·E·S·T ASIAN SERIES

THE BEST ASIAN SHORT STORIES 2017

Monideepa Sahu, Guest Editor • Zafar Anjum, Series Editor

32 writers. 11 countries. One anthology of its kind in Asia.

The stories in this anthology by Asia's best known and well-respected contemporary writers and promising new voices, offer fresh insights into the experience of being Asian. They transcend borders and social and political divisions within which they arise. While drawing us into the lives of people and the places where they come from, they raise uneasy questions and probe ambiguities.

Explore Asia through these tales of the profound, the absurd, the chilling, and of moments of epiphany or catharsis. Women probe their own identities through gaps between social blinkers and shackles. A young Syrian mother flees from war-ravaged Aleppo into a more fearsome hell. The cataclysmic Partition of India and its aftershocks; life and death in a no-man's land between two countries; ethnic groups forced into exile; are all part of the wider Asian experience.

Life flows on in the pauses between cataclysms, bringing hope. Fragile dreams spread rainbow wings through the struggle to succeed socially, earn a living, produce an heir, and try to grasp at fleeting joys and love. These symphonies of style and emotions sweep across Asia – from Jordan and Syria to Pakistan, India, Bangladesh, Singapore, Malaysia, the Philippines, Thailand, Japan and Korea. Crafted with love, they continue to resonate after the last page.

THE BEST ASIAN SHORT STORIES 2018

Debotri Dhar, Guest Editor • Zafar Anjum, Series Editor

This is the second volume in the series which contains well-crafted stories with innovative characters, gripping plots, diverse voices from 24 writers in 13 countries.

While Rakhshanda Jalil is a seasoned writer known to many in South Asia, Aditi Mehrotra is an aspiring Indian writer whose story delightfully juxtaposed textual passages and news clippings on women's empowerment with everyday life vignettes of domesticity from small-town India. Martin Bradley's story highlighted the intersecting themes of travel, historical memory, and communication across differences. Today, when latitudes shift, cultures collide, and we are all travellers in one form or another, in ways perhaps unprecedented, these stories must be told.

THE BEST ASIAN SHORT STORIES 2019

Hisham Bustani, Guest Editor • Zafar Anjum, Series Editor

War, loss, love, compassion, nightmares, dreams, hopes and catastrophes; this is literary Asia at its best. From a wide range of geographies spanning from Palestine to Japan, from Kazakhstan to the Malaysia, mobilizing a wide array of innovative narrative styles and writing techniques, the short stories of this anthology, carefully curated by one of Asia's prominent and daring writers, will take you on a power trip of deep exploration of local (yet global) pains and hopes, a celebration (and contemplation) of humanity and its impact, as explored by 24 writers and 6 translators, many of whom identify with many homes, giving Asia what it truly represents across (and beyond) its vast territory, expansive history, and many traditions and languages. This book is an open celebration of multi-faceted creativity and plurality.

The Best Asian Short Stories 2020

Tabish Khair, Foreword • Zafar Anjum, Editor

From the mountains of Uttrakhand in India to the Rocky Mountain in Canada, the stories in this volume represent the multitude of Asian voices that capture the wishes, aspirations, dreams and conflicts of people inhabiting a vast region of our planet. While some contributions deal with the themes of migration, pandemics and climate change, others give us a peek into the inner workings of the human heart through the prism of these well-wrought stories. This volume is the expression of a community, "a community of Asian writing that stands on its own two – no, its own million – feet!", as novelist and critic Tabish Khair says in his 'Foreword'.

THE BEST ASIAN SPECULATIVE FICTION 2018

Rajat Chaudhuri, Guest Editor • Zafar Anjum, Series Editor

Between singing asteroid stations with a secret, and chilling visions of dystopia, between mad sorcerers with an agenda and time-travelling phantoms perplexed by the rules of afterlife, this volume of stories offers a unique sampling of flavours from the infinite breadth of the Asian imagination. If science fiction, horror, and fantasy are the genres you swear by, but miss Asian voices and settings, then this anthology is your oyster. Call these stories speculative, sff, or by any other name, they are really tales well told, and they always take off at a tangent from the big, blustering 'real'. Here the imaginative spirit is aflame, casting a rich lovely light. Tales from sixteen countries of Asia plus the diasporas. Freshly minted, told by seasoned writers and new talent—a smörgåsbord of Asia's finest speculative imagination.

This volume features stories from 34 stories from 16 countries.

THE BEST ASIAN CRIME STORIES 2020

Richard Lord, Guest Editor • Zafar Anjum, Series Editor

Fittingly for a crime collection, this debut anthology offers thirteen stories, stretching from India to Japan, with key stops along the way in Singapore, Malaysia and the Philippines. Some of the authors whose work is being showcased in this anthology are Priya Sood, Carol Pang, Timothy Yam, Lee Ee Leen, Wendy Jones Nakanishi, Ricardo Albay, and Aaron Ang, among others.

THE BEST ASIAN TRAVEL WRITING 2020

Percy Fernandez, Guest Editor • Zafar Anjum, Series Editor

Stories from the inaugural edition of *The Best Asian Travel Writing* offer you glimpses into the curious, strange and wonderful experiences in Asia through the eyes and words of our writers. They travelled to find the roots in Cherrapunji, discover the wonders of Bamiyan, volunteer in the high Himalaya, looking for Malgudi among others that offer a frisson of excitement and expectation.

CPSIA information can be obtained
at www.ICGtesting.com
Printed in the USA
LVHW032342080122
708099LV00003B/52